Alone, On Foot, in the Midst of a Blizzard

The train kept coming, wheels turning, chains rattling, snow whirling around it in a cloud.

Susan took a few steps closer to the tracks . . . And then she was blind. No, not blind, there was something holding her, holding her head and covering her eyes. She gasped, froze, skin prickling all over. She could feel gloves, thin, soft material like cotton against her face.

"No!"

She clawed frantically at the gloved giant hands. And then, as suddenly as they had come, they were gone.

Susan spun around.

There was nobody there.

Nothing.

Only the darkness and the wind-driven snow, biting at her eyes and her face.

DEAD WHITE

by Alan Ryan

TOR

A TOM DOHERTY ASSOCIATES BOOK

Copyright© 1983 by Alan Ryan

A Tor Book

Published by Tom Doherty Associates, 8-10 W. 36th St., New York, New York 10018

First printing, November 1983

ISBN: 0-812-52541-8
CAN. ED.: 0-812—52542-6

Printed in the United States of America

Distributed by Pinnacle Books, 1430 Broadway, New York, New York 10018

For Marie

A sad tale's best for winter.
I have one of sprites and goblins.

—*The Winter's Tale*

SUNDAY
January 16

4:45 P.M.

The second time the green Datsun skidded on the ice, Susan Lester thought she was going to die. Her hands froze solid to the steering wheel and locked there for an instant, while her own voice shrieked in her head to turn into the skid. She released her breath, and a cloud of mist puffed from her mouth in the cold interior of the car. Christ, turn into the skid!

Then her fingers unlocked, and the instant of time fell away behind her in a blur of white-covered trees and blowing snow. Fat wet snowflakes slapped against the windshield and ran like tears before the wipers whisked them away.

Susan gritted her teeth, made some wordless noise, and hauled the wheel into the skid. The front tires slid away, slowly, slowly, coming around in line with the rear end of the car. For an instant, the Datsun threatened to go sliding off the other way but, just in time, Susan caught it, brought the wheel back a little, deliberately loosened her grip enough to feel the play in the steering, and, tentatively, the car righted itself.

A bead of sweat trickled from under her red knitted cap, hesitated at her thin eyebrow, then ran, stinging, into her right eye. She squeezed the eye shut and managed another thirty or forty feet of slow progress on the

treacherous road before she felt safe in lifting a hand
from the wheel to wipe at her eye.

Slowly, fearfully, the car made its way along the
road, lurching heavily into deep puddles, like a frightened, living thing testing each foot of space before trusting itself to proceed.

Then, suddenly, the wind shifted from behind the car
and hurled a rattling gust of snow against the window
beside Susan's head. The car rocked for a moment, then
settled back uneasily to its slow progress.

"Oh, come on, world," Susan murmured. "Give a
girl a break, willya?" She was leaning forward over the
wheel, eyes rigidly fixed on the snow swirling across the
hood, squinting to see through it to the road ahead.

She'd been driving this road—New York State Route
7 west from Cobleskill toward Oneonta thirty miles
away—for six years, ever since she'd gotten her license
just after her sixteenth birthday, and she knew it as well
as she knew anything else in her life. But now it was hidden behind shifting clouds of white and the ineffective
slap of the wipers.

The snow had started early that Sunday morning,
eased off for a while at midday, then grown furious late
in the afternoon while Susan visited friends in Cobleskill. When she saw the storm gathering strength again,
she'd thought of leaving then to get home safely to
Deacons Kill, but the friends still had their Christmas
tree up—they still had a pumpkin from Halloween, too
—the wine was good, the talk cheerful, she had stayed
too late, and now the storm had grabbed her.

The snowfall had revised the landscape, buried and
blurred the familiar lines and angles and made them into
soft and shifting shapes that had never been there
before. In one place along the road, a drainage ditch at
the edge of a field was nothing more than a thin blue

shadow. In another place, the curve of the road melted into the landscape of a hill, a lawn, a driveway, and the road that stretched to home had disappeared in the gray, cold lace of living snow.

"Come *on!*" she said under her breath, and hit the wheel with the side of her fist.

The car moved sluggishly forward, tires slipping on old ice beneath the new slush. Susan squinted through the blowing snow, hunting along the side of the road for the turnoff to Deacons Kill.

Then she saw it, the road curving away to the right, sloping upward between the trees. Carefully, she rolled the wheel over, feeling the car shift direction beneath her, lose its grip for a shivery second, then catch again. Slowly, she eased it into the turn and headed for Deacons Kill.

"Dummy," she muttered softly to herself. "Learn when to go home. You're a big girl now, all alone in the world. Better learn how to take care of yourself."

The car groped its slow way through the blinding whirl of snow, its headlights snatching ineffectually at the swirling cloud ahead.

The road north from Route 7 to Deacons Kill climbed through the hills, twisting and turning like a thing alive. On the right, snow-shrouded woods flashed momentarily into view as the headlights swept across them on a curve. Then, as the car swung back the other way, the lights disappeared across an empty gray expanse of dead and frozen fields.

"Stay calm, Susan, my girl," she told herself. "Just stay calm. Home sweet home is straight ahead."

She tried not to picture herself and the car sliding off the road into a ditch, but her imagination ran away with her and, in her mind's eye, she had a vivid picture of the little green car overturned, wheels still sadly spinning, herself pinned in the wreckage with a broken leg, slowly freezing to death as the night wore on and the wet snow soaked in against her skin.

"I am cursed with a lurid imagination," she said distinctly into the cold air of the car, and watched her words puff out before her face and disappear.

She tried not to think of her father.

Danny Lester, owner of Danny's Diner on Route 7 just west of the Deacons Kill road, had died the previous summer when the driver of a huge trailer rig had lost control of his truck on the wet road in a rainstorm. The truck had slammed through the diner just at the busiest part of breakfast time. Her father had landed face down on his own grill and had suffered for three endless days in the intensive care unit of Fox Memorial Hospital in Oneonta before giving up the fight.

Susan tried not to think about it, not to think about any of it, not to think about the wreckage of the diner that had been more home than place of business to her widower father, not to think about the bloodstains everywhere, especially not to think about the dead body of the truck driver or the smashed cars the monster truck had shoved aside like toys.

"Oh Christ," Susan breathed. "Get a grip on yourself."

Orphaned now and just graduated from the State University campus in Cobleskill, Susan had set about making her way alone in the world. When the insurance check finally arrived, she went out and bought the Datsun. She hadn't driven a car since her father's death. Onward and upward, she'd kept telling herself, and had grimly gone out to drive the mountain roads in the rain that fall, determined not to be afraid.

"Almost home. Just a little bit more."

Then, so suddenly that her tense hands had no time to

react, the car was sliding sideways off the road, teetering on the edge of the hard surface, and slipping slowly into the drifted snow in the shallow ditch at the side. Almost with a sigh, it settled heavily into the ditch and moved no more.

Susan sat gripping the wheel a minute longer, waiting for the pounding of her heart to slow down and her lungs to resume breathing. When she finally loosened her hold and forced tense muscles to relax, she slipped sideways in the angled seat.

"Great," she said out loud. "Swell. Absolutely terrific."

She raised her fist to hit the steering wheel, then thought better of it, fearing the car might slip farther down the side of the ditch. With the snow slapping wetly at the windows, she couldn't see enough to judge how securely it was balanced. The one thing she knew for sure was that she'd have to walk the rest of the way to the Kill.

"Look at it this way," she said. "Now you won't have to go on one of those awful Grand Canyon trips. Think of the money you'll save. You can develop your survival skills right here at home."

She threw her head back and stared at the ceiling of the car.

"Oh God, Susan, now you're talking out loud to yourself."

She exhaled deeply, sighed, and began pulling her coat collar up around her throat and her knitted cap down on her face. When she had her wool scarf settled snugly across her mouth, she took a deep breath and opened the door.

Icy wind made her eyes water instantly and snapped at her cheeks like ferocious teeth. The door was yanked from her hand and flew open, the wind rattling it back and forth on its hinges. A white cloud of snow rushed into the car and swirled around her head as the sudden cold took her breath away. She could feel the rough wool of the scarf already growing wet and icy against her lips.

She moved slowly, carefully, afraid the car would slide away beneath her, as she eased herself out and sought something solid to put her weight on beneath the drifting snow. She found gravel, got her balance, and stepped out of the car.

She was only two feet or so below the surface of the road and, in three careful steps, she was up and out of the ditch. She stopped for a second to catch her breath and look down ruefully at the car. It looked sad down there, helpless. Well, she'd be back for it. One of these days. Maybe in the spring thaw. If there ever was another spring. Oh hell.

She turned away and started up the road toward the Kill.

The wind seemed to pinch at every part of her body. Snow lashed at her eyes, penetrated the cloth around her throat and touched cold fingers to her neck. Winterdead trees at the side of the road keened sadly in protest at the storm. Beneath her feet now there was only snow, no more wet puddles, snow that blew and drifted and shifted into a different shape with every step she took. Above her the heavens were white with the snow, then dark with the blackness of night, then gray, and all-enveloping white again. She hunched over against the wind, hands shoved deep into her pockets because she'd left her gloves ("God, Susan, what are you using for a brain?") in the car. The scarf slipped down from across her mouth and bunched up uncomfortably at her chin. She left it that way because she didn't want to expose her hands to the wind. She could feel their stiff, dead-white bloodlessness in her pockets.

Corpse fingers, she thought. Oh God. Keep walking.

Finally, breathing heavily and squinting against the blowing snow, she came to a section of old stone wall beside the road and knew she didn't have too far to go. The road curved sharply left here, ran straight for a bit, then looped around to the right, crossed the bridge over Deacons Kill itself, the mountain river that gave the town its name, then ran straight up a little farther directly into the village square. Home. Warmth. Dry clothes. Not too far. Just hang in there, girl.

She was slogging her way to the top of an incline in the road, just before it turned left, when she thought of something else. On her right was a flat open field, covered now with eddies of snow that seemed to dance and caper across its surface. The market field, people in the Kill still called it, although it was only rarely used in the old way anymore. In recent years, it had been used for a very rare livestock market, more often as a Saturday vegetable market during the summer, occasionally as the site of a traveling carnival. On this side it bordered the road, which in the old days had given the farmers easy access for their livestock. Off to Susan's right, she knew, it stretched away to where it ended at the edge of the woods. And on the far side, as she looked across it now, were the abandoned railroad tracks and the immense dark shape of the old warehouse that, in the last third of the nineteenth century, had helped to make Deacons Kill temporarily prosperous when the railroad lines had spread out from Oneonta and reached back deep among the hills.

The field itself was level, even though Susan couldn't see its surface beneath the snow, but it should be easy to cross—it certainly couldn't be any harder than remaining upright against the wind out here in the middle of the road—and just beyond the warehouse and the old railroad station were Depot Street and Railroad Street. And a couple of blocks beyond them was the square. And just beyond the square was home.

Susan turned to her right, stepped off the road, and started across the field.

It was different out here, she realized almost at once. The field was immense, infinitely bigger in the rapidly growing dark, with only the vicious whirling snow to fill its emptiness, than it had ever seemed in the sunshine of day. The wind, set free in the open space, howled madly across it, turned back on itself, and snapped at its own tail. Like a wicked magician, it held up a lacy, shifting veil of white around Susan's head, obscuring her view, confusing her direction, making her gasp. Beneath her feet, cold and wet now from the snow, the frozen earth of the field was hard and uneven, rutted, pitted, its traps slyly hidden beneath treacherous white.

She stumbled, almost lost her balance, and pushed on. The next time she stumbled, pain shot through her ankle and she gasped, drawing icy-cold air into her mouth.

She was about three-quarters of the way across the field when, at last, she could just discern the high, dark outline of the warehouse and the lower roofline of the old Victorian train station beside it on the left. She stopped for a second, breathing heavily, to take the weight off her sprained ankle.

Then, testing each footstep, but hurrying as much as she could to escape the biting cold, she continued toward the railroad tracks and the station.

The sound came suddenly out of the night, a long high wail, sad and piercing, lasting longer than human breath.

Susan stopped. The wind picked at her clothing.

Gooseflesh crawled up the back of her neck.

The sound came again, a high keening whistle out of the dark and the blinding snow. From over there. From the left.

Once more it came, like a machine strained by agony and shrieking its pain at the darkness.

And then she saw the light. It was like a solid thing, a shaft of yellow piercing the dark, spearing individual snowflakes and making them dance in its beam. Coming toward her. Coming toward her with another sound now, powerful, heavy, machinelike, rhythmic, pounding.

Susan stood alone in the field, engulfed by snow, and watched the light come near her, its beam crossing her path. The wind plucked at her scarf and pulled one end of it loose to flap crazily at her back.

She held her breath and watched.

Out of the cloud of snow appeared a locomotive, black and wet and gleaming in the dim light of its own lanterns, giant wheels turning slowly, pistons plunging, steam spraying from beneath the engine as it slowed at the station. Tangled black piping that didn't touch the hot boiler was already being etched with snow as the huge engine slowed just in front of Susan. A patch of brilliantly lighted snow glowed in front of the single headlight. Metal clanged on metal, rattled, as the cars the engine pulled slowed behind it. Susan could make out a coal tender in back of the engine, tall and black as night, its top crested by a mantle of snow. She looked up toward the cab of the locomotive. Faint light glowed there behind a small cloudy window, but there was no arm, no shoulder, no face. Wasn't there a driver? He must sit on the other side, Susan thought.

The engine kept coming, metal straining, couplings rattling behind it. The train loomed up from the cloud of white, swelled and grew larger than life.

Then the front wheels of the engine clacked over a long-dead switch and the locomotive, drawing the train behind it, rattled slowly, steadily, off the main track and onto a siding alongside the dark square bulk of the abandoned warehouse. Following heavily behind it were two boxcars and . . . Susan waited, watched, holding her breath . . . two coaches. They were old, like the locomotive, something out of a railroad museum come to sudden nighttime life.

But they can't be here, she thought. In the first place, no train would be running with this much snow accumulating on the track. And this track is almost totally abandoned. And it's a Sunday night in January. And besides, the train is so old, it must be some sort of antique. Oh God, I'm imaging things. The cold is freezing my brain.

But the train kept coming, wheels turning, chains rattling, snow whirling around it in a cloud.

Susan took a few steps closer as the coach cars rolled past. She could just make out some dim lettering and elaborate scrollwork on the sides. She tried to read the words . . .

And then she was blind. No, not blind, there was something covering her eyes, there was something holding her, holding her head and covering her eyes. She gasped, froze, skin prickling all over. Someone had come up behind her and put hands over her eyes. She could feel gloves, thin, soft material like cotton against her face.

"No!"

She snatched her hands from her pockets and clawed at the gloved hands. Her fingers were stiff with the cold, but she could feel the hands, the fingers, as icy as her own. The hands tightened their grip and she thought she was going to scream. She clawed, pried frantically to loosen the grip of the hands, giant hands that seemed big enough to hold her whole head. And then, as suddenly as they had come, they were gone.

Susan spun around.

There was nobody there.

Nothing.

Only the darkness and the wind-driven snow, biting at her eyes and her face.

She turned her head quickly, breath catching in her throat, and looked all around.

Only the snow.

"Bastard!" she yelled at the night.

She backed up a few steps, still searching, searching, but whoever it was had melted away behind the blowing white curtain. Determined not to sob out loud, she finally turned away, took a few steps, then stopped. The train had come to a halt, the second of the coaches, the last car of the train, on the siding before her.

Pushing the toe of her right foot through the snow in front of her to feel for the ties and tracks, Susan inched forward. She reached the first rail of the main line and stepped over it, then the other rail. The coach was in front of her.

A row of windows glowed faintly with yellow light hidden from the night by drawn drapes. Elaborate woodwork—Victorian?—framed the rippled glass. The train was stopped now, deadly silent, the only sounds Susan's own breathing and the keening of the snowy wind.

Her breath came in cold gulps from the fright. She took a step closer to the train and leaned one cold hand on the wood of its side to support herself. Below her hand, boldly elaborate colors spelled out words on a banner. The faint light from the window above reflected from the snow, and Susan moved her head back to see if she could read what it said. She slid her numb fingers over the wood as she made out the words.

STANTON STOKELY'S STUPENDOUS CIRCUS.

She stared at the words.

Circus. A circus train—did they still have such things?—using these antique cars on this abandoned railroad line on a bitter-cold January Sunday night.

Something rattled faintly above her head. Like fingernails on glass. Susan looked up.

The heavy drapes had been pulled aside, and there, at the window of the coach, its bulbous red nose pressed flat against the glass, was the grinning white face of a clown.

5:37 P.M.

Elbert Warren, M.D., was watching the snow from the window of his office on Hill Street. Doc had kept his regular office hours today, just as he did every Sunday through the whole winter, and he'd been busy with patients all afternoon. He wasn't going to keep these Sunday hours in summer anymore, the way he always had, but that was the only concession he'd make to his advancing years, seventy-plus of them, and never mind just how many the plus represented. Besides, nobody was ever so sick on a Sunday in summer that they couldn't let it wait until Monday. People had better things to do with their Sundays when the days were long and the sun was shining. But he kept the Sunday hours in the winter months, and he was seldom there alone.

The wind was blowing the snow horizontally across his field of vision. An instant later, it changed direction and came directly at him, spattering against the small panes of glass in the window.

Terrible snow and wind, he was thinking, a deadly storm, for sure, and he'd seen all the bad ones in the Kill for years gone by. This was going to cost some power lines, telephone lines, fine old trees—how he hated to see the old trees go, they were such sturdy friends through all the decades of a long life—and maybe a few

23

of the old-timers too. And broken bones, of course; there were always broken bones in this weather.

"Well," he said softly to the empty room, and dipped his head again to look over the top of his half-glasses at the snow outside. For a moment, the wind let up or dashed down some other street or waited around the corner and, for that moment, the heavy flakes of snow drifted lightly to the earth and touched it gently. They floated softly downward in the cone of light from a streetlamp at the corner of the square, just beside the Centennial Hotel. Doc looked at the upside-down cone of floating snow and remembered how the snow looked that first time each year when you were a kid. Yes, it could be terrible but, God, it was lovely too, and he smiled a little at the thought and the memory of all the winter snows he had survived.

But of course there'd be broken bones in the morning. There were always broken bones in the morning.

Then the wind, its strength renewed, lashed again at the side of the building, flinging snow hard at his face.

"Same to you," he muttered pleasantly, and turned away from the window.

He took his time dressing for the weather. He buttoned up his vest, then pulled a heavy wool sweater over his head and settled the thick turtleneck collar high against his throat. He already had his long johns on beneath his trousers, but nobody had to know about that, did they? He sat at the chair in front of his old rolltop desk to pull on his galoshes, fold his trousers inside, then snap them tightly closed. Then came the wool scarf—it had seen him through sixteen winters now and he supposed a new one would be warmer, but he still liked this old red one best—and then the long overcoat. He slipped his reading glasses into the inside pocket of the coat, pulled on his cap, settling the wide flap around his ears and the back of his head, closed the top of the desk, looked around the office once more, and snapped out the light.

A few seconds later, he was making his way down Hill Street, past the sheriff's office with the three cars outside with their motors running, heading toward the square and the front of the Centennial Hotel. The cold and the wind took his breath away, but he walked as upright as the wind in his face would permit, breasting his way through the storm.

5:44 P.M.

Susan had to stop halfway across the square to catch her breath. God, the wind was fierce. Her ankle hurt from running through the snow after she'd seen the clown at the window of the train, but she'd kept running anyway, at least as far as the south side of the square. Then she had to slow down and move more cautiously, favoring the injured ankle. And she was beginning to think she'd never catch her breath again. God, what would it be like to get old if she felt like this at twenty-two? She leaned against the War Memorial in the middle of the square and rested her forehead against her arm.

When her breath came a little easier, she straightened up and tested the ankle gingerly. She thought it would be all right if she didn't forget about it and put her whole weight on it immediately. She could be home now in five minutes. Get across the square, over to the Centennial Hotel, around the corner into Hill Street, and another minute or two would bring her home. Just hang in there. Her face was wet with snow and the tears the wind brought to her eyes. She squinted, pressed her lips together, and started off again.

5:45 P.M.

Richie Mead scribbled the information down as quickly as he could. He kept saying "Yeah" into the telephone as he wrote, and thought that if he heard himself say it one more time, he'd go batty.

He switched to "Uh-huh" the next few times, then forgot about it as the import of what he'd written down struck him hard.

At the desk on the other side of the office, Deputy Frank Carpenter sipped coffee from a paper cup and watched him over the rim.

"Okay, thanks," Richie said into the phone. He listened a little longer to the emergency information officer at the New York State Highway Patrol in Albany. "Right," he said. "Hey, keep in touch, okay?" He listened again, then said, "Right. But we're pretty isolated here, you know. And I'm new at this." Then he listened again and had to say "Right" again. When he hung up, he sat back in his chair, stared sourly at the phone for a few seconds, then said, "Right, right, right."

"What did they say?" Frank Carpenter asked over the rim of his cup.

Richie looked up at him. "Are you going to hog all the coffee?"

"Yes, *sir!*" Frank said. "You'll be pleased to know I made a whole pot." He got up from the desk and went to the electric coffee maker on its little table in the corner, then returned with two full cups.

They sipped at the steaming coffee in silence for a minute.

"Enjoy this one, Frank," Richie said. "That's probably the last peaceful cup of coffee you're going to have for a few days. Albany says this storm is going to be just exactly as bad as it looks. The weather guys struck out on this one. The thing seems to have changed direction and now it's heading—you guessed it—right this way."

"How bad?"

"Very cold temperatures. High winds. Drifting snow, and more of it on the way. If we're lucky, it'll only snow for three or four days."

"Look for the high ground," Frank said drily.

"Forget it. You'd be blown away. Besides, you couldn't tell it from a snowdrift."

"So they think the Kill will be snowed in?"

"They guarantee it. Maybe till Thursday or Friday. Also, radio communication is very bad and telephone lines are going down already, so the phones are unreliable. The Thruway's been closed for an hour, the whole Mohawk section, and south from Albany as far as New Paltz."

"Christ," Frank said.

"He says they're getting all sorts of confused reports about secondary roads, so we should consider them closed and the town cut off."

Frank finished the last of his coffee and tossed the cup into the basket beside his desk. There were three others in it already. "Okay, sheriff, lead the way."

"Acting sheriff," Richie said automatically. As long

as John Chard was alive—whether he was sitting here at his desk in the Kill or spending three months with his brother-in-law in California while he recovered from the near-fatal heart attack he'd suffered the first week in November—the town would have only one sheriff. Somebody else could fill in for a bit, sure, but he'd be doing nothing more than acting the part. Richie really didn't think he was just imagining the looks on people's faces that kept reminding him he was only the *acting* sheriff in Deacons Kill. "Oh, yeah," he added tiredly, "and that fellow in Albany reminded us all to take good care of John Chard's town." He shook his head and leaned heavily against the desk. "And I guess that's what we'll have to do. I just hope this thing doesn't get too bad."

He looked over at the small window beside the front door of the office. He could just make out the snow blowing past, but he had no trouble hearing the wind.

"It will," Frank said.

"Thanks a lot."

"Don't mention it. Listen, Rich, do you mind if I talk honestly for a minute?"

"As opposed to the way you usually talk? No, go ahead."

Frank arranged his big, plain face into a deliberately casual expression. "Well, if you don't mind me reminding you, the sheriff left you in charge because he knew you could take care of anything that came up. You know how he feels about this place. So just go ahead and do the job. And I hope you don't mind me saying so."

Richie smiled at last. "No, I don't mind, you dumb bastard. As a matter of fact, I've been waiting for weeks to hear somebody say that. I'll even settle for you. You know, all I've heard since he left is how much everybody misses John and how the town just isn't the same without him." He resolutely pushed himself away from the desk and stood up. "Thanks for the good word, Frank."

"Sure."

"Well. Okay, then. The first thing to do is think about getting word out that people should be ready for the worst. The farmers know what to do with their livestock, but we better get ready to start keeping tabs on all the other important stuff, especially things like milk. If we really are snowed in completely, we'll have to inventory food supplies in the stores, and then keep track of it all. Ever think of going into the grocery business?"

"Lots of times," Frank said easily, trying to catch Richie's slightly lighter tone. "I'm thinking of it right now, in fact."

Frank pulled a yellow pad in front of him and began scribbling notes.

"Call Bob and Phil and get them in here. And tell them to come prepared to stay for a while."

"Till this blows over, you might say."

"You might, if you wanted to make a bad joke. Check with Doc Warren, too. See if he's home or in town or what. And ask him to get in touch with the nurses who live here. There are three, right?"

"Three."

"Okay. And call everybody on the emergency committee. Start with Al Vredenburgh. And get everybody you call to call somebody else for you. The phone lines may not last long, the way it's blowing out there."

He had started pulling on his coat while he was still talking.

"I'm going over to the hotel to see who's in town and look around a bit. I want the emergency committee to meet there at eight o'clock. But I also want everybody in this town who has any sense and who can make it to meet there at eight, in the ballroom."

His hand was on the doorknob when Frank said, "Do you think you could—"

"I'll see who's around and send somebody over to help with the phones till the other guys get in."

"You know, that's exactly what I was going to ask you."

"Get busy, Frank."

"Yes, sir," Frank said, with not a trace of irony in his voice, as he pulled the telephone over beside his pad.

"I want everybody who can get there at the hotel by eight o'clock," Richie said again. "Everybody."

Then he opened the door and went out to measure the size of the monster.

5:46 P.M.

An instant after Susan realized the curb must be here somewhere under the soft snow, she had stepped off it, lost her balance on the wobbly ankle, and fallen in the road. This is getting to be too damn much, she was thinking, when suddenly there was a figure bending over her.

"Are you all right?"

"Oh, I'm perfect," Susan said as she struggled to sit up. "I just thought I'd lie down here to rest for a while."

Oh God, Susan, you have a stupid mouth sometimes, she thought.

Doc Warren scowled down at her. "Don't you dare be fresh with me, young lady. I've spanked your bottom before this, and I'll do it again."

"Oh gee, I'm sorry, Doc. Yes, I'm okay. I sprained my ankle before, so I guess it's a little weak."

"Everybody's a doctor these days," Doc said. "You get right home and put some ice on that ankle."

A gust of wind suddenly circled around them and snow danced and hovered between their faces.

"Okay, Doc, I will, I promise. And, I know, I shouldn't have been out in this weather in the first place."

"That's right," the doctor said sternly, then reached out and put his hand on her shoulder for a second. More gently, he said, "Put ice on it."

Susan smiled. "I will, Doc. Thanks."

As she moved away, she concentrated all her efforts on walking as steadily as she could manage.

6:02 P.M.

Alice Bissell looked out at the snow and didn't even know she was smiling. In all her nine years of life, she had never seen so much snow. Out there in the yard, it blew and danced merrily in the light from the living room window and the one streetlamp Alice could see. She thought it kept making wonderful shapes and figures that appeared for only an instant in the fluttering snowflakes, then flew dizzyingly apart. And every now and then, the wind was stilled for a moment and the snowflakes, stunned by their sudden freedom, hung uncertainly in the air—just hung there for a frozen instant—before dashing wildly away. Everything was covered now—the lawn, the driveway, the street—all hidden by the soft white carpet. The limbs of the trees in the yard were etched in white too, their stark lines softened and pretty.

Alice had slipped in behind the couch to get to that window so she could see the front yard. Her thin arms were folded on the cool windowsill, and her chin rested snugly on them. Her smile broadened as the snow seemed to race in a circle around one of the trees. It must be so cold outside. Alice reached out one tentative finger and touched the tip to the pane of glass. The icy touch sent a shiver of delight through her body. She

wished she could stay up late and go outside to play in
the snow. She wished she could go out and build a snowman. She wished she could at least open the window and
put her head outside and feel the snowflakes on her eye-
lashes and catch them on her tongue.

"Get away from that window!"

Alice jumped in fright, and her knee cracked painfully against the wall. Knowing full well she was guilty,
but not knowing exactly what it was she had done
wrong, she turned around fearfully to face her mother.

"Come out of there!" Sally Bissell snapped. "And be
careful of those drapes. You'll have them down around
you. I spent three days working on them and never mind
the cost, and I don't want the likes of you tearing them
down with your clumsiness. I said, come out of there!
Get a move on! I swear, you're set on driving me
crazy!"

Alice, her eyes cast down to the floor from force of
habit, came slowly—trembling and taking care not to
trip over the cord of the lamp—out from behind the
bulwark of the plastic-covered couch and stood silent
before her mother.

Sally Bissell was a small, bony woman, with thin but
powerful fingers, dark bags beneath her intense dark
eyes, thin and lifeless hair pulled into a wispy clump at
the back of her head, and endless tension etching lines in
her face. She wore a yellow housedress with a white
T-shirt beneath it, and over it a bright green cardigan
sweater that belonged to Leon, her husband. The sleeves
were rolled and pushed up on her forearms, and the
buttons were fastened almost to the neck.

"Honest to God, I swear, you'll be the death of me!
What are you up to now? What were you doing at that
window?"

"Looking at the snow," Alice said very softly. It

sounded very stupid to her.

"Oh, you were looking at the snow, were you?" Sally's hands were on her hips and, although she was a small woman, she looked very tall to Alice.

"Is that it? Is that what you were doing?"

That was a trick Sally Bissell used all the time on both husband and daughter, making them repeat something —usually the simplest, most innocent sort of admission —until it took on the gravity and import of guilt.

Alice nodded.

"Don't you nod your head at me, Alice Bissell! I didn't raise you up so you could answer me like that."

"I was looking at the snow," Alice whispered.

"So!" her mother said, and threw her hands up in the air, exasperated. "Well, that's just fine. That's just what we need. You know what'll happen if you go near that window? Do you?"

Alice shook her head, then instantly regretted it, but her mother, intent on getting on with what she had to say, let it go.

"You'll be sick again, that's what'll happen. You'll be sick again and have to stay in bed again like you done before. Is that what you want? Is it? Answer me!"

"No."

"No. Who do you think is gonna take care of you when you get sick again? Do you think I'm gonna do it? Do you? Well, you're wrong on that one, I can tell you that. I'm done with it. I've had enough. Do you think it's easy having a sick child in the house for months and months? I've done my time, I can tell you."

"I'm sorry, Mommy."

"You're sorry. I'll bet you are! You spent two months, two whole months, lying there sick, and me with nobody to help around here with anything. And now you say you're sorry!''

She was pacing back and forth now, really getting into it.

"And all that time missed from school. And me having to pay that fresh college girl to come in here and give you lessons. Like you was something special or something. Is that what you're looking for? Is that what you want? Well, you won't get it, I'll promise you that right now. So just forget all about it. And stay away from that window! You'll get a chill and then you'll get pneumonia, I suppose, and then—''

"Aw, Sally,'' Leon Bissell said from the doorway. He had just come up from the basement where he'd been working on the furnace, trying to coax a little more heat from the relic to fight the winter wind. He wore his overalls, and both they and his hands were black with grease and soot. "Aw, come on, Sally.''

"Aw, come on, Sally,'' she repeated. "And you, you're as bad as she is. I thought I only had one child to look after, but no, I have to do all the thinking around here for everybody. Is that furnace fixed? Is it?''

"Wasn't broke,'' Leon said. "Wasn't broke in the first place.''

"I *know* that,'' his wife said, summoning her infinite patience. "Is it giving out any more heat? Because I certainly don't feel it. We'll probably all freeze in our beds in the night. Just freeze up right to death and at least I'll have some peace *then*. And you''—she swung toward her daughter, who was looking now at Leon—"get into bed this minute. This minute, do you hear me? And God help you if you kick those covers off, so just remember. Get going, Alice, can't you hear me, are you deaf now too?''

Alice moved quickly past her mother toward the

door. When she came near her father, he dropped to his
knees with a smile and Alice came into his arms.

"You get yourself right into bed, honey, and I'll be
there to tuck you in." His arms encircled her and felt
warm still from the heat of the furnace. Alice buried her
pale face against the coarse skin of her father's neck.

"Get away from her! Look at you, all covered with
dirt and grease, and now you've got it all over her. *Will
you get into bed?* And *you,* well, you can just do the
laundry yourself, because I promise you I won't do it.
God, why did I have to marry such a dumb ox? Why?
Get in there and take a shower. Go on, Leon, I'm telling
you something!"

She threw her hands up in despair again, then stalked
past him back to the kitchen and swung the door closed
to remove him from her sight.

Alice hurried off to the bedroom. Leon remained
standing where he was for a minute, head hanging.
Then he moved slowly across the room, looking toward
the window. He could see the snow outside. As soon as
he got close to the window, he could feel the cold
coming from around its edges. He hoped the furnace
would produce at least a little more heat now; otherwise
Sally would be angry. He hesitated, glanced over his
shoulder, then knelt on the couch, the plastic covers
crunching and hissing beneath his knees. He hesitated
again at the sound, then quietly leaned his arms on the
back of the couch, pushed his face close to the glass,
and smiled as he watched the snowflakes dancing by.

6:07 P.M.

Doc Warren was sitting in the lounge of the Centennial Hotel. The fine old room glowed brown and gold. Light from the brass lamps reflected warmly on the polished oak paneling and the long bare planks of the floor. The bar itself, running the whole length of one wall and then curving around a corner, would have been the pride and joy of any fashionable big-city saloon. Here it simply stood strong and solid, like the hotel itself, as permanent and natural in this quiet setting as its wood had been when the trees stood still and tall on the hills around the Kill. Shining glassware glittered above the bar, and candles in brass sconces flickered along its length. The booths and tables showed the softened outlines of decades of steady use.

When Richie Mead came strolling in, he looked around, then walked over to Doc's booth.

"Keeping off the weather, Doc?"

"Nope," Doc said. "As a matter of fact, this is the first liquor I've had in, let's see, sixteen days. That was my New Year's drink. I have one on Christmas too. And on my birthday. And . . ."

Richie waited a few seconds, then said, "And . . ."

Doc sipped briefly from his glass, set it down again, and said, "And on certain ceremonial occasions."

"Weddings and christenings?"

"Depends on whose wedding and whose christening. And wakes sometimes, too."

"Does that also depend on whose wake it is?" Richie asked, smiling in spite of himself.

"You bet," Doc answered firmly. "That more than the others. You have to be nice with the people you live among, see every day. But with the dead, you have to be honest and deal with them straight."

"Otherwise they come back to haunt you?"

"I wouldn't rule it out."

"What's the drink for today?"

Doc Warren cocked his head and studied Richie's face. "Ceremonial occasion," he said.

Richie looked puzzled.

Doc took another sip from his drink. There was still half of it in the glass, the melting ice cubes diluting it and the color fading. "Come on," he said. "I'll show you."

He slid out of the booth and reached for his overcoat.

"Doc, we have to talk about this storm. I'd like to check on medical supplies and such."

"I know that," Doc said. "We will. Plenty of time yet. You just come with me and I'll show you something."

Richie, looking puzzled, fixed his scarf under the collar of his blue parka, and followed Doc out of the lounge.

In the lobby, about a dozen men were standing talking in small groups. Most of them still had their coats and caps on, still white and wet with snow.

"It's a regular winter wonderland out there," one of them said as they passed.

At the front doors, Doc suddenly stopped and spoke quietly to Richie. "Are you ready for this, Richie?"

Richie raised his eyebrows. "Working on it, Doc," he said.

"Good," Doc said.

Snow had blown onto the porch of the hotel, whipped up against the wall by the wind. The cold air was like a knife blade, slicing through clothing, slipping in through crevices at neck and wrist, penetrating to lungs and heart.

Doc Warren, his head bent sharply forward, felt his way slowly down the wooden steps to the street. The steps were several inches deep in snow. Without looking back, Doc started across the street toward the square.

They moved slowly, buffeted by the wind and trying to pick their steps carefully, the white landscape changing and shifting its contours with every step they took. One instant, the wind howled at their faces, driving icy snow into their eyes and blinding them as it pushed them back. The next instant, the wind raced around and shoved them hard across the shoulders, pushing them forward faster than they could safely walk.

Doc didn't stop until he was a little distance into the dimly lighted square. Above their heads the ancient trees creaked and groaned as they struggled with the wind howling at them out of the night. Their trunks were coated with white that adhered to their bark, hurled at them from all sides by the wind. The wind itself, like a mad musician, whistled and thumped at the branches, raced away for an instant's silence, then returned, its strength renewed.

Like two animals suddenly trapped on a stormy mountainside, menaced by the night and the storm, Doc Warren and Richie unthinkingly huddled together, shoulders touching, heads down, mouth to ear.

"Look at it," Doc shouted. "Look at it!"

They raised their heads together. Above them, a

cloud of snow dropped endlessly, endlessly, enveloping their heads, their bodies, their feet, and dropping endlessly still. It swirled about their heads, both soft and fierce, ferocious as animals and gentle as mist, the wind it rode on prying with icy fingers while at the same time pushing them together.

Doc's eyes were wide open. His face was red with the cold, his lips parted, and Richie caught a glimpse of tears, started by the cold, running down his cheeks.

Doc clutched at his arm, pulled him closer so he could say something to him. "This is the occasion," Doc shouted, "for the drink."

Richie nodded but said nothing.

They stood there a moment longer. Snow stuck to their clothing, coating it white like all of the town.

Then, without speaking further, they turned, linked arms together for support, and started back to the hotel. When they went inside, the sudden warmth of the lobby made their faces tingle.

6:30 P.M.

Susan finally gave up and used the hair dryer. Her long auburn hair was naturally a little dry and thin, and she normally just let it dry by itself after a shower. When she'd come into the house and pulled off her clammy clothing, she rubbed it lightly with a towel, then wrapped the towel around her head like a turban. But after a while, when it was still wet, she'd lost patience with it and the cold, wet feeling at the back of her neck. She wanted to be warm and dry—that wasn't too much for a girl to ask, was it?—so she'd pulled out the hair dryer and used it, on the low setting, until her head felt dry at last and toasty warm.

She'd changed into fresh jeans and a navy sweatshirt that said NEW YORK CITY BALLET—she'd seen them at Saratoga early last summer—but she still didn't feel snug enough against the storm outside. She went back to the bedroom closet and took out a green terry-cloth bathrobe. It was thick and soft, a present from her aunt on her twentieth birthday, and the perfect thing to snuggle into on a cold winter's night.

She felt better now as she headed for the kitchen and put a kettle of water on the stove to make tea. While she waited for the water to boil, she pulled the curtain aside from the little window over the sink and looked out at the night. God, the storm was still going strong.

It felt good to have the solid little house around her. And it felt good to be on her own and making a go of it.

She had rented the place last September, after her father's death, which had left her pretty much alone in the world. She had carefully considered her choices—nervously, but carefully—and had made up her mind that she was going to make it on her own. No charity for her, and no excessive sympathy and kindness. No, thank you. She'd get along just fine by herself. There were two aunts who immediately offered her a place to live—one up in Cooperstown and another over in Lee, Massachusetts—but that meant living indefinitely in a single room in what would always remain somebody else's house. It would mean no privacy, no lots of things. Most of all, it would mean she wasn't really on her own. She had carefully considered her financial situation, consulted with Tom Trenchard at the bank, who had looked after her father's accounts, checked with the insurance company that had covered her father, and decided she would do it. Find her own place to live and just go ahead and do it.

The house was small, really just a cottage, but it was enough for her—big enough to feel substantial, small enough to be cozy. Besides the one bedroom, it also had another small room that she grandly thought of as her office, although so far she had only used it to store junk, and the living room had an ell that formed a separate dining area. Susan had only lived here for a few months, but she had spent much of her free time working on the place, selecting curtains and drapes, throw rugs, new bookcases and lamps. Most of her furniture had come from her father's house, but she saw to it that her own place had enough new things in it to mark it as her own. And thank God her father had kept so much insurance; Tom Trenchard had made it clear to her that she'd never have to worry about money again.

Her determination to find her own place to live had had a great side benefit too. Dale Michaelson, the real estate agent in the Kill who had helped her settle on a place, had taken a liking to her and then offered her a position as an assistant and indicated that he'd be willing to take her on as an agent if she was interested. She had agreed immediately and signed up at once for the necessary courses that would lead to getting her license. Things were looking good. She was on her own. Just barely, she thought sometimes—mostly just muddling through and making it all up as she went along—but on her own nevertheless.

The teapot whistled and she poured the water.

Seated at the dining room table, with a hot cup of tea in front of her, she began to feel as if she were in control of things again. That was stupid today, going to Cobleskill in the first place with the radio saying there was a chance of a terrific storm. And, sure enough, it hadn't missed the Kill after all. Of course, you couldn't stay cooped up all the time, couldn't live like a prisoner just because it was going to snow, or might snow, so maybe she shouldn't really blame herself for that. But staying too long, when she knew it was snowing and could see the sort of storm it was going to be, *that* was stupid.

Oh God, the car. She still had to deal with the car. She hated anything like that, anything that made her look inadequate or dumb or clumsy, and now she'd have to go to Bob's Service Station and ask them to go fish her car out of the ditch. Crap! Well, at least it wouldn't be the only car like that. With the roads in that condition, there'd be plenty of others.

But then, walking across the field. *That* was dumb. Oh, was that dumb!

And the train.

And the hands over her face when no one was there. When no one could possibly be there.

And the face of the clown at the window.

Dumb, dumb, dumb!

You're losing your mind, Susan, my girl, she told herself. Going, going, almost gone. The cold is freezing your brain cells, turning them into raspberry sherbet and just about as useful.

There could not possibly have been a train on those tracks tonight, no more than there could have been the face of a clown grinning insanely at her from a window. No more than there could have been somebody sneaking up behind her in the storm to frighten her. Uh-uh. No way.

She sipped the hot tea.

Nope, no way. She was sure of it.

Except that she had felt the hands on her face and heard the train and seen the clown.

Oh God, raspberry sherbet, for sure, that was the only explanation.

The ringing of the telephone saved her from further lamenting the loss of her mind. She'd had the phone installed in the living room rather than the bedroom when she moved into the house; now that she was an independent adult human being, there was no more time for spending hours and hours lying on the bed talking on the phone. She carried the tea into the living room and set the cup on a copy of *Ms* magazine on the glass coffee table.

"Hello?"

"Susan, you're home safe?"

She knew Doc Warren's voice instantly. Almost everyone in the Kill knew his voice instantly on the phone.

"Yes, Doc, I'm home safe. No more falls." She smiled to herself at the thought of the doctor worrying about her. She might have been annoyed with anyone else, but she had welcomed his watchful eye on her since her father's death.

"Well, I just want to be sure, that's all. Did you put ice on that ankle?"

"I did," she said, wincing at the lie. Once inside the house, she had forgotten all about the ankle. "It's fine now, really."

"No swelling?"

"Nope, nothing but beautiful slim ankles down there."

"I hope so," Doc said. Susan couldn't tell from his tone whether he believed her or not. "Well, you be careful with it. I'm not going to have time for girls who go around carelessly spraining their ankles."

"What do you mean?"

"The storm," Doc said. "I'm at the hotel. Looks like we're going to be snowed in for a few days. Something to keep us all busy, keep us from being bored with a nice quiet winter. It's a very bad storm, Susan. There's an emergency meeting tonight for all those who can get in here. I thought you'd want to know."

"Yes, I do," Susan said quickly. "What time?"

"Eight o'clock. At the hotel, of course."

"I'll be there."

"You dress warm."

"I will, Doc."

"And be careful with that ankle."

"I *will*, Doc."

"All right, then. I'll see you at the meeting."

The cup of tea was getting cold already, and Susan realized the house wasn't as warm as it had seemed when she'd first come in. She walked back to the kitchen to make a fresh cup.

So the storm really was as bad as she had thought.
And the Kill was going to be snowed in. She could remember a few times when that had happened before,
but all it had meant to her those times was a few days
off from school. But things were different now. Now
Doc Warren called her to let her know about an emergency meeting. And she was expected to be there. She
rather liked that thought.

Yes, she did rather like that thought.

She smiled to herself as she poured the tea.

7:15 P.M.

Deacons Kill, like a sleeping child, lay silent beneath the growing storm.

The town lay in a fold of the hills, a sloping valley that might have been the result of a primeval cataclysm that melted rocks and reshaped the land, or it might have been cut by the kill itself that still ran through the town, starting in a mountain cavern and splashing its way over rocky beds to the lower ground. However it was formed, the valley often shielded Deacons Kill from the worst of the weather. Only rarely did storms seem to seek it out and nestle there, blowing and roaring, filling it with their icy breath, liking it there and lingering.

This storm was settling over the Kill to stay.

It flung snow at the clapboard walls of houses, and the snow, its own life dependent on the whim of the wind, clung there, afraid to move. It clung to trees, filling the notches of branches and crevices of winterdead bark. It froze the kill itself solid, then piled rippling drifts of snow atop the ice, as if the river had never lived. It covered bales of hay scattered in the fields, until they looked like lonely white beasts cast adrift and frozen solid as they lay on the ground. On the hillside farms, it drifted up the curving sides of silos, up the wood-slatted sides of barns, until the livestock within

49

complained with guttural grunts and moans, and only
the repeated patting of the farmer's gloved hand on a
chilly flank could still the worry of a nervous beast.

Farmers stood in the doorways of barns and looked
up at the night sky, wondering how long the storm
would last but knowing it would last too long. Wondering if the big silver milk truck would make it up the
road in the morning and knowing it would not. Wondering how much milk would go to waste and knowing
to the penny the daily amount of loss. Wondering if the
storm would cost any lives in the Kill and knowing that
it would. Old folks, even when they stayed strictly indoors through the worst of it, seemed always to recognize a signal in a storm like this, and often died, figuring
the time had simply come.

On the north side of the square, the streets of the
town and the roads that led upward into the hills were
quiet, anticipating the worst. Around the corner from
the square and the Centennial Hotel, on Hill Street, the
three police cruisers sat humming to ward off the cold.
Farther up the street, snow had blown onto the front
doorsteps of houses where no one had set foot since returning from church in the morning. Out past the town,
where Hill Street turned into Deacons Road and rose
among the hills, the gravel of the road was iced through,
solid, rock-hard beneath the drifting snow. The wind
danced among the trees on one side of the road, leaped
across to the other side and made those trees join the
dance, then raced up the hill and into a brittle sloping
field where corn had once grown and into another rocky
one where cows had browsed, and all that once had been
seemed now dead and gone forever.

White. Everything was white. Roads, fields, yards,
flower beds, vegetable gardens, driveways, cellar doors,
cars carelessly left outside, garage roofs, windowsills,

signs over shop doors, street signs at the corners, the movie marquee in the square—everything was white and silent.

Only the wind had a voice.

It snapped harshly at the brittle branches of trees, dry and chortling as it pulled at them. It buffeted loud and strong at the sides of houses, pushing hard to knock them down, backing off and coming back, breathing hard, to push again. It swung, creaking, on storefront signs, creaking this way, squealing that. It slipped silently around corners, then shrieked down yet another street.

Up on Deacons Rise, high above the town, where the woods grew thick and the rocks held the secrets of the mountain, the wind whistled up the snow-clad slopes, whirled around boulders, danced on the icy summit, gathered more snow, then raced back down to the town and renewed its stern assault.

Here and there throughout the town were a few small noises of human beings. A venetian blind rattled at a window as one more resident of the Kill looked out to see if the storm was still at it, still just as bad, as strong, and, yes, of course, it was. Here and there, someone issued forth from the warm inside, armed with a shovel, to clear a path down the driveway in hopes the task would thereby be easier come morning. The shovel dug and scraped against black asphalt now turned white. Here and there a window shutter yielded to the wind, came loose from its rusty hook, and slammed, banged against the wall, banged again and again, until a door opened and a man with a curse on his lips came out to do battle and restrain it. Here and there a few people walked, boots crunching in snow, breath coming hard and sharp against the wind.

On the north side of the square, where the Centennial

Hotel stood big and stout and three stories tall against the wind and the night, the storm seemed to focus its anger, hurling snow up the steps, battering at the double doors, whitening the wooden porch, rattling the glass, and howling its fury in the trees of the mute and frozen square.

They came in small groups, twos and threes and fours, through the wind-filled streets, heading for the meeting at the old hotel, men in parkas and overcoats, big with sweaters and caps and thick gloves, saying little outdoors, needing their breath to fight the wind that would steal their words away. They walked doubled over, stumbling through the snow, thick dark shapes against the swirling, blinding white, and would have cursed if the wind had left them breath.

7:20 P.M.

"Sure thing," Evan Highland said into the telephone. "Count on me. Eight o'clock? I'll be there. Yeah, and thanks for letting me know. I'll pass the word up this way. Right."

When he hung up the telephone, he stared briefly at it for a moment, then said curtly to the empty room, "Fuck."

He stalked across to the wide picture window and yanked on the cord at the side. The drapes swung back. Evan looked out at the snow for a minute, shook his head in disgust, then yanked the drapes closed again.

"Double fuck," he said again, and went back to pacing the length of the living room.

He looked at his watch. Seven twenty-one.

Where the hell was she? Why the fuck didn't she call? It was almost like she was doing it deliberately. And he wouldn't put it past her.

Janice, his beloved wife of twelve years, had left the house early that morning in the station wagon to drive to Albany. To visit her sister, she said. Funny how all of a sudden in the last few months Janice had gotten awfully goddamn chummy with that wisemouth sister of hers. And it was even funnier how she was always so mysterious about her visits there. How's your sister?

53

Okay. What did you do? Nothing much. Anything new? Not really. Evan figured she had a boyfriend over in Albany and she was probably screwing her brains out with him at this very minute while her loving husband froze his ass alone here in the Kill.

Of course, it was only fair in a way, if Evan had been in a position to admit it, which he definitely was not. After all, he did have his own little sideline number simmering nice and cozy over in Richmondville.

Except that they were both going to do their simmering alone tonight—wasting a perfect opportunity—if Janice didn't call soon and let him know where in the goddamn hell she was. The telephone lines could go down any minute. The storm was getting worse by the second. And he couldn't even call Valerie because it might mean missing Janice.

Seven twenty-three.

If she didn't call soon, he'd have to give it up and just go on to the meeting at the hotel.

The telephone rang.

Janice.

"Christ, I've been worried about you," he said at once. "Where are you, at your sister's?"

She was at her sister's and she was going to stay the night. In fact, the way it was looking now, she might be stuck in Albany for a couple of days. She understood Route 7 was closed, and a lot of other roads too. Yes, she'd take care of herself, and, yes, he'd do the same. She'd call him tomorrow and she hoped the storm wouldn't last too long.

Evan sighed aloud, puffing out his lips, when he'd replaced the receiver. He hurried back to the window and opened the drapes again, getting close enough to feel the chill and to steam the glass with his breath. God, that was a major-league prizewinner of a storm. Well, Trailways wouldn't exactly be crying for their drivers in this weather, so at least it would mean a couple of days off. And a couple of days without Janice. He pressed closer to the glass. Bad news. The roads would be murder with that wind and drifting snow. He studied the scene outside a little longer, hesitating, debating with himself. Make up your mind, buddy, it's now or never. Wait much longer and there won't be any decision to make.

Okay, then. If he could wrestle a Trailways bus through some of the storms he'd been caught in, he could sure as hell get that mother of a Buick, all decked out with brand-new chains, from here to Richmondville. And think of the reward, buddy, just think of that sweet little reward. Janice, I hope you're nice and warm in Albany, because I'm sure as hell going to be nice and warm in Richmondville tonight.

He yanked the drapes closed and got going.

7:35 P.M.

"You still awake, honey?"

Alice Bissell nodded her head on the pillow. Her father could just see the movement in the dark. He sat carefully on the side of the little bed and touched his rough hand to the soft skin of her face.

"Aw, you know you're supposed to be asleep."

"I know, Daddy. But I'm not sleepy."

They were both whispering in the dark, both fearful that wife and mother would catch them.

"You have to."

"But I can't." She moved her face against his hand.

"But you have to," Leon said, stolid but gentle. "You're still a baby, so you have to go to sleep."

Alice giggled, and covered her mouth with her other hand. "I am not a baby. And I want to see the snow. Oh, Daddy, I love the snow."

Leon thought about that.

"I could open the curtains," he said at last.

"You mean the drapes, Daddy," she said.

"All right," he said. He was used to being corrected. "Would you like that?"

"Yes," she said, her voice intense in the dark.

Leon rose from the bed and moved cautiously through the darkness to the windows. He found the edge of the drapes and pulled back one side, then the other. Gray, snow-clouded light filtered into the room. Leon made his way back to Alice's bed.

"Thank you, Daddy."

"Do you like that?"

"I love it." She reached for his hand and pulled his face down to her pillow, her arms sliding around his neck. "Thank you, Daddy," she whispered. "I love you."

He kissed her and stood up. "I love you too. Now you sleep tight," he said. His mother had always told him to "sleep tight" when he was little, and he loved the sound of the words.

He left Alice watching the snow outside the bedroom window. Then he walked quietly out to the kitchen and started the laborious task of pulling on his boots.

7:45 P.M.

Susan got as far as the point where Hill Street touched the northwest corner of the square before she hesitated. She stood uncertainly for a minute, clutching her scarf close about her throat. The wind that flung prickling snow in her face reminded her again of the train and the frightening touch she'd felt in the field. She hesitated a moment longer, then, instead of crossing Hill Street toward the Centennial Hotel, she crossed the other way. When she reached the front of the movie theater, she ducked quickly into the lee of the entrance to catch her breath and think things over again.

Did she really want to go slogging through the storm just to prove to herself that she was crazy? Because that's what she'd be doing, right? There wasn't any train down there.

But she'd seen it. And she'd seen the face of the clown at the window.

Dummy, she told herself, you're doing it again. Make up your mind, for God's sake. Either get moving and get on down to Depot Street and see if there really is a train sitting on the tracks, or forget the whole thing and just go to the meeting. Put the whole thing down to galloping juvenile senility.

She beat her arms against her sides to keep the circulation going. When she looked toward the front of the hotel, she could just make out a few dark figures heading for the entrance.

Okay, so she had to be satisfied. One quick trip down to the station, only as far as necessary to get a glimpse of the track. Resolutely, but annoyed at her own uncertainty over what she had or had not seen, she lowered her head into the wind and started down the west side of the square.

Across the street, trees sang a creaking song in the wind. Snow whipped at her legs and clung to her jeans. Beneath her boots, it crunched and squeaked at every step. One moment it was like sand in her face, and the next like pellets of ice. She ducked her head lower and kept moving.

At the south end of the square, she crossed to her left. Another few streets and she'd be down the hill to Railroad Street, and right after that was Depot Street, and then she'd be able to—

Someone grabbed her shoulder.

She gasped, sucking ice-cold air into her lungs. Her knees turned instantly to foam rubber and her feet threatened to go flying out from under her. She flailed her arms for balance and the hands snatched at her again.

"Oh my God, you scared the hell out of me!"

Richie Mead, bundled up in his blue parka and with a dark blue cap pulled down almost to his eyes, was still holding her arm to support her.

"Oh, Susan," he said, but he had to snap his face away when a gust of wind filled his mouth and choked him.

Together, they turned their backs against the blast.

"I didn't mean to scare you."

"I didn't mean to jump like that."

"You okay?"

"Yeah."

"Where are you going? This is no weather to be out."

Susan dug her hands in under her arms and thought fast. "I just wanted to see how bad it was."

"It's bad," Richie said, raising his voice against the ceaseless roar of the wind in their ears. "I'm doing the same myself."

"What?"

"Seeing how bad it is."

There was a moment's silence, only the wind whistling between them.

"You sure you're okay?"

"Fine. Cold, but fine."

"You know about the meeting?"

"Yes." She nodded her head vigorously, as much to keep warm as to answer.

"Eight o'clock. Pretty soon."

"I know."

"You coming?"

"Yes."

"Well, come on, then."

So much for that, Susan thought. He already thinks I'm nutsy just for being out here. I must look really smart, not knowing enough to come in out of the snow. All I have to do now is tell him I saw some weird kind of train rising up out of the storm like some sort of illusion, and he'll lock me up for sure, just to keep me from hurting myself.

But at least it was Richie, and not somebody she hardly knew. Not that she knew Richie all that well. Three casual dates in four months didn't exactly reveal a person's innermost being. Some courtship: Richie hesitant to ask her out so soon after her father's death, then Susan not expecting to hear from him while he was busy filling John Chard's oversized shoes. Grand sum: one clumsy romance. But they had gotten along just fine on those three dates, and maybe he'd come calling again when this was all over. That is, if he didn't think she was using tapioca pudding for brains.

"Susan?"

"Coming."

With the wind mercifully at their backs for the moment, they started off across the square toward the lights of the hotel.

8:15 P.M.

Here, in this little-known part of the northern Catskill Mountains, where Route 7 curves and twists its way from Cobleskill westward to Oneonta, Deacons Kill had lived while other towns died or simply failed to grow. The land itself was rough—hilly and rocky and tough to clear—but farmers for two centuries had cleared enough to live on, a little more each season, and the dairy cows always found enough to eat between the loose stones and boulders of the hills. Then, in 1865, the new and expanding railroad system reached exploring fingers into the Catskills and touched Oneonta, and from Oneonta the tracks spread farther, curving around mountains, following the lines of river valleys and racing the rushing water.

People in the Kill reacted. A market field was cleared on one side of the track, and on the other a huge warehouse was built, big enough to hold and store any modern marvels the new industrial age and the steam railroad might care to bring to town, and big enough too to handle lumber, corn, grain and feed, barrels and tins of maple syrup, apples. A lovely, ornate railroad station, its white paint glowing gold in the light of oil lamps, all gingerbread carving and frosted glass, was raised beside the track.

The produce of the mountains, tins and crates and barrels of it, passed through Deacons Kill. Stores and businesses were started. Homes were built, many of them, mostly in the handsome, tree-lined streets on the northern side of the square, large enough for the boisterous country gentry of the time. It was then and, though faded, is still now a pretty place to live.

The Kill had only four possible rivals in these northern mountains. Oneonta in the west, with its straight and dull main street, offered little in the way of polish other than fine stone churches, and a man could only rejoice in one of them for an hour or two in the week. Cooperstown to the northwest, with its shining Glimmerglass and the hovering presence of old Judge Cooper's famous son, was poorly situated as a center of trade. To the northeast, Sharon Springs, a tiny village in the higher hills, offered healing mineral waters, a green-and-white bathing pavilion, and decorous evening music to its fortnightly visitors seeking the cure. And Cobleskill, east of the Kill on the main road, simply acted less quickly and missed its chance.

The Kill changed, of course. Wars took its sons. Marriage took its daughters. It grew smaller. Some of the big houses were divided, making room now for three families where one had lived before. The railroad put a stop to passenger service in 1951, and freight service ended only six years later. But the town, quieter now, lived on, and the Centennial Hotel lived on with it.

"You can't kill the Kill," people said even in the nineteenth century, and there was truth in what they said.

The men and women of the town were gathering now in the hotel's lobby. Richie Mead was there, with deputies Frank Carpenter, Phil Aymar, and Bob Carroll. Tom Trenchard from the bank was normally pink-

faced; now he looked red and wind-seared from his bout
with the storm. Al Vredenburgh, a big man in a flannel
shirt and down vest, who ran a big dairy farm up on
Deacons Road, said little and only spoke in answer to a
question, then went back to listening. Doc Warren was
there, talking quietly to old friends. Susan Lester was
there, talking near the stairs with former classmates
from high school. Steve Mercer was there, and Tom
Planck; Jeff and Joan Prisco, who ran Prisco's Pizza on
the east side of the square; Bob Booth, of Honest Bob
Booth's Home of Good Used Cars; the Kennedys; the
Whitmores; Paul Senderoff, who had recently opened
the Kill's first video shop; Andy Birkett; Joe Esty and
his sprawling family; Norman Kite, who owned Kite's
Kampground; Reverend Sydney Grant and his wife,
Minerva; Rosemary Stell and her daughter Paula, who
ran the Miller Bookstore; old Ed Shalvey; Don and
Leanne French with their bratty kid; George Yoshioshi
and his family; the Ptaceks; the Gardners; the Quigleys
. . . Slowly, the town was gathering at the hotel, drawing
itself together and measuring its strength.

Richie Mead looked around the lobby, making a
quick count. "About sixty or seventy," he muttered to
Frank Carpenter. "There should be more by now."

"Awfully hard getting around out there. We had a lot
of people on the phone, and I'm sure we covered everybody in town, one way or another."

"Phones still okay?"

"As far as I know," Frank said, but he looked doubtful.

Richie looked at his watch. "I'm going to hold off
another twenty minutes or so, give people more time to
get here."

"Good idea," Doc Warren said beside him.

"Hello, Doc."

Talk was growing louder in the lobby, and the air was filling rapidly with smoke. Every few minutes the front doors opened and another few people slipped in, bringing with them a stinging lash of cold. A small puddle of brown water was forming just inside the door. Along the walls on either side, flanking the doors to the lounge and the Dining Room, the wooden pegs for coats were all covered and a second layer was being started. Richie Mead made another quick count, and this time he came closer to ninety or so, with more in the lounge.

The doors opened again and Leon Bissell came in. Several people greeted him as he pulled off his coat and one of the sweaters he was wearing. Leon grinned back and said hello. He made his living by doing odd jobs around the town, and there were few people in Deacons Kill who hadn't employed him at one time or another. Leon stamped the snow from his boots and added to the puddle at the door.

"Meeting upstairs?" he asked the group nearest him, which included pudgy Paul Overholt, the owner of the Centennial.

"Yep," Overholt said. "In the ballroom."

Leon nodded thoughtfully. "That's good," he said. He looked around. "Yep, that'll be big enough. You got the heat going up there?"

"Oh, cripes," Overholt said. "I never thought of it."

"Hey, Paul," someone said, "you want us all to freeze our chops up there?"

"Hell of a landlord," someone else said pleasantly.

"You want me to do it?" Leon said eagerly. "I know how to do it."

"Sure thing, Leon," Overholt said. "Thanks."

Leon hurried off.

When he was gone, one of the men in the group murmured, "Poor half-wit has more sense sometimes than all the rest of us put together.''

No one objected.

The front doors of the hotel rattled loudly, then rattled again. People turned to look, but there was no one there, only the storm trying once again to come inside.

8:42 P.M.

The ballroom of the Centennial Hotel filled half of the third floor of the building. Although it was usually closed for most of the year now, the doors in the stairwells locked tight, it had once been the showplace of the town, a focus for the social life that, in the late-nineteenth century, thrived here among the northern Catskill Mountains.

The southern Catskills had their nineteenth-century showplaces too, the famed Catskill Mountain House with its bracing breezes, and the rival Overlook Hotel, high atop Overlook Mountain, a little north of Woodstock. Both of them, readily accessible by horse and carriage to the wealthy and sophisticated populace of New York City, had their brief heyday, then fell victim to careless management, unrealistic hopes, and consuming fires unfightable on the side of the mountain. Today all that remains of the Overlook is the stony ruin of the foundation, its broken, treacherous steps leading downward to a weed-grown bottom. Of the Catskill Mountain House, which once glared stolidly at the younger Overlook across a deep mountain gorge, while its guests laughed and flirted and sipped languidly at chilled glasses of lime water, nothing at all remains.

But the Centennial Hotel in Deacons Kill served its

town and its neighbors well through the years and
decades of two centuries, and outlived its more sophisticated cousins to the south.

The first hotel on the north side of the square was
burned by a band of drunken Indians in 1797. The
second one burned down in 1872, and a man named
Alden Gayle immediately set about planning the con-
struction of a hotel to be opened on the occasion of the
nation's centenary, a showplace hostel to serve the
needs of both townsfolk and stranger alike. The opening ceremonies, on July 4, 1876, were marred by a
strange disturbance, centering around the enormous
quilt, depicting scenes from the town's history, that
hangs still, fresh and bright, on the western wall of the
ballroom. But the hotel did open as promised and had
been filled with life ever since.

When Richie Mead decided he couldn't wait any
longer, he strode to the front of the ballroom and called
loudly for order. Slowly, in a wave sweeping gradually
from front to back of the room, the people of Deacons
Kill grew quiet.

Many of the men had taken up positions around the
walls, like sturdy frontier churchgoers, watchful for
sneaking Indians. They all looked thick and bulky in
flannel jackets and wool sweaters. Some still wore their
knitted caps. As they moved their feet, the metal clasps
on their boots tinkled lightly.

A large number of women, more than Richie Mead
had expected, filled the seats along with the men. While
he waited for the room to grow silent, Richie wondered
what that meant, assuming it meant anything at all. He
had always said, mostly to Frank Carpenter and Phil
Aymar, and mostly late at night, that women had a sixth
sense that men almost totally lacked. They could sense
danger in the offing—that, in fact, was one way it mani-

fested itself: a woman sensing that something was wrong—and God help the man or beast that threatened a woman's security when she was already forewarned. On the other hand, maybe it only meant that a lot of the women just didn't want to stay home and watch "One Day at a Time" tonight. Maybe there were no good movies on cable this week.

Richie, he told himself, for Christ's sake, cut the crap and get this show on the road.

Then there was a huge crash at the back of the ballroom. Leon Bissell, carrying an armload of metal folding chairs that was one chair too many for him, had lost his grip and dropped them all. People at the back of the room moved to help, and Leon, his face bright red, scrambled to set them all up quickly in hopes no one would notice it was him.

Richie sighed, and waited a little longer. His gaze met that of some of the people scattered around the room. Doc Warren was sitting on his right, near the side aisle, with Susan Lester beside him. Behind Susan sat Tom Trenchard, talking quietly with Don French, the carpenter, who had modernized most of the kitchens and finished most of the basements in the Kill, at least for those homeowners who weren't handy enough themselves. Rumor had it that French was as sly with a dollar bill as he was with a bottle of beer and that he had any number of little enterprises going on the side. Richie watched French talking with the banker and thought maybe he should have gone into the carpentry business himself. It had to mean a lot less acid indigestion than this job did.

Another dozen or so newcomers all arrived at the same time at the back of the ballroom, and that meant a further delay. Then Don French's nine-year-old son, Jimmy, came running down the side aisle, looking for his parents. Don's wife, Leanne, made her way over to the aisle, took Jimmy firmly by the hand, and led him out into the corridor.

Richie's eyes met those of Frank Carpenter, standing with his arms folded at the side of the room, near the front. Frank raised his eyebrows.

"Okay, folks, let's get going," Richie said loudly. "Quiet down, everybody." A little more quickly this time, the ballroom grew quiet, but Richie couldn't help thinking that John Chard, the man whose job he was filling—trying to fill—could have had silence in the room just by the simple act of standing up.

"Okay," Richie said, and immediately lowered his voice when he heard its loud, brittle tone bouncing off the hardwood floors and walls. "If anybody misses any of this, the rest of you can fill them in later."

Everyone was looking at him. The whole town, it seemed, was looking at him. Make it good, Richie.

"Now, as you may have noticed already, it's not exactly picnic weather out there."

There were a few laughs and murmurs of agreement, and someone repeated his words.

"But that's about the last joke we're going to be able to make about this storm until it's over and we add up the damage."

That got their attention and they were watching him now in a different way, waiting for him to explain the danger and tell them how to avoid it.

"Okay," he said quietly, and blessed the police instructor who had told him that you could always get attention by dropping your voice. "Here's the situation, and I want to spell it out very clearly, because it's very serious. This information is the latest I've had, just a few minutes ago. So far we have between eleven and thirteen inches of snow on the ground. But you already know that figure is deceptive because of the high wind. There's deep snow drifted all over the place. Last I heard, the temperature was sixteen degrees and dropping. But that's deceptive too, because with the winds running the way they are, the wind-chill factor works out to an awful lot below zero.''

No one moved. Richie took a deep breath and continued.

"That's not the worst part. You may or may not have heard this on the radio, but if you did, let me confirm it. The U.S. Weather Service office in Albany says the storm has changed its original direction. And what that means to us is that, instead of just mostly passing us by, the way we thought it would, it's going to stick around right here for a while, possibly through the week. And you may have realized by now that we're already just about snowed in. I suppose it might just be barely possible to get a truck or something through the roads around here, but I doubt it. Anyway, by morning it'll probably be out of the question.''

He paused to let all of that sink in.

"Now, the purpose of this meeting is to make very clear to everyone in the Kill just how serious this thing is. And, of course, to do some organizing. First, however, I want to ask Doc Warren to come up here and say something. Doc?''

Doc Warren rose, looking younger than his years suggested, and walked quickly to the front of the ballroom. With no preliminary remarks, he outlined succinctly the measures people should take to prevent frostbite, the signs by which to recognize it, and the treatment if they couldn't get to him. "I'll be right here at the hotel until this is over,'' he finished.

"Thanks, Doc. Of course, it goes without saying that those of you with livestock will have to take steps to protect them. You should also recognize the fact that you may lose some. I mention that because of this: if I had to make a choice between losing some livestock and losing a friend, I'd rather lose the livestock. I hope you'll all keep that in mind.

"Now, here are some of the things we're going to have to do. For one thing, if you know of anybody who's not accounted for—anybody at all in this whole area—I want you to give their names to one of the deputies here at the hotel. We'll be setting up a desk in the lobby, and there'll be somebody there at all times until this is over. That might mean some old folks who live in an isolated area. That might mean somebody who was simply out of town for the day and couldn't get back. Whatever. That's very important. Oh, and of course, all the schools are closed." Some of the children and young people cheered softly.

"Everybody's going to have to check their fuel supplies. Make sure you have enough heating oil. As much as possible, at least until the storm eases off a little, everybody who doesn't really have to go out should try to stay inside. As Doc Warren said, frostbite can be very dangerous. But we're going to need a lot of volunteers too, men and women both, and for as long as you're willing and able. There are going to be some people out there who got caught without fuel to heat the house, or who couldn't afford it in the first place. There are going to be people who got caught without enough food on hand. There are going to be people sick or injured. Doc is going to be moving some medical supplies in here, into the hotel, and Paul Overholt is going to make space available here for anybody who needs it."

He went on, outlining plans for organizing rescue teams if they should be needed, checking on the availability of snowmobiles, asking the food merchants and owners of eateries who were present to check on their supplies. Then he answered some questions. He ignored, as long as he gracefully could, old Ed Shalvey sitting all the way in the back, whom he knew always caused a needless stir at town meetings, always objecting and finding fault with the plans of others. Just what I need, Richie thought, nasty opposition for no good reason. But he had to recognize the old man at last.

"Mr. Shalvey?"

"Yes, I'll tell you what I'd like to know, young fella. How do you suppose John Chard would be handling this if he was here himself?"

Richie looked at Shalvey carefully for a long time, focusing the crowd's attention on himself, and when he spoke at last he used a normal tone of voice.

"First, let me point out to you very clearly, Mr. Shalvey, that John Chard is *not* here. Second, let me remind you that I'm the sheriff in Deacons Kill and that it's my responsibility to take whatever steps I think necessary for the good of this town and everybody in it, including yourself. I've already outlined what those steps are, and I look forward to cooperation from everybody." He looked around the room, scanning the faces carefully. "Are there any other questions?"

There were not.

"Okay, then. Now, there won't be too many of you going off to regular jobs in the morning, but I suggest everybody go on home and get a good night's sleep. Except those who have things to do here before they leave. Thank you all very much."

Chairs creaked and voices rose around the ballroom. A few people moved at once to the windows in one long wall of the room. The storm was as before: wind howling fiercely at the glass, snow blowing, inches deep now on the wide window ledges of the old building.

As people slowly began moving toward the corridor, Richie, with Frank Carpenter and Phil Aymar beside him, moved after them. They had to wait for the crowd to clear the doorway. Doc Warren came up close beside Richie and said very softly, eyes twinkling, "Not bad, Richie. Not bad at all."

Richie looked at him for a second, then grinned. "I thought not," he said. "Under the circumstances."

"Under the circumstances," Doc agreed. Then they moved slowly after the crowd and down the stairs to the lobby.

9:26 P.M.

Blanche Mackintosh, the stout black woman who was the only domestic help the Overholts kept on through the winter to take care of guest rooms, finally had a chance to mop up the muddy pool of water just inside the front doors. Leon Bissell usually took care of polishing the fine old hardwood through the summer season, but in winter Blanche took care of it herself. She always put two extra coats of wax on the floor just inside the entrance. She worried about the wood. It had been there for more than a hundred years already and, if she had her way with it now and somebody else took the same care of it after she was gone, it would be good for another two or three hundred years yet. She wrung her mop out over a bucket and surveyed the floor critically, humming "Hey, Jude" softly under her breath. Then she went off to fetch the rubber-backed runner she always put down in wet weather. It would protect the floor for a while, anyway, but she reminded herself to go over it again later when things had quieted down for the night.

Halfway across the lobby she stopped, and came back to where Richie Mead and Phil Aymar were studying a large map of Deacons Kill spread out on a card table, while Bob Carroll worked on a list of names of the elderly people in isolated areas who should be looked in on.

"Excuse me, sheriff."

Richie looked up. "Yes, Blanche?"

"I just want to tell you that you did a fine job tonight and everything's going to be all right."

"Thank you, Blanche. I appreciate it."

"That's all right," Blanche said. "But just to be on the safe side, I'm going to say an extra prayer just for you tonight. It never hurts to have a little credit stocked up with the Lord."

Richie smiled. "I don't mind that at all."

Blanche was smiling warmly as she started to move away. But her expression was more serious when she looked back at him and added, "You say one too."

9:32 P.M.

Evan Highland was finally beginning to feel the warmth from the car's heater. He was concentrating so hard on his driving—the way the roads were, it was more like sledding than driving—that it was a few minutes before he became aware that his face wasn't as cold as it had been. Thank God, the heater was beginning to make some headway against the bitter cold. He breathed with relief and, holding the wheel carefully, pulled off one heavy glove, then the other. He hated driving with gloves; you had better control of the wheel with your bare hands.

The windshield wipers slapped back and forth rapidly across the glass, but all they afforded was a momentary glimpse of the road ahead. And not very far ahead, either. Christ, he'd thought he'd be there by now. This was going to be one memorable bitch of a snowstorm.

First, he'd lost twenty minutes while he let the car's engine run to warm it up. Then, when he'd thought he was finally on his way, the Buick, chains and all, had slid right down the goddamn driveway and all the way across the road into a snowdrift. By the time he got it shoveled out again, he was so damn frozen he had to go back in the house to warm himself up. More time lost.

And now here he was, tooling along a back-country

road in a blinding snowstorm, at the dizzying speed of
six or seven miles per hour, wrestling grimly with the car
just to keep it on the road. He had chosen this route
because the narrow road was lined a good part of the
way with heavy forest growth that he'd hoped would
keep the road clear from some of the snow and drifts. It
hadn't.

And for what? he asked himself. To get laid? To get
even with Janice? Christ.

"Evan Highland," he said out loud, "you are getting
entirely too old for this shit."

The hollow sound of his own voice in the car startled
him. He stretched out his right hand and turned on the
radio. There was nothing but crackling static. He
pushed a couple of buttons, trying other stations, then
finally gave up and switched it off.

He tried humming for a minute. Then he gave that up
too and returned his full attention to the treacherous
road, so that he'd live a while longer to be foolish again.

The only sounds that kept him company were the
buffeting of wind against the car, the slush of snow beneath the tires, the slap of the windshield wipers, and
the jingly clatter of the chains.

9:45 P.M.

"Jesus Christ, this is frustrating!" Richie Mead said suddenly. He threw down the pencil he'd been toying with and stalked off across the lobby to the front doors. The brass doorknob was icy cold to the touch, but he grabbed it and yanked the door open anyway. A blast of frigid air, furious wind, and blowing snow hit him hard in the face, taking his breath away. He stood his ground for a second, then slammed the door shut.

"That's a goddamn monster out there."

Frank Carpenter, watching impassively from the table at the side of the lobby, said nothing.

"I'm telling you, it's a goddamn monster. It just roars into town, starts knocking things around, probably hurting people too, and all we can do is sit here and wait for it to go away. Look at this!" He came striding back to the table. "Look at this. All we're doing is pushing around pieces of paper." He ran his hand through his hair.

"Maybe," Frank said quietly, "if you're going to talk like that, you should go back to the station where only the flunkies can hear you, and not the taxpaying citizens."

Richie stared at him a moment, not caring that the anger showed in his face, then looked away. After a moment, he said more quietly, "Have you had a chance to eat tonight?"

"No, but I can wait. If I get hungry, I'll eat some of this paperwork. Go get something."

"No, I—"

"Richie, if you fall down dead from hunger, then *I* have to take over, and I don't want any part of it. Will you please go get something to eat?"

Richie drew in a long, slow breath. "You're supposed to call me *sir* when you tell me to eat my dinner."

"Sir," Frank said very seriously.

"I'll be back," Richie said, and crossed the lobby to the Dining Room.

9:45 P.M.

Doc Warren had borrowed a pad of paper, and now he was sitting in the Dining Room making a list of medical supplies that had to be brought over from his office to the hotel. He'd been through a good number of winter storms like this in his years in the Kill, and he'd often heard his father, who was the doctor in the Kill before him, tell tales of what the blizzards were like in the old days. ("Now, *there* were storms to talk about!" his father had always said.) Doc knew what supplies he'd be needing, but he was methodical and he wrote it all down anyway.

It distressed him to think of what lay ahead in addition to the usual run of winter colds and flu. He sat here listing various kinds of splints and bandages, for instance, knowing they'd be used, but knowing too that the very ankles and legs and elbows and arms to which he'd be applying them were, at this moment, still whole and healthy, unharmed and free of pain. And no way to prevent any of it, no way to prevent the storm. All he could hope to do was minimize the hurting.

He stopped writing, thought a little more about it as he scanned the paper again, and decided the list was finished. His eyes were beginning to bother him, and he rubbed them lightly as he sat back in the chair.

Richie Mead came into the restaurant. He stood uncertainly for a moment as he looked around the room.
There were still several groups of people there, eating or
drinking coffee or just talking. Tom Trenchard's car
wouldn't start when he'd gone outside—he should have
known better than to bring it into town, Richie thought
—and he'd decided to stay the night at the hotel. He was
talking with Fred Hesler. Don French was there too, sitting with two other men. The others both lived close to
the square, but Don lived up near Castle Road and apparently he'd decided not to risk the drive home. His
wife Leanne was at another table talking with a couple
of women. Their son Jimmy was drawing with his finger
in sugar he'd poured onto a nearby table. Kid's up too
late, Richie thought, they always let him run around too
much.

"Hey, Rich!" Don French called.

Richie waved a hand and nodded, but headed toward
where Doc Warren sat by himself.

"I hope you're planning on a good night's sleep,"
Doc said as Richie took a seat across from him. "You're
going to need it tomorrow."

"I was planning on it, Doc, but I don't expect to get
it."

"Last chance."

Richie sighed. "Doc, you're a real inspiration tonight, do you know that?"

"Just being practical."

"I know," Richie said, and looked across the room at
nothing in particular.

"Big job," Doc said quietly after a moment.

Richie said nothing, only mouthed "coffee" to
Peggy, the waitress.

"You'll do fine."

Richie looked at him.

"You will."

Richie held his gaze for a moment, then said, "Yeah, I suppose I will. I just don't feel that way right now. It's this waiting. All I can do is watch it snow and wait for more and wait to see what happens. I talked to the state troopers after the meeting. They wished us a lot of luck."

Doc nodded. "That was very nice of them."

Peggy brought the coffee. "Can I get you something to eat, sheriff?"

"No, just the coffee for now, Peggy."

"Doc, how about you? Something else?"

"I'm fine."

She went away, shaking her head.

The two men were still sitting in silence when Susan Lester walked in. She did the same thing Richie had done at the door, surveying the people in the room, then heading for Doc's table.

"Well," she said when she was seated, "this is a solemn little group."

"Just thoughtful," Doc said.

"Yeah, I know what you mean. This storm would make a brick thoughtful." She turned to Richie. "You run a good emergency. And I liked the way you put old Mr. Shalvey in his place."

"Don't be disrespectful, young lady," Doc said mildly.

Susan blushed and, for the briefest of instants, looked angry. Then the moment passed. She looked at Richie again. "Well, let's say you asserted authority where it needed to be asserted." Then, in a different tone of voice, she asked, "Is there anything to be done tonight? Can I help with something?"

"Not really," Richie said. "You live close in, so you can sort of stand by. But there isn't really anything to do, at least tonight. We're working on a list of people in outlying areas, old folks and so on who might need help, people with babies. But for the most part, we won't really know the most important things we need to do until . . . well, until we need to do them. What I'd really like to be doing tonight is bringing in some of those people, the ones who might be in danger, but there's no way it can be done at night, and with the storm like—"

Richie looked up quickly as Frank Carpenter appeared beside him.

"Phones are out," the deputy said. "Phil just came over. Said he can't even get a dial tone on the line he's been using. And the other lines have stopped ringing."

Richie's lips tightened. "Anything else?"

"Not at the moment."

"Okay," Richie said, and Frank went back to his papers in the lobby.

Richie looked at the doctor and made a gesture that indicated "of course."

"Well, we expected that, I suppose," Doc said. "Good thing there's a number of snowmobiles in town."

"I can drive one," Susan said.

"Not at night, you can't," Richie told her. "And not in the worst of the storm."

"I didn't mean that. Oh, I guess I'm just frustrated by all this sitting around."

"Well, then, you can get to work," Doc said. "Why don't the two of you start bringing over some of those supplies from my office? The fact is, you're getting on my nerves, both of you. You need something to do. Here's the list." He pushed the pad across the table and tapped a long index finger on the yellow page. "That's everything except medicines I can't let you handle.

You'll be able to find most of that stuff in the big closet in the hall. It's not locked up. Just check off what you bring over and I'll pick up the rest of it myself in the morning.''

Susan took the list and was standing already. "Okay," she said.

Richie moved more slowly, but he looked obviously relieved at having something concrete to do.

"Come on," Susan said. "Don't worry about a thing, Doc." She hurried off toward the lobby.

"When in doubt, work," Richie said as he stood up. "Is that the prescription?"

"Works for me," Doc said.

Richie managed a smile. "What will you be doing, Doc?"

"I'm not in any doubt," Doc said. "The kindly owner of this establishment has given me a room for the duration, and I'm going upstairs to bed."

"I should have been a doctor," Richie said, and followed Susan out to the lobby to put on his coat.

10:02 P.M.

Blanche Mackintosh lived in a room on the second floor of the hotel. During the summer, she was relegated to a small room at the rear of the building, but during the winter months, with most of the hotel empty, she moved over to a more pleasant guest room at the front, facing out on the square.

She moved gracefully for a woman her size as she lowered herself to her knees at the bedside.

She debated for a moment, wondering if it would be all right if she didn't read from the Bible tonight. She usually read for half an hour before saying her prayers and going to sleep, and it was normally a great comfort to her. But tonight she felt a heaviness in her eyes and a weariness in her body. It had been a long day for her, and there had been all the extra fuss and bother of the meeting. And the worry.

Blanche hated snow. She didn't like to hate anything the good Lord had made but, oh, she hated snow. Snow had taken away her husband Edward eleven years ago, dead of a heart attack while he shoveled the driveway after a winter storm, and Blanche hoped the Lord would forgive her for hating part of His handiwork but, oh, she hated snow.

She leaned forward at the edge of the bed, her face

low enough to smell the clean, homey aroma of the pink
chenille spread.

"This is going to be a bad one," she whispered into
her clasped hands. "I know it is, Lord. I can feel it. I
can just feel it. Don't do anything too bad to us, Lord,
because we're trying our best. We are, Lord, we're
trying our best, so please don't let this one be too bad."

She prayed a while longer, lips moving, until arrows
of pain shot up from the floor through her knees. Then
she puttered briefly around the room and at last, with a
great sigh, climbed into bed. But she lay awake almost
another half-hour, sighing occasionally and moving her
head from side to side on the pillow and staring at the
dark, because tonight, of all nights, for no reason she
could tell, and with a storm raging outside, she wondered if the Lord had been listening.

10:41 P.M.

Richie Mead turned away from the closet. His arms were filled with blue-and-white packages of Ace bandages.

"These?" he said.

Susan consulted her list. "Yep," she said. "I think that's the end of it."

Richie set the packages down on the floor beside the other things they had accumulated. Three boxes toppled out of his arms as he bent foward. "Shit," he said under his breath.

Susan reached for the loose boxes and stacked them neatly on top of the others.

"It's really getting to you, isn't it?" she said as she busied herself checking items against the list.

"What's really getting to me?" Richie was kneeling on the floor, facing her across the clutter of bandages, splints, unfamiliar packages in unfamiliar shapes.

Susan looked up at him.

"What's really getting to me?" This time his voice was constricted, the muscles in his face taut.

Susan held his gaze for a moment, then dropped her eyes and sat back on her heels. She carefully placed the yellow sheet of paper with Doc Warren's list beside her on the floor.

"I was only trying to help, Richie. I just thought if you had a chance to talk about it . . . Look, I know you probably don't *want* to talk about it. I know it's hard to—"

"Hold on a minute," Richie said. "What exactly is it that's so hard for me to talk about?"

Susan opened her mouth but he cut her off.

"What are you," he said, "the town psychiatrist, all of a sudden? The town shrink? Did Doc send you over here deliberately to make me feel better?"

"No."

Richie scowled at the floor and took a long, slow breath.

"Don't you *want* to feel better?"

He studied her face briefly, then got to his feet and crossed the room to look out the window. He had to hold the curtain aside with one hand. The snow was still flinging itself at the Kill. It rattled and clawed at the window before his face.

"All I want is for this goddamn storm to stop," he said more quietly.

"That's all anybody wants right now."

A long silence filled the room, broken only by the cold rattling of the window and the noise of the wind outside.

"I think I want it more than anybody else," Richie said. Behind him he could hear Susan begin piling the medical supplies into the large carton they had brought over from the hotel. He stood a minute longer at the window, feeling the cold creeping in around its edges. When he turned to look at Susan, the carton was filled.

"I packed it," she said. "That means you have to carry it."

"Story of my life," he murmured. He bent over for the carton.

"I don't understand," Susan said suddenly.

Richie was still bent over, his fingers beneath the bottom of the box. He looked up at her from under his eyebrows.

"I don't understand why you're so upset," she said. Richie set the box on the floor. When Susan spoke again, her voice was softer. "Come on, Richie, we know each other pretty well. We can talk, right? I'm only trying to help. In the first place, there's nothing you can do about the storm. I mean, you can't wish it away and you can't make it stop. And in the second place, you know what you're doing. Don't you? You know everything you're supposed to do. I know you're sheriff and you have all the responsibility and everything, but the storm is enough of a crisis by itself. . . . You don't have to make it seem worse than it is."

"I'm not—"

"You are."

"I—"

"You are," she said gently.

For an instant, Richie was about to respond with another denial. Instead, he clamped his lips tightly together and hefted the carton to his chest, looking at her across the top of it. Again, he opened his mouth to speak but then thought better of it. He shifted the box for better balance.

"Honest, I'm only trying to help," she said softly.

After a moment, he said, "I know," his voice as low as hers had been. Then his tone changed, became deliberately lighter. "You just have a few things to learn," he said. "Like the proper way to speak to an officer of the law." He got a good grip on the carton and turned away toward the door.

She let him reach it before she spoke.

"Sheriff, sir?"

He turned back, looking elaborately exasperated. "What now?"

"You better put your gloves on before you go out there, sheriff, or you'll freeze your trigger finger and *then* where will you be?"

Richie snorted. Susan came and took the box from him and held it while he pulled on his gloves.

"You know, for a second there," Susan said, "you almost smiled."

"Almost," he reluctantly agreed. "But that's all. Only almost."

"Almost is a lot."

"Come on," Richie said. "Let's get back to the hotel. I have work to do."

"Almost is a lot," Susan said again, as she held the door open for him and they went into the snow and the nighttime wind.

10:56 P.M.

Blanche Mackintosh still couldn't sleep, because now she heard something moving in the hallway outside her door.

She had heard it for the first time a few minutes ago, and now she heard it again. It was only a small sound, even a tiny sound, but in the stillness of the hotel it reached her ears and brought her back from the edge of sleep. There was something moving stealthily in the hall.

She heard it again. A board creaked. She knew exactly which floorboards in the hallway creaked when you stepped on them, so she knew exactly where the thing was. It was right there on the other side of the door, just a little to the left, on the side where the doorknob was—and the lock that she always left open—with only an inch of wood between her and it.

The doorknob turned slightly. The tiny metallic sound rattled in her ears and filled the room. The flesh on the back of her neck prickled, and she felt a drop of perspiration roll icily down her side. The wind outside banged at the window. Blanche clutched at the covers and pulled the chenille bedspread up tight around her throat.

The doorknob rattled again.

Blanche waited.

It rattled again.

That was too much. Blanche breathed a hasty prayer to the Lord into the darkness and, moving as quickly and quietly as her size permitted, she sat up, moved to the edge of the bed, and felt with naked feet on the cold floor for her slippers. She shivered but fought the chilliness of the room with another quick prayer for the Lord's protection. Her dark blue robe lay across the foot of the bed for extra warmth—her feet were always cold, even in summer—and she quickly pulled it around her shoulders.

As she stood up, the doorknob turned.

Blanche drew her breath in sharply. She never locked the door of her room. She'd had a friend once who had died in a fire, and Blanche had recurring nightmares about a fire starting in the hotel in the middle of the night and herself trapped by a locked door as her room went up in licking, searing flames. She pulled the robe around her and took five silent steps toward the door.

As she reached it, the handle turned again, louder this time, and stopped abruptly. All Blanche could hear now was the rushing of blood through her own body and the heavy hammering of her heart.

Help me, Lord, she breathed silently.

She reached for the doorknob and, before fear could freeze her hand, yanked it open.

Little Jimmy French, startled, his eyes wide, stared up at her.

Blanche reached for him. He jerked away.

She reached for him again, and then he was running down the hall toward the stairs. Halfway there, when he knew he was safe, he stopped, turned, and stuck his tongue out at her.

"Fat, fat, fat!" he shouted. Then he turned and high-tailed it for the stairs.

Blanche leaned back against the doorjamb, one hand to her chest, until she could catch her breath. When the pounding of her heart had steadied a little, she closed the door softly and made her way back to the bed.

"Oh Lord," she sighed. "Oh Lord, oh Lord, oh Lord."

11:27 P.M.

Susan Lester had wanted to spend the night at the hotel, so she could be on hand if she were needed, but Richie Mead had made it perfectly clear that she should go home and leave him alone while he made the rest of the preparations for the morning. Not that there was all that much to do. Frank Carpenter had still been sitting in the lobby with another of the deputies, Phil Aymar, both of them shuffling papers and looking infinitely patient, and a couple of people were still sitting in the lounge, drinking beer and talking quietly. Susan stayed with them for a while and drank one bottle of Genessee. But they were all older than she was, the Frenches and another couple, Al Vredenburgh and two other men. She was welcome to sit with them, but she definitely felt herself on the outside looking in at that conversation, and besides, she couldn't stand the Frenches anyway. Besides, after all the excitement of the evening, and the sheer physical effort of battling the wind and the snow just to get across the street, she was feeling very tired. The beer finished her off. By the time she was three-quarters of the way through the bottle, she could feel her eyes growing heavy. She said goodnight to the people in the lounge and headed home.

The lobby was empty and beginning to get cold as she

passed through. Richie and Frank must have gone back
to the office around the corner. She stopped, bundled
herself up carefully, then opened the door.

As soon as she turned the corner into Hill Street, she
could see the yellow lights of the sheriff's office through
the swirling snow. She hesitated for an instant as she
passed across the street from it, then quickly decided to
go on home. The storm, she thought, had grown worse.
Wet snow lashed at her face and she had to double over
to try to avoid it. The wind clutched at her jeans, pulled
at her coat, and ran cold fingers down the back of her
neck. The inside of her nose felt tight, its fragile membranes frozen. She had to open her mouth to breathe,
but the wind took her breath away and the air was so
cold it made her teeth hurt. Walking, especially doubled
over like this and battling the buffets of the wind, was
treacherous. There was ice, slippery and uneven, hidden
under the snow. The snow itself, she saw, had covered
the sides of buildings where it was driven against them
by the wind, and the trees were white. She stumbled
where she thought the curb must be and sank knee-deep
into a drift. Her knitted cap had slipped up and she
thought her ears were going to drop off with the cold.
Icy tears crackled at the corners of her eyes.

When at last she reached home, her face and ears
burned hot and painful with the heat. She took off her
gloves, scarf, hat, coat, sweater, and went to the bathroom to look at her ears. The pain was terrible, and,
sure enough, they were a fierce red and tender to the
touch of her fingers. She winced and walked back to the
living room. She stood near the window a moment,
almost fearing the bitter cold that howled outside, then
finally went closer and held the white curtains aside.

The snow seemed to be coming from every direction
at the same time, whirling and capering on demented

wind. It rushed up, as if spewed from the earth, then twisted and hurled itself back down, then veered and rushed right to left, left to right.

After that treacherous walk home, doing battle with a determined wind that seemingly meant to carry her away and keep her for itself, she had a hard time seeing the snow-shrouded street as pretty or picturesque or all those other Currier-and-Ives sorts of things. The image of the clown's grinning face snapped into her mind. Crazy. Dumb and crazy. She shivered violently and felt her nipples stiffen with the combination of cold and a moment of sudden fear. She wrapped her arms tight across her chest and turned away from the window and the storm.

When she went to bed a few minutes later, although the house was warm enough, she pulled an extra blanket from the closet and put it on the bed just to be sure.

11:31 P.M.

Leon Bissell was lying wide awake in the darkness beside his sleeping wife. He was listening to the storm. It made him think of ghosts and he sort of liked ghost stories, as long as they weren't scary. Someone had once told him that all ghost stories are scary—it's in the nature of the beast, Leon—but he wasn't too sure about that. All he knew was that he sort of liked ghost stories, as long as they weren't too scary.

In the next room, just on the other side of the wall behind his head, he heard Alice's bed move and the floor creak. He jumped, shivered, turned his head quickly to see if his wife had heard. She didn't move. He heard the floor creak softly again in Alice's bedroom. She was up out of bed. Or could it be a ghost? He shuddered at the thought. Then he thought, my little girl, and, moving stealthily, slid out from under the covers and stood on the freezing floor. He watched his wife for a moment, as well as he could see her in the gray light that filtered in from the snow-covered world outside, but she was still sound asleep, unmoving. He sighed with relief and tiptoed toward the hall.

When he opened Alice's door, he was trembling with cold and fright and fear that something was wrong with his little girl, or that ghosts were in the room and would get them both, or that Sally would wake up and yell at him again. He closed the door behind him and squinted into the darkness of the room.

"Daddy," Alice whispered.

She was standing near the window. Leon could just make out her shape.

"Come look, Daddy," Alice said, keeping her voice low. "It looks so pretty outside."

Leon crossed the room and knelt beside his daughter and held her tight against him.

"Alice, you shouldn't be out of bed."

"I just wanted to get a better look out the window. I wanted to see the snow. The trees are all covered and everything looks so pretty."

Leon still hugged her. He could smell her hair. He loved that smell.

"I know, honey," he said, "but it's nighttime now and it's cold, and you're supposed to be in bed."

"Just look, Daddy," Alice said. "Just look."

She turned away from him, and this time he let her go. Together they looked out the window.

The snow had covered the big maple at the side of the house and blanketed the top and sides of the bushes that Sally had insisted on so their property would be clearly separated from that of their neighbors. It *was* very pretty, Leon thought. The world seemed to glow with an eerie whiteness, deadly and so pretty at the same time. Alice shivered suddenly, and Leon pulled her closer against him.

"It's real pretty, honey," he said, "but you better get back into bed now. You don't even have anything on your feet."

"Daddy, could we open the window just for a minute?"

That frightened Leon, and he wished with all his

might that he hadn't been thinking about ghosts just before. What if there really were ghosts? And what if they got in?

"Just for a minute? I won't be cold, I promise."

"Alice—"

"I want to catch a snowflake on my tongue."

Leon held her and remembered catching snowflakes on his tongue when he was a little boy. He remembered how they prickled.

"Please?"

"Just for a minute," Leon said. "But you wait right here. You're gonna be cold."

He left her, but instantly he was back with a blanket that he wrapped tightly around her.

"Now don't make no noise," he said.

"I won't," Alice breathed, her voice charged with excitement.

Carefully, so it wouldn't make a sound, he felt for the catches on the storm window, released them, and pushed up.

The storm raced into the room, and wind and snow touched them. Alice giggled.

"I can't reach, Daddy. Lift me up," she said, and she stretched her arms.

Leon gripped her around the waist and lifted until she was balanced on the windowsill. Alice suppressed a giggle and turned her head quickly toward him as he stuck his head out beside her.

Snow touched their faces and hair and hands. Alice squirmed into a better position. Leon kept one hand on her back to protect her and help her keep her balance. The collars of their pajamas flapped against their necks. Together, with the wind howling at their heads and making their eyes water, they lifted their faces to the night and caught snowflakes on their tongues.

11:42 P.M.

Evan Highland thought it was all over. He had never seen a road like this, never seen so goddamn much snow, never had such deadly driving. The road was so slippery, the visibility so terrible, the rushing snow so impenetrable, and the wind so fierce, that he had been forced to stop more than once to think things over. Each of the times he'd stopped, touching lightly at the brake pedal and pumping cautiously, he'd instantly felt the car sliding out from under him and had to fight to keep control. Even so, he'd already ended up with the car sitting sideways in the road three times, and now it was threatening to do it again. That would make a perfect ending for this fiasco, leaving him stranded way the hell out here in the hills with the nearest house a few miles back down the road. He was hunched forward over the wheel, gripping it tightly with bare hands— thank God, at least the heater was keeping out the worst of the cold—but his back and neck and shoulders were aching with tension and the strain of his position.

When he once again felt he had control of the car— for the time being, at least—he managed to sneak a look at his watch. Good thing it had a little light in the face. Almost midnight.

"Christ," he said out loud. How long had he been on

the road? It felt like all his life.

The car started grinding its laborious, slippery way up an incline.

Point of no return, Evan thought bitterly. He'd come too far now, too long, to turn around and go back. What was that his grandmother had always said? In for a penny, in for a pound.

The town line was just ahead. Goodbye, Deacons Kill. Hello, Richmondville. Hello, icebox. Hello *graveyard,* would be more like it, he thought.

When he was three-quarters of the way up the hill, he thought he saw a figure in the road ahead. For one frightening instant, he thought he was hallucinating. Then he saw it again and it waved its arms at him.

Evan leaned even farther forward over the wheel. Who the hell would be out in a storm like this, and in the middle of the night? Only some damned fool, he thought. Which makes a grand total of two of us. Oh, Christ.

The figure ahead moved awkwardly from the center of the road over to the right side. It was still waving its arms at him to stop, but Evan couldn't make out through the darkness and the snow if it was a man or a woman. Somebody stranded, he thought. Or hurt. Maybe there was an accident ahead, somebody gone off the road. *That* was easy to believe. The figure was standing still now, slowly moving its right arm back and forth, signaling him to stop. Evan strained to make out the road ahead. He could see the crest of the hill now. The figure was standing just this side of it, a few feet in front of the sign that announced you were leaving Deacons Kill and entering Richmondville. Evan thought he could stop right at the top, if he did it carefully, then hope to hell that, when he started again, the goddamn car didn't slide all the way down to the bottom or the other side.

He was coming close to the figure by the side of the road now, but the rushing snow and the smeared windshield and the slapping, useless wipers still prevented him from seeing the person very clearly. The figure moved forward as the car approached, heading for the door on the passenger side. Evan touched the brakes and the car slowed, then stopped. He leaned across to open the door on the right side.

The figure pulled the door open and tumbled into the car with a whoosh of wind and snow and icy air. When the ceiling light flashed on for an instant, Evan caught a glimpse of a black hood pulled high around the person's face. Then the door was slammed shut and they were back in the dark.

"Some night!" Evan said. "Good thing I came along." He was already touching a tentative toe to the gas pedal, eager to be on his slow way to the end of this damned journey. The car began to move and slowly crested the hill, chains clanking beneath it.

Out of the corner of his eye, Evan could see the hunched black figure on the seat beside him. Outside, on the right, he suddenly caught a glimpse of the green sign that said, "Come Back to Deacons Kill." And it was green. Not white, snow-covered, the way everything else in the world was covered with snow, but green, a swatch of metallic green that looked like a hand had swept across it and wiped the snow away.

"Hey!" Evan said, and took his eyes quickly from the road to look at his passenger.

As he turned, the figure beside him suddenly lifted black-clad arms and pushed the enveloping hood back from its head.

"Hey!" Evan shouted. *"Hey!"*

The figure beside him leaned toward Evan as the car went out of control and slid off the road toward the trees. The last things Evan Highland saw were the grinning, wide-eyed, red-lipped face of a clown and gigantic white hands that were reaching for his head.

12:00 MIDNIGHT

Deacons Kill lay silent and sleeping beneath the snow. The wind shrieked around it, above it, rattled its windows, battered its trees, made the livestock stamp and snort and its residents toss uneasily in their sleep.

Drifts formed against the sides of buildings, at the bases of trees, then blew away and took up new positions somewhere else. Branches creaked painfully beneath the weight of snow and the ceaseless hammering of the wind. Somewhere in town, in one of the streets leading out from the square, a window shutter was torn loose and banged threateningly against the side of the house until the owner awoke at last and, swearing and shivering, went outside to tie it down. In the square itself, hanging store signs above the street swayed and swung before the wind. Snow stuck to the sides of the theater marquee, wiping out the words. It swept into doorways and began to pile up. It covered sidewalks and roads and dirt paths and the remains of frozen grass in the square and the places where flowers had once grown in front of houses and the places where vegetables had once grown in the back. It penetrated, infiltrated, everything, and where the snow couldn't go itself, its ally, the wind, could.

On the south side of town, just below the square,

where the road began to slope downward, the wind whistled past the gas pumps of the Arco station, swept around Honest Bob's used cars, smothering them with snow, then raced off toward the old railroad depot. It battered at the weathered old wood of the warehouse, hurled still more snow at its sides, covered the empty, splintered depot platform with a light dusting at the edge and a foot of snow up against the wall, then curled and danced and leaped at the train that stood still and silent on the siding.

Snow was beginning now to turn the train white, picking out details of wood carving and ironwork, white highlights where before had been only shadows. The tracks behind the train and before it were almost hidden now by snow, leaving no sign of the train's passing and no route for it to leave.

Dim yellow light spilled from a curtained window in one of the coaches, casting its pale color on the snow that whirled by outside. There were sounds within the coach, voices, and merry peals of laughter that flitted quickly away on the wind.

MONDAY
January 17

6:10 A.M.

Dawn came slowly, reluctantly, to Deacons Kill. The pine-wooded hills surrounding the Kill were gray, marked only by the spiderweb tracery of dark-shadowed trees, frozen firs, their needles dark green beneath the clumps of snow on every bough, and bare maples, their limbs spindly and cold. A thin line of light took form slowly atop the hills to the east, stretched to north and south, and, imperceptibly, the sky moved from blackness to a gray that matched the hills, a gray that crept down the hillsides to Deacons Kill itself. Somewhere on a farm outside the town, a cow lowed at the morning's gloom, a dog barked and then was still, a horse kicked once, hard, against its stall.

In the town, all traces of human movement had been erased by the falling snow and the silent darkness of night. Dawn pulled its grayness through the yards, past the frozen lawns, across the square, around the snow-muffled buildings, against the tight-closed windows, along the silent streets. There were no sounds and nothing moved. All traces of human life, human movement, human effort, had been erased. Not a footprint marked the snow. Here and there a skeletal shape rose from the ground, clothed in a white blanket, a bough pressed and torn by the weight of snow from the tree

above.
   All was silence.
   It was still snowing.

6:25 A.M.

The Centennial Hotel was beginning at last to stir. The big silent building creaked occasionally in muffled protest at having to awake, especially to a day such as this. Paul Overholt was in the big kitchen behind the Dining Room, setting up for breakfast and wondering if he'd have almost no one at all today or if the whole town would be sitting out there looking for oatmeal and eggs. He shivered, pulled his sweater closer around him and wished he'd worn the heavy turtleneck instead of the cardigan, then pulled out another round box of oatmeal and another tray of eggs. Better to be ready, he thought. He checked on the coffee. The sounds of bubbling from the urn did a little to make him feel better. Yep, better be ready for anything. He looked at the trays of eggs he'd stacked on the gleaming counter near the long silver stove and wondered if there'd be any eggs left for tomorrow morning. Good thing he always bought way ahead on these things during winter. Many's the time he would have been caught short on staples by a storm if he hadn't. He shivered again, and, just as he shivered, the steam pipes began to rattle and snap and hiss. Thank God, he thought, and pushed through the swinging double doors to go upstairs and change into a warmer sweater.

6:28 A.M.

Deputy Bob Carroll had been on duty at the station all night, by himself. When Carl Yasnowski had finally come to relieve him—Carl, bless his punctual heart, had been right on time, since he lived only a few streets away in town, but it felt to Bob like *finally* after that long, cold, and lonely night—they had sat talking quietly, sleepily, for a few minutes. Then Bob had bundled up as best he could—he was definitely breaking out the long johns as soon as he got home—and hurried across Hill Street and around the corner to the Centennial Hotel.

At least the wind had let up, but, apart from that, Bob couldn't find anything else to be grateful for as he took a hurried look around the unbroken white face of Deacons Kill. He shoved his hands deeper into the pockets of his leather jacket. God, it had been a long night.

Snow had almost completely obliterated the outline of the steps to the hotel's porch, and Bob had to kick awkwardly at it, step by step, before trusting his footing. Inside, the lobby seemed hollow and nearly as cold as outdoors. I could have taken my vacation now, he remembered. I could have been at Disney World *right now,* me and Janie and the kids, and I could have read about this storm in the newspapers. Jeez.

He went into the Dining Room. The lights were on, and the familiar, friendly glow of wood paneling, brass fixtures, and gleaming silverware made him feel better. There was no one around. He pushed through the swinging doors to the kitchen, checked the coffee urn and saw that it was ready, took a cup and saucer from the stack beside it, and poured himself some coffee. He sipped cautiously at the steaming cup and shook his head sadly. I could have been at Disney World *right now*.

6:32 A.M.

Blanche Mackintosh was dreaming that she was lost, running barefoot and freezing through the dark woods around the Kill, and snow-covered trees were somehow flaming with fire all around her and closing in, trapping her, but then she heard the blaring, screeching horns of the fire engines coming to the rescue and the ringing of the alarm clock finally woke her up.

"Oh Lord," she said out loud to the cold room, "it's going to be another day like that."

6:37 A.M.

When Doc Warren woke up, he was fully alert at once, the result of a lifetime of midnight calls and crises, late-night fevers and middle-of-the-night deliveries. On such occasions, he sometimes remained the rest of the night wherever he was, so the strange surroundings of the hotel room did not disturb him. He glanced toward the window without lifting his head from the pillow. Gray. And still snowing. He sighed, glanced at the clock-radio on the night table beside his head, and decided to treat himself to exactly ten more minutes of rest with his eyes closed.

Four minutes later, he sighed again, resolutely pushed the covers back, and sat up.

6:49 A.M.

Richie Mead slapped clumsily at the Little Ben clock when it jangled noisily at him. Then, before he could give in to temptation, he forced himself to sit up straight and open his eyes.

Still half-asleep, he used the toilet, shaved—trying not to look too closely at the strained lines around his eyes—washed up, and got dressed. God, the house was cold. I should have turned up the thermostat last night, he thought. This is no weather to be economical.

He was reaching for the telephone to call the station to get a report on the night when he recalled that phone service was completely out. He hesitated for a second, lips pressed together, then picked it up anyway. The telephone was cold to the touch and absolutely silent, like a dead thing, and after a second he put it down.

He went to the kitchen window and looked out at the silent length of Franklin Street. Still snowing, but it looked like the wind had let up. Well, that was something, at least. But it was snowing hard, steadily, determinedly, big fat flakes driving straight down out of a solid gray sky, and the whole world beneath them was already gray-white and smooth and featureless.

Richie turned from the window, took a saucepan from the stove, and started to run cold water into it at the sink. Then he dumped out the cold water, switched over to hot so the boiling would have a head start, and filled the saucepan again. While he waited for it to boil, he stared out the window at the blur of falling snow and tried to keep himself from thinking of anything unpleasant. When the water began bubbling, he dumped a teaspoon of instant coffee into a mug, then filled it with water from the spitting saucepan. He added a little milk to cool it from a container in the refrigerator, then carried the cup to the table and warmed his hands around it. After a moment, he got up, carried the cup across the room, added another teaspoon of instant coffee to it, tasted it, grimaced, but drank it down as quickly as he could. When it was gone, he glanced at his watch, thought for a moment, and got up to make another.

With the second cup in front of him, he leaned forward on the cool table and tried to think through what had to be done today. His thoughts were a mess. Everything he thought of reminded him of three other things, every one of which had to be done first. At least, Phil Aymar would be around full time now. His fellow deputy had had a few days off last week, getting over a bad cold, but he'd been okay last night and now he'd be around again. Richie was glad of that.

And then he was thinking about Susan Lester. That was a pleasant thought, and Richie even found himself smiling a little. He was glad she'd been around last night, even though he was convinced she didn't realize how serious a storm like this could be. And he wished he hadn't been such a shit to her. He had to admit he liked her a lot. They'd had a nice time on those three dates and if circumstances hadn't gotten in the way, the three might have been a lot more. He'd have to try to be nicer to her today. Christ, wasn't she one of the few people in the Kill who was really helping him out?

Come on, sheriff, he told himself, get on with it.

He gulped down the rest of the coffee and stood up, leaving the empty cup on the table. Then he walked quickly back to the bedroom, strapped on his gun, pulled on the rest of his clothes, and left the house.

7:08 A.M.

Susan Lester had been up for almost an hour.

She had showered, washed her hair, dried it, brushed it, and made a hearty breakfast already, interrupting the pleasant morning routine only by long looks out the kitchen window over the sink and trips to the living room to look out the window at the snow-covered street in front of the house.

Everything outside was white and beautiful, glowing pearly-gray in the dim morning light. The limbs of the trees were softened by white cushions of snow; the lawn was a soft white carpet, the roadway a broad, clear, unobstructed river of white. She thought it was the most beautiful snowfall she had ever seen.

A few weeks ago she'd been hoping for a white Christmas, but Christmas had come and gone with only a promise of flurries and nothing more than slushy snow mixed with mud underfoot. But this January storm was making up for it with a vengeance.

That thought disturbed her a little, and she frowned as she dried her cup and saucer and carefully put them back in the cupboard. The storm had seemed indeed to have a kind of vengeance to it. At least, it had certainly seemed that way last night. She shuddered as she remembered the force of the wind pushing at her and clutching at her clothing. She closed the cupboard door and walked briskly out to the living-room window.

It was still pretty dark outside, but she could see the snow clearly as it fell past the window. It was coming straight down, heavy and steady, and there was clearly no wind. That was a relief; the snow was all right without the wind.

And there was plenty to do. No one—except maybe the diehards—would be going to any regular jobs today. Probably only the people who owned foodstores would open up their shops, unless Richie wanted to organize the food supplies somehow. The other storekeepers, she guessed, wouldn't bother. Besides, if somebody needed something desperately, he could probably see the store owner in town anyway, or just call him at home.

No, come to think of it, people couldn't call, could they? The phone lines were all out. Well, even so, not too many people would have an urgent need for greeting cards and such things today. Too many other things to think about.

She checked her watch. Better get going. Richie had said he'd be at the hotel early, and if there was something going on, Susan wanted to be there to lend a hand. With the phones all out, everyone in town should stay close to the hotel.

She put on her outer clothing and her boots, took a last, long look around the house to see that everything was in order—she prided herself on keeping a pleasant, proper home—then opened the front door and went out into the cold.

She kicked a high, smooth drift for good luck as she made her way down the snow-covered pathway to the sidewalk, then kicked it again for good measure.

7:52 A.M.

"Frank, will you make sure about the snowmobiles?" Richie Mead said. "I think I remember Sam Hollander bought one for his kid a couple of months ago. If you can't find Sam, Norman Kite might know."

"Will do," Frank Carpenter said. "But if Hollander does have one, we'll have to send two people with one of the big ones out there to get it."

They were sitting in one of the side booths in the hotel's Dining Room. Richie leaned back into the corner against the wall.

"Right," he said. "I'm aware of that. So just do it, okay? Just do whatever needs doing. You leave the heavy thinking to me and I'll leave the fine details to you."

Frank pursed his lips briefly, then said, "Sho nuff, boss. But it sho is early in the mawnin' to be talkin' so tough." He slid out of the booth.

"Frank," Richie said quickly.

They looked at each other.

"I'm sorry," Richie said.

Frank nodded, then went off quickly to hunt up Sam Hollander or Norman Kite.

"Christ," Richie muttered under his breath, and told himself he was going to have to do better.

9:05 A.M.

An hour later, things seemed a little better organized, a little more under control, a little calmer.

People who lived within a reasonable walking distance of the square were all gathering now in the lobby and Dining Room of the Centennial Hotel, filling its wood-paneled interior with talk of snow and drifts, branches broken from trees, impassable roads, frozen motors, worried talk about food supplies and the careful use of heating oil, and names of families in outlying areas, on remote farms among the hills, who were now cut off from town. But there was less of the nervous excitement that had given a sharp edge to conversation the night before.

Plans were being made. Measures were being taken. Things were being done. A group of people, including Susan Lester, had gone off to make a survey of perishable foods and other supplies on hand in the town's foodstores. Others were checking on home heating fuels, trying to anticipate which of the Kill's families would be in the greatest danger if the town remained cut off for more than another day or two.

There was some disappointment and concern when only a few of the larger trucks currently in town could be started in the bitter cold, and more concern when it

proved impossible to move even those that were fully
winterized and equipped with snow chains. Because of
the blowing winds the night before, a few streets here
and there were almost clear of snow, while others were
buried under two feet of it. The town had one snow-
blower, kept at the Arco station on the south side of the
square, but Fred Ramsey, the bearded mechanic who
had gone off to try it again, had returned on foot an
hour later and embarrassedly explained to Richie Mead
that the damn thing wouldn't move any more today
than it would on Sunday afternoon. The only form of
transportation, then, would be snowmobiles.

Richie sent off a small group of men, recruited from
those in the lobby, to trudge through the hip-deep snow
to get all the snowmobiles they knew of that could be
reached on foot and bring them into the square.

Doc Warren had eaten his hearty breakfast, including
two bowls of steaming oatmeal, in the Dining Room,
then had recruited two of the men in the lobby, Bob
Booth and Norman Kite, to accompany him to his
office on Hill Street while he gathered up the medicines
he needed. He was now busily establishing an emergency medical center in a small office just off the lobby that
was never used in winter.

Upstairs, Blanche Mackintosh was opening guest
rooms that had been closed and locked for the winter
months, making up beds, and readying the rooms for
people who would be staying in town until this whole
thing was over.

Every now and then, someone in the lobby of the
hotel strolled to the front doors and looked out at the
white-sheeted town. And every time the door opened to
admit a newcomer, no head failed to turn to catch a
glimpse of the continuing storm.

It was still snowing.

9:18 A.M.

"Strangest thing I ever heard," George Yoshioshi was saying. He was working his way along the meat case of the Superette, clipboard in hand, taking inventory. He had volunteered to do this part of the task because he could, more readily than most of the others, evaluate what would be most useful if the town had to ration food for a couple of days. George had moved to the Kill a year before with his family and opened a Japanese restaurant down on Route 7. To the surprise of everyone in the Kill and the surrounding towns, it had turned out to be a great success, and George had become as much a part of the life of the Kill as many people whose families had been there for two hundred years. He checked the list on his clipboard once more against the contents of the meat case, then looked over at Steve Mercer, who was counting loaves of bread. "Really strange," he said.

Susan Lester looked up from the egg cartons she was counting.

"A train?" Steve said. He kept his hand between two loaves of bread to mark his place.

"Yep. A train. Jud said it was a train. Locomotive, coal tender, boxcars and coaches, the works. You know, a train."

"Yeah, I know," Steve said impatiently. "But, in the first place, those tracks have been abandoned for years. The only time they're ever used at all anymore is when the repair yard over in Oneonta runs a locomotive on them to test it out. And I don't think they're even much good for that anymore. Couldn't tell you the last time a train came through the Kill. You sure Jud said he actually *saw* it?"

George nodded.

Steve shook his head. "What time was this?"

"I think he said last night."

Steve shook his head again. "Well, if he says he saw it, I guess he at least *thinks* he saw it. But in the first place . . . No, in the *second* place, I don't think any train would be running in that storm, the way the snow was blowing and drifting last night. No way a train could get through that. And besides, what was Judson Taylor doing down that way anyhow last night? He lives 'way off on the other side of town. Maybe you should have smelled his breath or given him the old balloon test."

They laughed together and got back to counting the foodstuffs.

Susan Lester turned back to the eggs, but her mind was far away. All the sudden fright of the night before came rushing back to her and made a tight knot form in her stomach. She remembered first the icy roads, the car skidding and sliding beneath her, then going off the road, the savage wind pulling and clawing at her, the walk across the market field in the howling dark, then the hands—she was sure they'd been there and she was sure they'd been real—that had covered her eyes, and she remembered the circus train that had come clanking and rattling out of the storm, and the red-and-white painted face of the clown that had leered grotesquely at her from the window. She shuddered and drew back from the food case. Her hands, she noticed, were red from the cold, and hurting.

She told herself firmly that she had imagined the whole thing. She must have imagined it. And Judson Taylor had imagined seeing a train there too. For one silly moment, she wondered if you could see mirages in a snowstorm as well as in a desert. Mirages of circus trains, complete with clowns. She tried to smile at herself but could not. She'd seen the train, seen the clown at the window, felt the hands across her eyes. That goddamned train was as real as real could be.

"You done there yet, Susan?" George Yoshioshi asked from over at the meat case.

"Yes," Susan said quickly. She stood up and handed him the list of milk, eggs, butter, cheeses.

Steve Mercer was finished too. They took another look around the store to see if they'd forgotten anything important. Steve made a note of some bags of charcoal in a corner and a stack of artificial logs for fireplaces.

When they were at the front door and George was locking up—most of the Kill's shopkeepers left a spare set of keys in town for just such emergencies—Susan cleared her throat and said, as casually as she could manage, "I'll see you guys back at the hotel, okay?"

"Where are you going?" Steve Mercer asked.

"Enjoying the wild beauty of nature," George said, smiling.

"Some beauty," Steve said.

They ducked their heads into the falling snow and started trudging toward the hotel.

Susan waited a minute, until the two men had disappeared behind the shifting curtain of white, then turned and started walking the other way, toward the south side of the square and, beyond it, the railroad tracks and the depot.

As she pushed her way through the deep snow, she kept telling herself this was stupid, the whole thing was stupid, everything was stupid, especially herself, for seeing things, for believing them, for not believing them.

She bent her head lower to keep the snow from striking her face, and kept on walking.

9:35 A.M.

The train was still there.

Of course.

So she wasn't crazy, after all.

Susan had deliberately taken a route that would bring her down from the square past Railroad Street and Depot Street to the far end of the abandoned little station, a route that would hide the far side of the huge old warehouse, the side facing the tracks and the market field, until she was right down to the point where the tracks curved in against the platform. There were no tracks visible now. The place where she knew they ran was a solid blanket of white, stretching unbroken from where she stood across the vast open field beyond.

She came to the corner of the depot and stopped. The snow had drifted hip-deep here, and she had to reach a gloved hand out against the bare wood of the building to steady herself. Then, slowly, she moved out of the depot's shelter and stood beside the end of the platform. Not really wanting to do it, she raised her face into the snow and looked toward the warehouse.

The train was still there.

"Oh brother," she said out loud, and felt cold snow-flakes touch her lips.

The train stood still and silent beside the warehouse.

Thick snow had accumulated on the roofs of the cars and on the small platform at the end of the last coach. All around it snow had drifted up against the wheels and under the cars, and into the space between the warehouse and the train. None of it was touched. Not a mark disturbed it.

Susan took a deep breath and began climbing carefully up the six wooden steps at the end of the platform. Then the face of the clown loomed suddenly in her memory. She caught her breath, tasting the coldness of the air, hesitated, then turned and made her way back down the steps and away from the depot.

9:37 A.M.

As Susan hesitated at the far end of the depot platform, a figure moved in the last coach of the train. It
held aside ever so slightly the heavy draperies that
shrouded the glass of the narrow window at the end of
the car. It watched Susan, saw her stop, change her
mind, then go back down the steps.

The figure smiled, moved back, and let the draperies
fall heavily into place. It cocked its head to one side,
and its smile broadened.

It wore a black top hat, white tie with high white
collar, and black tails. It carried in one hand a black
baton with a silver tip that gleamed cruelly in the light
from a gas lamp.

The figure bent slightly forward again, held the
drapery aside with one crooked finger, and peeked out
once more. Susan was gone. The depot platform was
empty.

The figure moved away from the window, used the
silver-tipped baton to push the top hat back farther on
its head, then suddenly slapped its white-gloved hands
to its knees and doubled over with rollicking, silent
laughter.

9:37 A.M.

"What train," Richie Mead asked. "What are you talking about?"

George Yoshioshi told him again what Judson Taylor had said about seeing a train coming into town the night before and stopping at the depot.

Richie shook his head and rubbed the side of his face. "That doesn't make any sense."

"I *know* it doesn't make any sense," George said, unperturbed. "I just thought you should know."

"Yeah, right, you did the right thing," Richie said. "Okay, George, thanks. I'll look into it. Listen, if you run into Jud around anywhere, ask him to come see me."

"Sure thing," George said.

Richie wiped a hand across his eyes. He'd been up a while now already—how long? three hours—but he still felt as if he'd just rolled out of bed after a very, very bad night. He stood up from the desk in the hotel manager's office, stretched, and pressed his hands into the small of his back. Through the doorway, he saw Frank Carpenter coming toward him across the lobby.

"Did you find out about Hollander's snowmobile?" Richie asked as soon as the deputy had come through the doorway.

131

Frank grimaced. "Yeah. He doesn't have one. He decided not to buy it after he saw his kid's first report card this term. That gives us a grand total of six."

"Six. Terrific."

"Richie," Frank said mildly, "Deacons Kill is not exactly the United States capital of winter sports. I mean, we're not holding the Olympics here or something."

"Six."

"Right. Six."

"Okay, okay. Get teams together to go out and check on the folks on that list, the old folks and people with babies. I'd like the owners driving their own machines. They'll take better care of them, and there'll be fewer chances of an accident. This is no time for joyriding, so don't let any of the kids take them out. And if any of those people are having problems with food or heat or whatever, or if they're sick, the guys will just have to bundle them up and bring them in. Strap them across the snowmobile, if they have to. And check with Doc Warren before anyone leaves. He'll know if there's anyone out there who needs special attention. And tell everybody to take it easy with those things. I don't want any injuries. We've got our hands full as it is. I don't want to spend time rescuing the rescuers."

"Phil is getting them together now," Frank said. "Do you mind if I make a run myself?"

"No, go ahead. Better to be moving than just sitting around here."

"Do you want to go yourself? Phil and I can watch things here for a while."

Richie thought for a second, then shook his head. "No, I want to stay close in for right now. Maybe I'll take one out this afternoon and have a look around. Just keep your eyes open while you're out, okay?"

Frank left the office, and Richie rubbed his face again. He searched his brain to see if there was anything still left to do, but he thought everything was covered now. The hotel was ready to shelter people, checks were being made on food and fuel, rescue operations were starting, Doc had an emergency center set up in the hotel. Coffee. That was what else. It probably meant choosing between being bleary-eyed all day, at a time when he most needed to be alert, and being a little more clearheaded but having indigestion. He chose the indigestion and headed for the Dining Room.

In the lobby, several people greeted him, but he thought some of the others standing around eyed him curiously as he passed. He gave them all a general greeting. Then, in the middle of the lobby, he changed direction on impulse and walked slowly toward the front doors. Through the glass in the windows, he could see the snow still falling.

Always know your enemy, he thought, and reached for the door to pull it open.

The door swung back in his face and Susan Lester burst in.

"Richie," she said, "I need to talk to you."

9:45 A.M.

The snow in the square was deep and cold, muffling all sound. Except for the crunching of their boots and the sound of their own breathing, they moved through a great white cloud of silence.

Susan had told Richie about the train, told him about seeing it pull into the station, told him about its being a circus train, and told him about being frightened. She hadn't told him about the white-gloved hands that had covered her eyes or about the grinning face of the clown at the window. Those things would have been too much.

"You should have told me last night," Richie said, his breath puffing out white from his mouth. He had told her that in the office.

"I know," Susan said. "I'm sorry. Really, I am." She had said that in the office too. "I just didn't . . . I just didn't think it was that important. And then there was the meeting and everything, and I forgot."

They walked a few more steps, heads bent against the snow.

Richie said, "George Yoshioshi told me Jud Taylor saw the train too."

"I know," Susan said, so low that Richie barely heard her.

134

He stopped and looked at her. "How did you know that?"

"George was telling us while we were at the Superette."

Richie puffed out his cheeks and exhaled a long breath. "Are there any more secrets people are keeping from me?"

Susan met his irritated gaze. After a moment, she lowered her eyes and said, "Nothing that makes any sense."

"What's that supposed to mean?" The impatience in his voice was clear.

"Nothing," Susan said quickly. "Really. Nothing."

"Come on."

They pushed their way across the square where memory said the path should be, beneath trees straining with the burden of snow, past low bushes now nothing more than mottled white blocks. Their breath puffed out in little clouds before their faces with the effort of walking. The snow that struck them felt gritty, like tiny frozen pellets, and Richie prayed that the temperature wouldn't drop any lower.

When they were heading downhill and coming close to the depot, the same route Susan had taken a little while before, Richie stopped and took hold of her arm. His face was red with the cold and his eyes were watering.

"Tell me again," he said. "Are you sure you didn't see anybody get off the train?"

Susan shook her head and, for an instant, debated telling him the rest of it. But Richie was already walking again and she had to hurry to catch up. She didn't want to be left behind. That train, imaginary or not, made her awfully nervous.

They reached the end of the platform, and Richie climbed the steps where Susan had stopped before. He was standing with his gloved hands on his hips when she came up beside him.

The train looked the same as it had before.

"I don't believe it," Richie said. "I mean, I believe it, but I don't. It must be . . . I don't know. I guess I was a kid the last time a train like this came into the Kill."

"It's a circus train," Susan said.

"I suppose you saw a giraffe with its neck sticking up through the roof," Richie said. He didn't take his eyes from the train.

"It says so on the side." It came back to her now. "Stanton Stokely's Stupendous Circus."

"Never heard of it," Richie said. "Well, come on, if you want to. Let's go find out why the circus has come to town. In the dead of winter, at that." He started along the platform.

Susan thought of the clown again. "And why nobody came up to the hotel last night," she said softly.

Richie turned back to look at her. "To make no mention of how the train got here through the storm in the first place."

"That too," Susan said.

Richie stamped his feet to get the circulation going again and said, "You're making me nervous, do you know that? Come on, if you're coming."

"Grouch," she muttered under her breath. She saw from the angle of Richie's head that he'd heard her, but he chose to say nothing.

They pushed their way through the snow on the platform, past the weathered and cracked door and the boarded-up windows. At the other end, they climbed down and walked slowly toward the rear of the train.

"It's a circus train, all right," Richie said softly as they came close to it.

"Didn't you believe me?"

Richie didn't answer. He was looking down the narrow, shadowed corridor of space between the left-hand side of the train and the loading platform of the empty warehouse. After a few moments, he moved across the snow-covered tracks to the other side of the last coach. Susan followed him, picking her steps carefully through the heavy snow. She shivered when she came in sight of the curtained window where she'd seen the face of the clown.

Richie was studying the side of the coach, scanning the windows for any sign of occupants. The wood of the coach was covered by snow, and he could only discern a little of the colorful scrollwork and a couple of the letters that Susan remembered so clearly. He stepped closer and wiped his hands across the wood, then stepped back to read it. His lips moved silently at the words.

"A circus, for God's sake," he said. "I wouldn't believe it if I didn't see it with my own eyes."

"Maybe you shouldn't believe it now, either," Susan said under her breath.

Richie glanced at her, then looked back at the side of the train. "What?"

"Nothing."

Richie looked to his right, down the length of the train, toward the black coal tender, covered now with snow, and the towering locomotive. Susan followed his gaze, remembering how the light from the engine's headlamp had pierced the snowy darkness. Could it have been only last night?

"Doesn't look like there's anybody home," Richie

said. He started off through the deep snow, half walking, half stumbling, toward the front of the train, squinting up through the falling snow at the curtained windows of the coaches.

Susan took two steps after him, then stopped. She looked up at the window where she'd seen the clown. There was no sign of life there now, nothing at all to indicate that anyone or anything had moved recently—or ever, for that matter—inside the coach. Snow had piled up on the narrow ledge of the window and on the thin wood frames of the small panes of glass. Some snow had adhered to the glass itself, further obscuring a view of the interior, but she could just make out what might have been a brocaded drapery of deep maroon. There was nothing to be seen at any of the other windows, and Susan stared up at them, blinking in the snow that struck her face, trying to sort out memories from imaginings. She *knew* she had seen a face. Or thought she did.

"You look like you're in a trance," Richie said beside her, and Susan jumped.

"This train gives me the creeps," she said.

"Well, it's pretty weird, showing up here at a time like this." He looked again at the train and frowned. "But what I'd like to know is, where the hell is everybody? This thing looks deserted, and we still haven't seen anyone in town."

He hitched his collar higher around his chin and tramped off through the snow toward the platform at the end of the last coach. Three iron steps descended from the platform. Richie brushed the snow off them before climbing up. When he was on the platform, he put his face close to the glass of the window and tried to see inside.

"Richie, be careful," Susan called up to him. She

held her breath as Richie glanced down at her, drew back from the window, and knocked hard at the door. They could hear it rattle against its latch, but there was no other sound at all.

Richie knocked again, but Susan could see from the way he stood that he didn't expect an answer.

"Hey! Anybody home?" he called, but he was already moving to the edge of the platform. He crouched there for a second, then jumped down to the ground, kicking up a spray of powdery snow.

He looked at Susan, and his expression was puzzled and worried. "This is really strange," he said. "And I've got enough headaches to think about right now. Let's go. They'll turn up sooner or later, and I don't have the time to go searching for people who are already in town."

Much to Susan's annoyance, her conscience had been bothering her about not telling Richie everything that had happened—or that she thought had happened—the evening before. Although the thought made her stomach flutter, she said, "Maybe you should break the door down or something."

"That's only in the movies," Richie said. "And in Russia. We don't do that here when nobody's done anything wrong. Come on."

Although the mystery of the train's presence here was no clearer than it had been, Susan was relieved to move away from it. She'd already seen it more times than she cared to. And it had frightened her each time.

They made their way across the tracks, past the end of the train, through the same irregular channel they'd kicked in the snow before. Susan suddenly was very uncomfortable turning her back on the train. She shuddered violently and clutched at Richie's arm as they reached the top of the steps to the depot platform.

"What's wrong?" he asked quickly.

"I . . . I guess I'm just cold. I should have put on another sweater."

Her teeth were chattering now, and she was shivering. Richie put his arms around her—a clumsy movement with all the clothes they were wearing—and said, nodding at the depot and its boarded-up waiting room, "Let's duck in here for a minute. It won't be very warm, but it might help a little. It's a long walk back to the hotel."

Susan looked dubiously at the gray wood of the old station, but she was shivering so hard that the prospect of a few minutes rest, out of the snow, was very attractive. They moved toward the door, and Richie took his arm from around her shoulders to try the lock. Susan hugged herself for warmth and clamped her jaws together to try to still the chattering of her teeth.

Richie turned the old-fashioned latch on the door. Nothing happened. He tried it again, this time pushing with his shoulder. The door groaned and moved inward a little. Richie stepped back for leverage, then shoved hard again. This time the door, protesting loudly with creakings and a loud snap, flew backward so quickly that Richie stumbled and had to grab at the doorframe to keep his balance.

"God, this just isn't my day," he said. "Come on in. At least it won't snow on us in here."

Susan followed him into the dark interior of the abandoned railroad station. Even in the cold, the air smelled musty and stale, and the floorboards creaked painfully beneath their weight.

"Richie," Susan managed to get out through clenched teeth. "I'm really sor—"

Behind her, the old door slammed shut with a loud

bang and left them in the dark. They both felt their hearts stop dead for an instant.

"Welcome," said a man's voice from the blackness at the back of the depot. "I'm so glad you've come."

10:02 A.M.

Alice Bissell was building a snowman at last.

Earlier in the morning, Leon had finally worked up the nerve to talk back—he spoke very mildly but, for Leon, it constituted talking back—to his wife. And at that, he only did so after Sally's repeated shrill refusals had left Alice sobbing and curled into a ball at the corner of the couch. Leon hated to see Alice in tears even more than he hated his wife's constant yelling and complaints, and that had finally done it. He'd told Sally that Alice really was well enough now—really, honest— and that it wouldn't hurt her to go outside for an hour to play in the snow if she put on all her heaviest, warmest clothes and didn't run around too much. Sally had yelled some more, of course, but Leon, trembling at his own nerve and worrying about what he was in for later in the day, had taken Alice by the hand and led her back to her bedroom and told her to get dressed. He'd stood there and helped and supervised personally to make sure she was dressed good and warm. Then they'd gone outside together to build a snowman.

Alice was trying to roll a ball of snow hard enough to make a nose for the figure, but her hands were too small and her fingers too cold, and the wool knit gloves were long since soaked through, although she wouldn't say a word about it to her father and she'd have to hide the wet gloves from her mother.

"Here, let's try like this," Leon said. He guided Alice's little hands on the snowball, but his own hands actually did the work. Both of them were covered with snow, and Alice got more on her as she slipped from her squatting position and fell sideways, laughing loudly and merrily at herself.

"This won't work," Leon said. He was trying to get the snowball to adhere to the snowman's face to form a nose, but he wasn't having any luck with it. He tossed the snowball aside.

"Wait a minute," he cried suddenly. "Hey, wait a minute! I know what'll work just fine! You wait right here, honey, don't go off anywhere, and I'll be right back!"

He rose, quickly dusted a little of the snow from his clothes, and dashed off, as best he could through the deep snow, toward the kitchen door. In the doorway, he hesitated for a second, fearing Sally's wrath if he tracked wet snow into the house, but then he went ahead anyway, grabbed a package out of the food closet, and ran outside and back to Alice in front of the house.

"What is it, Daddy?"

"Look!" Leon said, holding up a blue package. "Oreo cookies!"

They laughed together.

"Here," Leon said. "Use these." He eagerly pulled the package open and handed one to Alice.

"Could I eat one?"

Leon checked the bag. "Sure. We've got plenty."

Alice put the first one in her mouth, and Leon handed her another.

"Try not to break 'em," he said. "Just press it in real easy."

Alice pressed the dark brown cookie against the snowman's face and—presto!—he had a nose. Very carefully, she added two more for eyes.

Leon was frowning, biting his lower lip. Then he grinned broadly. "I've got it!" He pulled two more cookies from the package.

"What, Daddy?"

Very carefully, concentrating on the task, Leon broke the two Oreos into jagged halves.

"There you are," he said. "You can use those to make the mouth."

They laughed together again, and Alice, taking great care not to crumble the dark cookies on the white snow, carefully pressed them into place.

"Give him a big smile," Leon said. "I like it when they have a big smile."

"Me too," Alice said happily. "I'll give him the biggest smile in the whole world."

And she did.

All the while they worked on the snowman, laughing in the falling snow and sharing the Oreo cookies, Sally Bissell glared coldly at them from the living-room window.

10:02 A.M.

Susan gasped, and Richie Mead snapped, "Who's there?"

A floorboard creaked in the darkness. For an instant, the only other sound in the deserted depot was their own tense breathing. Then the voice came again from the darkness at the back.

"Oh, please, do not be alarmed. I certainly didn't mean to startle you." A floorboard groaned again, as if someone had taken a step toward them.

"Who is it?" Richie said. "Come out of there!"

There was a tiny scraping noise and suddenly the yellow light of a flame shot up through the darkness. It flared, flickered, then settled into the steady yellow glow of a wooden match. They could see the hand holding it out toward them; then, as their eyes adjusted to the sudden light, they made out the figure of a man behind it. He raised the arm higher, lifting the flaming match, and the light increased a little. The figure was tall, dressed in a black overcoat of antique cut, and wearing a shining black top hat. The flickering light of the flame was reflected in the man's eyes, dancing there merrily, and he was smiling.

"Be careful with that match in here!" Richie said. "Who are you? What are you doing here?"

With a sudden flick of his wrist, as if the flame had come too close to his bare fingers, the stranger extinguished the match.

Susan clutched at Richie's arm, then inched backward toward the door, groping blindly behind her for the handle.

Another match sprang to life, casting its unsteady light on the stranger's face.

"I said, *who are you?*"

"I am—"

Susan grasped the handle of the door and yanked it open. Gray light rushed in, bright in contrast to the darkness of the old waiting room.

"There," said the stranger. "That's much better." He flicked out the second match, tossed it away, and took several steps toward Richie Mead and the brighter light from the doorway.

"I am Stanton Stokely," the stranger said, smiling. "I am owner, proprietor, and, of course, ringmaster of Stanton Stokely's Stupendous Circus. And I am at your service." He bowed gracefully, theatrically, before Richie, then straightened up and looked with amusement into the younger man's face. "And I am deeply regretful if I startled you." His glance took in both Richie and Susan. "It was not my intention."

"*Startled* us!" Richie said. "You scared the hell out of us! What are you doing here?"

The stranger's smile faded slightly. "I was merely—"

"You're from the train," Richie said. "That's your train out there. The circus train."

"It is, indeed," Stokely said. "I gather you've already investigated. Are you the local representative of the law?"

"Yes," Richie said, "I'm the sheriff," and felt a slight flush rise into his cheeks at not having identified himself to the stranger at once. He felt Susan's touch on his arm again and summoned up his most authoritative tone of voice. "I'll ask you one more time. What are you doing in here?"

"Why," said Stokely, "the same thing I imagine you were doing. I was seeking shelter from the storm."

Richie thought there might have been a hint of amusement, or even mockery, in the man's words, but there was nothing he could react to. And as far as he knew, the man had done nothing at all that was wrong.

"When the door blew closed," Stokely continued, "I was quite as surprised as you were, I assure you."

Richie was tempted to murmur, *I'll bet,* but kept the thought to himself. Instead, he said, "Come over here by the door where there's light."

The three of them formed a close circle just inside the doorway, with flurries of snow blowing in on them and dusting their clothes. Susan stayed close to Richie and kept her eyes fixed on Stokely's face.

"How did the train get through the snow?" Richie asked, nodding sharply toward the train. "Nothing ever moves on that line, it's never used anymore. And I wouldn't have thought *anything* could get through the snow last night."

Stokely smiled broadly and, in the brighter daylight from outdoors, revealed a rosy, pleasant face, lined but kindly, with eyes that seemed perpetually to twinkle at some secret jest. "It wasn't easy," he said, "I can tell you that. The crew had all they could do to reach the town before the storm forced us to stop. Quite a storm, quite a storm, indeed," he said, looking past Richie and Susan, out the door and up toward the gray skies and falling snow. "Is the town still open, or are we cut off completely from civilization?"

"We're cut off," Richie said brusquely. He took a

step outside the door and blinked in the snow as he looked toward the train. "Where is everybody?"

"On board, of course," Stokely replied.

"All of them? The crew and everybody else?"

"On board," said Stokely, imperturbable.

"Look," Richie said, "we're in the middle of a crisis here and I don't have time to stand around playing Twenty Questions. So why don't you just tell me what's going on. What's that train doing here in the first place, who's on it, and why the hell are they *still* on it?"

Stokely's smile faded quickly into a solemn expression. "Of course," he said. "Forgive me. I didn't realize how serious the town's situation is. The town. This *is* Deacons Kill, is it not?"

"Yes."

"Ah. I thought so, but I'm afraid our maps are a little out of date. Well, then, let me get on with it." He grasped the lapels of his overcoat. "Stanton Stokely's Stupendous Circus is on a winter tour of the northern states. We have our own train, as you have seen, which is occupied by ourselves alone and operated by our own crew. We travel widely and make the train our home. We—"

"What were you doing on this line?"

Stokely looked momentarily embarrassed. He dropped his gaze to the floor, then lifted his head and looked past them again, out at the snow. He spoke more slowly and a lot less grandly. "Things are not now as they were before. Alas. In plain truth, I will tell you— and ask you to keep the information to yourselves, if you'd be so kind—that times are very bad for us, very bad indeed. We take such bookings as we can get. Very often, I am sorry to say, we find ourselves in rather remote areas. But, of course," he added hastily, "I'm quite certain that the Kill is a fine and prosperous town, and I am hopeful that we will be invited to give a performance here. In fact, I was just exploring when we met, and this warehouse beside the depot is the very—"

"I really don't think we're in the market for any circus performances just now," Richie said. "But why haven't we seen any of your people? Why did you spend the night in the train, in this weather?"

Stokely sighed. "Alas, again," he said heavily. "We have all been sick, both performers and crew, all of us. The weather was responsible, no doubt, and—"

"What do you mean, you've all been sick? What was the problem?"

"Nothing more exotic, I'm afraid, than the ordinary illnesses of winter. We were—"

"Flu?" Richie asked.

"Very likely. Of some sort. But it's almost done with now, sheriff, I assure you of that. There is absolutely no cause for alarm. I've been fortunate enough to be recovered a little ahead of the others, but my colleagues will be fine in a day or two. The crew barely had strength yesterday to operate the train, but they're coming along nicely now. Indeed, it's just as well that we're here. It will give my people a chance to recover before continuing on. In the meantime, we thought it best if we all simply remained on board the train. We are adequately supplied with both food and firewood for our stoves —this is a *very* old train—so we shall want for nothing. And we shall be no burden to the town in its time of crisis. Indeed, I should like to offer what little assistance we can. I put myself at your service, sheriff, and as soon as the rest of my company are up and about, I assure you that we will offer whatever sort of aid might be needed."

Richie looked doubtful. The whole damned thing sounded ridiculous, but this crazy character and whoever else was on the train had done nothing wrong, and apparently were going to keep to themselves and be no problem.

"I'll have the doctor come down, if you'd like," he said, already anticipating Stokely's answer.

"No, no, I couldn't put him to that trouble in weather like this when there's no need. But thank you."

"Do you have any clowns in the circus?" Susan asked suddenly.

Stokely threw back his head and laughed easily and loudly. "Why, of course, we do, dear lady." Then his expression grew more solemn. "In truth," he said, "we have *only* clowns. But Stanton Stokely's Stupendous Circus has the finest and funniest clowns in all the land." He chuckled again, and now there were tears, either of laughter or cold, in his eyes and running down his cheeks. "Dear lady," he said, smiling warmly, "a circus can survive without many things. But what would be the point of it all without clowns?"

10:31 A.M.

"Mommy, isn't he pretty? Isn't he?"

Sally Bissell kept her hands clasped tightly at her waist as she looked down at her daughter's face.

"It's ugly," she said. "Ugly. And you have no business being out in the snow. You'll be sick again, and then somebody'll have to take care of you. But it won't be me, I can promise you that. It won't be me! I've done my share. That dumb father of yours doesn't have the brains of that snowman, I swear to God he doesn't." Her voice was tight, almost short of breath with anger. Without unclasping her hands, she crossed the room to the window and looked out at the falling snow and the snowman standing in the front yard.

"This town isn't safe," she said. "Not in a storm like this. We should be getting out of here while the getting's good. That's what we should be doing."

She turned away from the window and looked at Alice.

"That's what we should be doing," she said.

11:15 A.M.

"The Kill," Susan said.

She was sitting across from Richie in his office, where they had gone after leaving Stanton Stokely and his circus train. The two of them had labored through the snow in silence, saving their breath for the effort of walking, each of them suspecting that the other was equally lost in thought. When they neared the top of the square, Richie had turned toward the corner of Hill Street, and Susan, since she was neither asked nor sent away, had followed.

She was thinking of the clown—that grotesque painted face at the window of the train—and the ringmaster's laughter when she'd asked if the circus had clowns. "Dear lady," he had said, "what would be the point of it all without clowns?" She could still hear his voice and his laugh. But something else had bothered her too, something he had said. She waited until Richie had finished checking with his deputies. When he finally came over and sat at his desk, where she was waiting, Susan took a deep breath and told him.

"What do you mean?" Richie said.

"When we were talking to that man, Stanton Stokely, he said, 'the Kill,' the way people do who live here."

Richie looked at her blankly. "So?"

"So that's weird, isn't it? I mean, he doesn't live here in Deacons Kill. He just sort of . . . blew into town, right? So why should he call it 'the Kill'?"

Richie looked weary. "Susan," he said, "I really don't know. All I know is that the town is still snowed in, it's *still* snowing out there, and it looks like it's going to continue snowing until, literally, and you should excuse the expression, hell itself freezes over." He leaned back into his chair and his voice softened a little. "Look, I admit we had a scare back there, both of us. First, that door slams on us, then this guy suddenly speaks up in a place that we thought was empty. Big deal. All it means is that our nerves are frayed. I know I can vouch for my own and . . . well, look, I'm sorry, I know I keep jumping at you. But I think your nerves are showing too, and I can tell you they don't look so hot. In fact, they look a little ragged around the edges."

"You don't think it's weird about the train?"

Richie looked toward the ceiling, imploring divine help from above, and for a moment Susan thought he was going to stand up and send her away. Instead, he made his voice even more patient, a tone that grated on Susan's nerves. But, annoyed as she was, she still had the face of the clown looming in her mind, along with the fact that she had, as yet, said nothing about it to anyone. She controlled her annoyance and listened as Richie answered slowly.

"Yes, I think it's *very* weird about the train. Very, very weird. Exceedingly weird. I don't understand why it's on this line in the first place, since this line is ninety-nine and forty-four one-hundredths per cent abandoned. I don't understand how the train got here at all, coming through all that snow, although obviously it did, so I suppose it just managed to get through before the snow got too deep on the tracks. I think it's strange that everybody in the train *stayed* in the train, although it's true that Stokely said no one needed medical attention. *That* bit bothers me—about them all being sick—but if the man says they all had the sniffles, it's none of my business. I'll be damned if I know what a circus train is doing wandering around abandoned railroad lines in the northern Catskills in the dead of winter. And, just to make the record complete, I thought our friend down there was himself exceedingly weird. In plain English, he rubbed me the wrong way, although he did offer his own assistance, if we need it, and the assistance of his people, as soon as they're well enough. And from the look of that storm and the way it doesn't look like stopping, we're all going to be cooped up here long enough to *need* their help and for them to be well enough to give it. On the one hand, it's true that they aren't exactly pitching in to help. On the other hand, we really don't need their help just now. On the other hand—which, come to think of it, is the *third* hand—they are neither asking for any help themselves, nor getting in the way, nor, I assure you, are they doing anything wrong. The only other thing I know is that, since it no longer requires my attention, I don't have time to discuss it any further. And that's what I think about the whole thing, circus train, ringmaster, the lot.'' He spread his hands wide, palms up.

Susan's first thought was to be annoyed at what she thought was a condescending tone. But then she told herself that Richie wasn't being condescending at all. He had stated the case very fully and very fairly. What else was there to say?

But there was something. "Richie, he said they were using firewood to heat the cars. Did you see any smoke coming from chimneys or whatever?"

Richie thought for a second. "I don't remember. I

guess there was.''

"But if—''

Richie leaned forward and said, "Susan," in the warmest tone he'd used to her all day. "Listen, I know I keep snapping at you and I really am sorry. I hope you believe that. But you have to believe me when I tell you that nothing's wrong down there. Strange, maybe, or unusual, or weird, but nothing wrong. I didn't like that Stokely any more than you did, but I can't lock him up for being weird.'' He shrugged and looked helpless.

Susan looked away from him, pressed her lips together, and closed her eyes for a second. Make a decision, she told herself firmly. Now or never. Speak up or forever hold your peace. She thought of how Richie would react, and how her words would sound to herself, if she told him about Sunday night. The face of the clown flared brightly for a second in her thoughts, then quickly faded away to nothing.

"Okay," she said, looking up at Richie. "I have nothing to add.''

12:10 P.M.

"Well, it's broken, all right. You did a good, thorough job of it, too. Snapped it right through." Doc Warren peered over his half-glasses, wrinkling his forehead, as he looked at Frank Carpenter.

"Oh, for Christ's sake!" Frank said. The pain was clear in his eyes, and sweat ran down the side of his face, but his expression was more one of annoyance and frustration and embarrassment than anything else. He turned his head to look up at Richie Mead.

"I'm really sorry, Richie," he said. "I really am. I—"

He winced as Doc Warren straightened out the leg.

"I'm really sorry."

"It's okay, Frank," Richie said. He had been beside Frank since the other men had carried him in while Doc Warren silently ran expert fingers over the leg. "We'll manage. Don't worry about it. Just do whatever Doc tells you to do. Right, Doc?"

The doctor looked across Frank at the sheriff's face. "I'm afraid he doesn't have much choice in the matter. I'm going to set the leg with a lightweight splint. If you have to break your leg, this is the way to do it, nice and clean. It won't be as painful as you might think, once it's set, but he's going to have to stay very still and be very careful with it for a while. Isn't that right, Frank?"

"Right, Doc," Frank said resignedly, and looked helplessly up at Richie.

"Right," Doc repeated brusquely. "Now, sheriff, if you'll just leave me here alone to do my job, you'll be able to get on with your own. Blanche, please give me a hand here." Blanche Mackintosh had offered to help the doctor any way she could, since none of the three nurses who lived in the Kill could be located at the hotel. They had either been out of town to begin with, or on duty at Fox Memorial in Oneonta, or they just couldn't get in to the hotel.

"I'll check up on you later," Richie told Frank, then left the room and went back out to the lobby.

"Is it broken?"

Richie turned to see Susan standing beside him.

He exhaled deeply. "Why do I feel like all of a sudden I have a shadow? Can you tell me that?"

"Because you do," Susan said, trying a smile and pleased to find it still worked. "Think of me as a guardian angel." Then the smile wavered. "Look, my nerves are on edge too, like everybody else's. I was . . . I was just trying to help."

"It's broken," he told her.

"Crap," Susan said, then lowered her voice when she saw Bob Booth and Tom Trenchard glance at them from the other side of the lobby. "That's too bad," she said more softly. "Well, as far as I can see, you've already done whatever there is to do right now."

"Come in here," Richie said, and led the way into the office he was using.

With the door closed behind her, Susan said quietly, "I was just trying to be around so you'd have somebody to talk to, especially now that Frank is out of commission."

Richie was silent for a second, then said, his tone as quiet as hers, "Susan, I appreciate having you around, but I don't have time to be social right now."

"I know—"

"Look, this storm we're having is a genuine, honest-to-God crisis, not some entertainment being put on to keep us all amused and busy. We already have one serious injury. We're going to have more. There are still people out there, old people and others, who are in very real danger, whose lives are actually threatened by the storm. And it's all up to me to keep the damage and danger to a minimum. As for that crazy circus train, it just isn't at the top of the priority list right now. Okay?"

Susan nodded. "Okay."

"I'm taking out one of the snowmobiles myself now to have a look around," Richie said. "If you want to be helpful, check with Phil Aymar or see if there's something else to be done here in the hotel. I'm sure there's something that needs doing. This place is going to be filled to capacity by tonight."

When he left the office, Susan stared after him a long time while he put on his coat and hat and gloves and went out through the front doors into the still-falling snow.

1:15 P.M.

Blanche Mackintosh had finished helping Doc Warren and had spent some extra time seeing to it that Frank Carpenter was settled comfortably in a room upstairs. Doc had given Frank something to make him sleep for a couple of hours, and he was snoozing away comfortably when Blanche stole quietly from the room.

Lord, she was thinking, if this is where it starts, where will it be ending? How many more people are going to be hurt?

Blanche was standing at the linen closet, checking her list to see which rooms still needed to be made up, when she saw Susan Lester coming toward her down the hall.

"Susan, child," she said at once, "why do you have such a long face?"

"Do I?" Susan said. "Sorry. I asked around downstairs to see if anyone needed help with anything, but everything seems to be taken care of."

Blanche lifted her eyebrows. "Is that why you look like that? Because everything is under control?"

"No, I just . . . Well, Mr. Overholt said you were making up rooms, so I thought I'd come up and see if you needed any help."

"Well, as a matter of fact, child, I could use some help. I could always use some help. In times like these, this place is a lot to handle for one old lady. You can help me, sure. Here, let's get this cart out here and we'll start on this hall.''

Blanche loaded the cart with sheets and blankets, soap, toilet paper and tissues, and together they wheeled it down the hall and started on the first of the rooms.

"You'll be all set for another job if the real estate business doesn't work out for you," Blanche said as she and Susan tucked in a sheet beneath the mattress.

Susan said nothing.

"Well, I suppose that's a poor sort of joke and doesn't deserve an answer," Blanche said.

"Oh, I'm sorry," Susan said. "I guess my mind is far away."

Blanche straightened up and put her hands on her hips. "Your mind is far away, all right. If you ask me, which you didn't, it's just exactly as far away as Sheriff Richie Mead has gotten by now on that machine."

Susan blushed and looked at Blanche.

"Now don't you be telling me it's otherwise, because I saw the way you looked at him and I even heard the way you talked to him when he was in the lobby downstairs. And if *you* didn't hear that tone in your voice, you better start paying attention to the way you're talking and the way you're sounding, because sooner or later, *he* will."

"I didn't mean to—"

"Maybe you didn't mean to, but you sure did, anyway, whether you know it or not."

"All I wanted to do was help."

"All you wanted to do was be near him. But there's another part to it too, I think. I was watching the way you looked out at the snow."

Susan looked puzzled. "What's that supposed to mean?"

"It means," Blanche said, "that you're all excited about the snow closing us off from the outside world. Well, I'm here to tell you that it's exciting, all right— that it is—but not the way you might think. This is not excitement like you might talk about otherwise. This kind of excitement is nothing more nor less than *danger,* and I think we should all keep that clear in our heads. I'm telling you, it's *danger.*" Despite her words, Blanche's tone softened toward the end of her speech. "Now, don't you say a word," she added. "You just think about what I said. Now let's get a move on. There's still lots of rooms to do up. I swear, at times like this, the rooms always seem to multiply, all by themselves."

They finished with the room they were in and moved on to the next one, working together in silence, quickly and efficiently, finding the rhythm of their work.

"Hey, Blanche."

They turned toward the door of the room and saw Jimmy French standing in the hallway.

Blanche scowled at him. "What are you doing up here? You're not supposed to be up here."

"I can go any place I want. You can't stop me. It's a free country."

"Jimmy, don't be so fresh," Susan said sharply. "Now go on downstairs."

"Aw, they told me downstairs to go someplace else. That's why I came up here, just to see what's going on."

"Well, *nothing*'s going on," Blanche told him firmly, "so get back down where you belong."

"Hey, come on, I'm not in the way or nothing. I'll stay out of your way, I promise."

"You stay up here, young man," Susan said, "and you'll have to help. Are you any good at making beds?"

"Nah," Jimmy said. He stayed out in the hall. "Hey,

I heard some guys saying there was a circus train down by the depot.''

Susan looked at the boy, and Blanche looked at Susan.

After a moment, Susan said, "That's right, there is, but it doesn't concern you, so just forget about it. Now, make up your mind: either go downstairs or pitch in and help."

"Aw, pitch in yourself," Jimmy said. He laughed at his own cleverness, then jumped forward, grabbed the door handle, and slammed it shut on them. They heard his laughter receding down the hall.

Through clenched teeth, Susan said, "That child could provoke a very serious crime. Like maybe murder. If we're all cooped up in one place here for very long, I wouldn't give a nickel for his chances. Little monster."

"That's no way to talk about a child, Susan," Blanche said as she went back to working on the bed. "Not even about *that* child."

They worked a few minutes longer in silence, then Blanche straightened up from the bed and rubbed her back to ease the stiffness.

"May the Lord forgive me for saying it," she said sadly, "but that child *is* a little monster. I swear, he'll be the death of me yet."

1:20 P.M.

"No, you can't!" Sally Bissell told Leon.

"But why not?"

"I told you why not! What good are you to your family if you're down at the damned hotel? This is your place, right here. My God, I have to tell you everything. Your place is right here, with your family, to protect us. Look at that! Look out that window!"

Leon looked where she pointed.

"What do you see?"

Leon squinted.

"It's still snowing, you moron. It's still snowing! That's what you see. That's why you have to be home to protect us, not running around with all your pals, having a grand old time. Anything could happen in a storm like this. Anything!"

Leon looked very worried, but he said, "All right, Sally, if that's what you want, I'll stay home and protect you."

"You bet your life you will," Sally said. "You bet your life. In fact, we're all betting our lives just staying here in this no-good, two-bit town, this no-good town we're *stuck* in because you're too dumb to make something of yourself."

Leon lowered his head and looked surreptitiously toward the bedroom. Alice's door was closed, and he hoped fervently that she couldn't hear any of this.

"Well, I *won't* be stuck in it," Sally went on. "I won't. Do you hear me? I won't be stuck here, because we're getting out. That's what we're doing. We're getting out."

Leon spread his hands out in front of him and said, "Sally," very softly.

"We're getting out," Sally said again.

1:35 P.M.

As soon as he had gotten away from the office and the Centennial Hotel, Richie Mead felt as if he could breathe freely for the first time in twenty-four hours.

Out here in the cold, whizzing along on the snow-mobile, cheeks frozen by the wind, he felt free of the confines of the town, the hotel, the lists of names, the thousand-and-one items to think of and do that wouldn't make any great difference to anything or anybody. He felt, in fact, more than anything else in the world, free of the waiting. All that sitting around, drinking endless cups of coffee. Trekking back and forth between the office and the hotel. Standing around, talking to the local citizens, keeping the worry out of his face and his eyes and the lines of his mouth. Finding excuses for things to do, things that would only pass the time, keep his mind occupied. Walking down to that damned depot with Susan, looking at that damned circus train, talking to that damned spooky ringmaster. All of it just excuses to try and escape the waiting. Walking up and down, and waiting. Looking out the door or the window and waiting, waiting endlessly for the snow to stop.

But out here he was doing something useful and posi-tive, checking on his people and the land he was responsible for. Out here in the white cold and the roads, the fields, the hillsides of Deacons Kill, with the blurred snow streaking past him on the wind, he felt free and strong. His heart raced at the speed he was doing, his breath came short, and for the first time since Sunday afternoon, he began to feel that maybe everything wasn't so bad after all.

Around him the world was white and still and silent. Only the snow moved. The single sound was that of the machine beneath him, a sound that, in the white stillness of the world, was strong and purposeful.

He had left the square by going around the western corner of the hotel and heading up Hill Street. He increased the speed a little where Hill Street started climbing and turned into Deacons Road, winding up higher and higher toward Deacons Rise. He had slowed a little when he drew near Sheriff John Chard's home on Deacons Road, but as soon as he felt himself getting thoughtful about Chard—who should have been here to run things, not leaving a deputy in his place to fill his very large shoes—Richie had gunned the engine and sped on by.

Now he was sailing up the road, past the old Ferrand place where that new couple from New York lived. He remembered Jack telling him they'd be down in the city for a couple of weeks, so there was nothing to worry about there. Then he was speeding past dark trees, white-covered, on either side of the road. The world, impossible though it seemed, was even more silent here. Nothing moved. Not a branch, not a bird, not a breeze. Only the snow continued falling.

He topped a rise in the roadway and, for one heart-stopping instant felt the snowmobile leave the surface and move through the air. It landed on the downhill slope of the snow-blanketed road, unmarked by tracks of any sort, only rippled a little by Sunday night's furious wind, and raced on down the hill. Snowbanks blocked any view for a minute. Then off to the left, a blinding white vista opened out: a farm on the far side of a hill, weathered red silo and freshly painted red barn, like smears of blood on the white hillside. Remember to look in on them on the way back, he reminded himself. A moment later the road cut to the right, and the farm and the valley were gone.

The house he was seeking was on the far side of the next hill, and Richie almost hated to be drawing close to it. He hoped the people there, a couple in their seventies, were all right, not in any danger from the cold. But he would have preferred to keep on going, keep on racing, keep on speeding through the blinding, blurring whiteness of the snow-covered world.

He reached the house and found the couple in fine shape, with at least a week's supply of food, and not at all perturbed by the storm, only angry because the telephone didn't work. When he left the house and went back to the snowmobile and started out of the yard, the snowflakes that were falling seemed, he thought, to have grown a little heavier still.

2:08 P.M.

Jimmy French had been spending his time listening.

He had heard several different people mention a circus train, but he'd caught only odd bits of information from the adults' talk and he still didn't know too much about it.

Earlier in the day, he'd been playing with Freddie Ellenwood, and twice he'd been on the verge of saying something to Freddie about the train. But he'd thought better of it and caught himself each time before he'd spilled the little he knew himself. Why should he tell dumb Freddie? Freddie would only go and blab about it to the other kids, and then they'd all know about it. Jimmy liked being the only one who knew, so he'd kept quiet. Freddie hadn't said a word, so Jimmy figured it was because he didn't know anything about the train. Freddie would have told him if he did, since Freddie was too dumb to know when to keep his mouth shut about a good thing.

After he'd ditched Freddie, Jimmy had wandered around the lobby for a while, keeping out of trouble and staying as quiet as a mouse, just listening. Then he'd sort of strolled through the Dining Room for a few minutes and then wandered through the lounge, pretending he was looking for somebody.

And he learned that there really was a circus train in town. Nobody knew too much about it, and only a few people—so Jimmy gathered from the odds and ends of talk he could catch—had actually been down that way and seen it, but he had learned the most important thing: there was a circus train down at the depot.

Jimmy was glad of the storm, because that meant that all the boring old farts, including his parents—he'd seen them sitting in the lounge, drinking beer with some of their friends, but they hadn't seen him—weren't going to go out in the snow just to look at an old train.

He had heard the talk in the bar. "Damn strange, a circus train, can you beat that?" one of his father's drinking buddies had been saying. "Well, it ain't no business of mine if they want to sit down there and freeze their asses. Leave 'em there all winter long, for all of me. Then we'll go down there in the spring and chop 'em up and use 'em for ice cubes." Everyone had laughed.

So, the way Jimmy saw it, he had a clear field. Nobody to stop him and nobody to chase him home. He was going to get himself a good up-close look at that circus train and see if there were any animals or clowns. Maybe he could play a trick on them or something.

He took another long look around the lobby, then slipped away up the stairs to get his coat. If he was really careful about it, he could get back downstairs again, and slip into the Dining Room and through the swinging doors into the kitchen. Then he could get out the back door of the hotel and be gone before anybody even knew he was missing.

2:23 P.M.

Susan remembered very clearly Blanche Mackintosh's voice and the woman's frown when they'd talked earlier in the day, but she said it anyway.

"When you go out again, Richie, would you mind if I go with you?"

Richie was eating a meatloaf sandwich at a booth in the Dining Room. He finished the bite he'd just taken and put the rest of the sandwich on the plate.

"Why?" he said, and looked her straight in the eye.

Susan could hear Blanche Mackintosh again in her thoughts.

"Because I feel useless, just sitting around here, doing nothing."

"Lots of people are sitting around here, doing nothing," Richie said. "Half of Deacons Kill is just sitting around here, doing nothing."

Susan caught the first words that occurred to her before she actually said them out loud.

"Richie, don't be so damned stubborn. And just because you're so worried about all of this, doesn't mean you have to be such a crab. I can help. Sure, half the town is sitting around here, doing nothing. There's a bunch of guys in the bar who've already been there half the day."

"Yeah, I know," Richie said sourly. "That crowd that usually drinks down at Eddie's."

Susan nodded. "Right. Well, I've already helped Blanche do up the rooms for anybody else who comes in, and that's about all there is. I'm sitting around here like you, just . . . I don't know, just waiting, and it's getting on my nerves too. I'd like to get outside and *do* something, something positive, anything not to be sitting around here anymore."

Richie looked thoughtful.

"Can you drive a snowmobile?"

"Of course."

"No, not 'of course,'" Richie said, but the edge was gone from his voice. "Nobody can drive a snowmobile 'of course,' not at a time like this. Not when you might have to give first aid and then transport somebody back whose life could depend on your driving."

"Well, I can give first aid and I can drive a snowmobile," Susan said. "I went with a guy at school who had one. I drove it all the time last winter."

"Can you drive one with a passenger who's immobilized?"

"I can do it as well as you can."

Richie put down the coffee cup he had just picked up. "And what exactly is that supposed to mean?"

"It means that you've probably never driven one yourself with a passenger who's immobilized. So I guess I can do it as well as you can."

Richie picked up his spoon and stirred the coffee, although the cup was now half-empty. Then he looked across the table at her, and his eyes met her steady gaze.

"Okay," he said at last. "You're on."

"Okay, then," Susan said, and carefully kept from smiling.

2:31 P.M.

Jimmy French thought he'd never been so cold in his life. He'd remembered to wear his gloves and his blue knitted hat, and he'd even tucked his corduroy pants into his boots. Halfway across the white, deserted square, he'd remembered that his coat had a hood. He'd stood there, in the falling snow, struggling with his gloves for the zipper on the hood, and before he'd gotten it over his head, the knit hat was soaked through and icy water was running down the back of his neck.

"Shit," he said out loud, and it made him feel a little better.

He hadn't remembered his scarf, however, and he wished he had it now. The cold just crept in around his collar, and even keeping his chin way down against his chest couldn't keep it out.

But he'd gotten away from that crummy, boring old hotel without being caught, and he wasn't about to turn back now until he'd had a good look at that circus train. Just wait till he got back and told the other kids about it before some of them even knew it was there! Those dumb kids never knew anything. He'd be the first, just like he always was.

He was shivering by the time he reached Depot Street, and his face was wet with snow. He went around to the

172

left side of the old station, and made his way through
the deep drifts between the station and the warehouse.
Then, just as he caught sight of the last car of the train,
he lost his balance, slipped, and fell face down. Chilling snow seeped instantly through his collar and down
inside his clothes. His teeth began to chatter uncontrollably, and he was shivering so violently in the cold that
his legs would barely support him when he struggled to
his feet.

"Shit," he said out loud, but this time it didn't make
him feel better at all.

He looked toward the train, but it was only a sort of
gray-brown blur through the falling snow.

"Shit," he said again through madly chattering teeth,
then turned and began trudging back toward the square.

Behind him, on the platform steps that faced the
warehouse, a dark figure moved, then stopped to watch
as Jimmy disappeared into the curtain of snow. When
he was almost completely out of sight, the tall figure
bowed, grandly and elaborately, and doffed a tall top
hat. Then it slowly moved away toward the interior of
the train.

2:50 P.M.

They sped away from the square on the snowmobiles, Susan's borrowed Kawasaki bright red and lovingly polished where the finish showed through the snow; Richie's Honda silver, now looking almost black in contrast to the brightness all around them. They drove carefully, leaving a safe distance between the two machines as they moved through local residential streets northeast of the square, taking a shortcut from School Street toward Castle Road and the hills. There were still several families to check on out that way, but Richie didn't anticipate that any of them would really need help, at least not with food and heat. People on Castle Road could afford to keep adequate supplies. But there was still the danger of illness or injury, and the lack of medical attention.

As soon as they pulled away from the front steps of the hotel, the sense of activity and motion and purpose returned at once to Richie's mind. As he drove, his eyes scanned the houses and streets for signs of any problems.

On both sides of them, the houses of the Kill lay couched in drifted snow and pale blue shadows, all of it blurred behind a curtain of white that still came silently falling. While they were still relatively close to the square, they saw a few people, but only a few, moving on foot outdoors. The snow was waist-deep in many places, and against the houses it often reached as high as first-floor windowsills. Garage doors were blocked. Where yards were marked by hedges, only the tops of the bushes showed above the blanket of snow, themselves crested by an uneven crown of white. The black boles of trees rose straight out of the encircling snow cover, and the few people who tried to move about looked as if they were trapped in its icy embrace.

Richie shouted and waved to Susan, pointing her in the direction of the next corner. She nodded vigorously, then gave her attention back to the white track of the road and began moving into the turn. Richie followed her, and a moment later they were moving easily along Fenton Street, with the skeletal branches of trees arching across it overhead.

Then Susan shouted and pointed ahead to their left, indicating that she wanted to stop. Richie slowed down and swung left, toward where he imagined the curb to be, and came to a stop. Susan's snowmobile slid up beside him and halted. Her cheeks were bright red from the cold and her eyes were glistening.

"Look!" she said, and pointed toward the house where they had stopped.

Richie looked and at once saw the big, gracefully made snowman standing in front of the house. Its outlines were a little blurred from the fresh snow.

"That's the Bissells' house, right?" he said to Susan.

"Yep. I'll bet Alice made that snowman. I'm surprised her mother let her, the old witch."

Richie looked back at the house. "I wonder where Leon is. I just realized he hasn't been around all day."

"I sort of tutored Alice with her homework for a couple of months while she had pneumonia. Her mother's a real pain, hardly ever lets the poor kid out to play. She's probably keeping Leon in, too. She does that, you know." Susan raised a gloved hand and wiped snow from her face.

"Can you wait for a minute?"

Richie glanced up at the white sky, then looked at Susan. "Why?"

"I just want to look at the snowman so I can tell Alice I saw it. I'll just be a minute."

"Okay," Richie said, "but just for a minute. It'll be getting dark in no time. Make it thirty seconds, in fact."

"Okay, okay," Susan said. "God, what a grouch." She climbed out of the snowmobile and pushed her way through the knee-deep snow, holding her arms out for balance. Richie watched her from the road.

Susan made it to the snowman and crouched down to examine it. At the same time, Richie saw a curtain pulled aside at the front window. He could just barely make out the little girl's face—he thought it was the little girl—and saw Susan wave toward the house, stand up, and start back toward him.

"Was that the little girl?" he asked as Susan got back into her snowmobile.

"No," Susan said. "It was her mother. God, I hate that woman. I really feel sorry for Alice. And her poor father too. Anybody else would have thrown her out a long time ago."

Richie was looking oddly at her.

"Why are you looking at me so funny? The woman's a bitch."

"That doesn't sound very liberated," Richie said. He was almost smiling.

Susan shrugged. "A bitch is a bitch," she said. "It has nothing to do with being liberated."

"Okay," Richie said. "Well, come on, let's go. It'll be getting dark in an hour."

They started the machines again and swept on down the road. Richie took the lead and Susan stayed close behind.

3:00 P.M.

"They're watching us," Sally Bissell said as she dropped the curtain and moved away from the window.

Leon, sitting on the edge of a straight chair near the doorway to the kitchen, looked up and blinked at her.

"What do you mean?" he said. "Who's watching us?"

"That boy sheriff," Sally said. "I knew it would come to this."

Leon blinked again. "What do you mean? Why would he be watching us?"

"I don't know!" Sally snapped. Leon recoiled from the sound of her voice. "I don't know and I don't care. Probably for some damned stupid thing *you* did."

Leon went on blinking, but said nothing.

Sally paced the room in silence, kneading her hands tightly together although the house was plenty warm enough.

Leon scrunched up on the chair and hugged himself, waiting for the rest of it. There was always more when Sally paced up and down like that.

She paced a full minute longer, then suddenly changed course and stalked toward the front window. She yanked the curtains back, holding the edge crunch-

ed up in her hand, and glared out at the falling snow.
Then she whirled and came toward Leon.

"Get moving," she said. "Come on, get moving!
We're packing up and getting out."

Leon glanced toward the window. The curtain had
caught on the back of the sofa, and he could see the
snow falling heavily outside. He looked up at her, his
eyes wide and worried.

"It'll be getting dark soon, Sally. Where are we
going?"

"Out of here!" Sally said. "My God, you don't understand anything, do you?" She planted her fists on
her hips. "For the first time in your life, you're going to
do something to take care of your wife and family.
You're going to get us out of this godforsaken town and
out of this snowstorm and off someplace where it's safe.
Can you understand that, Leon? Can you? Someplace
where it's safe!"

"But—"

"Get inside and start packing what we'll need."

"But, Sally—"

"Get inside and start packing what we'll need!"

4:30 P.M.

As darkness reached the town, the Centennial Hotel was getting crowded. Many of the people who lived close to the square had spent all day Sunday in their homes, watching the snow accumulate outside and drift higher and higher against walls. Those of them who had come to the meeting in the ballroom on Sunday evening had gone hurrying home before the storm grew any worse, and most of them hadn't gotten any closer to it afterward than their living-room windows, where they stood watching the snow continue to fall and shaking their heads, wondering how long it could keep coming down that hard. But by midafternoon on Monday, most of them, who were in normal times busy and hard-working people, were tired of sitting around the house, doing nothing. True, it was still snowing—*still* snowing—but the wind had let up at last, so a few of them, and then a few more, began cautiously leaving their homes in the surrounding streets and plowing their way into the square and the hotel.

The lobby was warm and loud with talk, and gray with cigarette smoke. The bar was filled with laughter and, in the Dining Room, three of the women had been pressed into emergency duty to take the pressure off Peggy, the overworked regular waitress. In the manager's office, Richie Mead was trying to make a show of looking busy, but, if the truth be told, there just wasn't much to do. Phil Aymar was over at the office, ably filling the gap left by Frank Carpenter, and his orders were to try the telephone at least every half-hour. If and when he ever got a dial tone again, he was to try a variety of area codes, just to be on the safe side. So far there was still no dial tone.

A couple of the women, one of them a local schoolteacher, had rounded up the young children, all of them restless at being kept indoors all day long, and had organized games and amusements for them in the ballroom upstairs, where at least there was room to run around. The women were working that detail in shifts, because they had agreed right from the beginning that, with the children so restless, nobody could handle it for more than a couple of hours at a time. Even so, there was an inordinate number of fights and shouting matches among the children, and there was never a moment when at least one child wasn't in tears.

Around four-thirty, Jimmy French's mother, Leanne, rose from her seat in the bar and made her way, laughing at her own unsteadiness, through the crowd toward the ladies' room. She was in there quite some time, and, while she was there, she had a chance to think and realized that she hadn't seen Jimmy for hours. In fact, she hadn't seen the little bugger all afternoon, and she began to wonder where he might have gotten to and what sort of trouble he might be in. The kid was always getting into some sort of trouble. She remembered that most of the children had been taken off to the ballroom, so, holding on carefully to the polished wood of the banister, she made her way upstairs to look for him there.

The little Kennedy girl's mother was there—Leanne

couldn't remember her name—and George Yoshioshi's wife, Michiko, whom everybody called Mikey, and a couple of other women. None of them had seen Jimmy.

Leanne went to look in their room, but Jimmy wasn't there either. She went downstairs and took a good look around the Dining Room from the lobby doorway, but she still didn't see him. And he wasn't in the bar when she got back there and resumed her seat.

Well, she thought, he'll turn up sooner or later, someplace or other. The little bugger always turns up, right? Right. Her glass was empty and she poured a fresh one from the pitcher on the table. She poured carefully and only spilled a little.

4:40 P.M.

"Get in, I said!"

Alice looked up at her father, but he looked as frightened as she felt.

Leon licked his lips, then instantly regretted it when the cold struck them. He looked from Alice to his wife and almost whined out loud with the pain of indecision.

"Get in there!" Sally said. "Now!" She yanked open the door of the van and, with the other hand, gave Leon a powerful shove in the middle of the back.

"But . . ." Leon said as he stumbled against the step. "But the truck won't move, not in all this snow! And it's dark now." He was almost crying.

"It'll move if you really want it to move. If you want to save your wife and child from this storm," Sally said. She took Alice's arm and pulled her forward. "Get in there," she told the trembling child.

The van was equipped with new snow tires and good chains and a heavy-duty suspension, because Leon knew all about that sort of thing, and miraculously he was able to get the car backwards down the driveway and into the road. When he switched into drive, however, it bogged down in the snow and wouldn't budge. Leon looked sideways across Alice's hooded head at his wife. The way she was watching him made him try again, and

this time the truck ground forward about eight feet
before coming to a stop. Leon, frightened of both the
snow and his wife, slammed it back and forth a couple
of times and got it going again. Then he found a kind of
channel in the snow, where it lay flat and low, blown
that way by Sunday night's wind, and the van got as far
as the corner before bogging down once more. Leon
could feel Alice shivering beside him, and he tried to
edge a little to his right on the seat in hopes of giving her
more warmth.

The truck kept stopping, trapped by drifted snow,
and Leon pleaded with his eyes for Sally to ease up and
let them go on back home. But she was on her way now
at last, and she'd do nothing of the sort. After a while,
he gave in and just kept his eyes fixed forward, squinting at the snow flying past the van's headlights. It built
up so rapidly on the windshield, despite the wipers that
slapped noisily back and forth, back and forth. Now
when the van lurched to a halt, Leon just put it in
reverse and tried again, seeking ahead of him for a
clearer path through the uneven drifts. Slowly, slowly,
the van lurched away from the house, from Fenton
Street, from the square, from Deacons Kill.

And just as the falling snow and deepening evening
swallowed it up, a dark figure emerged from the greater
darkness of the night and strolled jauntily toward
Alice's snowman in front of the house. It paused for a
moment before the figure, leaned forward with hands
on knees to examine it more closely, then straightened
and walked all around it to see it from all sides. When it
had made a full circle and returned to the snowman's
face, it raised its long fingers to its lips and blew a
wonderful big kiss to the snowman. Then it fell to the
ground, arms wrapped around itself, rolling and thrashing in the throes of silent laughter, and kicking its
enormous floppy feet in the air.

4:45 P.M.

Jimmy French was down by the railroad station again, looking at the train, and this time he'd remembered his scarf. He'd also remembered to put on two pairs of socks and two sweaters, and now he wasn't freezing the way he'd been before.

He never would have admitted it, but the combination of cold and darkness and swirling snow—it was getting windy again—made him a little nervous. He slogged resolutely through the passage between the station and the warehouse, the same way he'd come before, but all signs of his tracks from the earlier venture were gone, buried deep beneath fresh snow.

He reached the corner of the warehouse, hesitated for a second, looked all around and over his shoulder, then took a few tentative clumsy steps out of the building's shelter. The snow here came all the way up to his waist, even a little higher in places, and he had to hold his arms out at his sides to keep from falling.

He stopped and looked toward where the train had been, and saw nothing, only whiteness and the endlessly falling snow. It was coming down heavier now, and he reached up and tugged his hood as far forward as it would go to keep the fat, wet flakes out of his eyes. He took another couple of steps and halted again, breathing deeply with his mouth open.

There were no lights here, only the pale, diffused eeriness of early evening and falling snow and an overcast sky. All was silence, except for Jimmy's breathing. Nothing moved, except for the snow.

He took three more awkward steps through the clinging snow. And then he saw it. The train stood silent and unmoving, a patch of darkness against the gray. Jimmy inched closer.

He realized suddenly that he was holding his breath. When he expelled it in a great white cloud, then gulped in more, the air was bitter cold, icy and metallic and painful in his mouth.

He stood there, uncertain, then slowly kicked his way closer through the untouched drifts.

The train was bigger than he'd imagined, looming over him, rising massive into the night. He came close to the platform at the rear end of the last car, all of it covered with snow, its fancy black ironwork outlined with a tracing of white snow against the wooden door, snow against the windows. Once more, Jimmy looked all around to make certain he was alone. Only the snow moved around him, falling in silence. He raised his right arm slowly and reached out to touch the train.

Something tapped him sharply on the shoulder.

4:45 P.M.

"The wind's picking up again," Phil Aymar told Richie when he came into the office.

Richie nodded toward the door to the lobby. Phil went back and closed it.

"That's fine," Richie said. "For a while this afternoon, I thought it was starting to let up."

"I thought so too. It looked promising for a while there."

They were silent, and Phil Aymar sat down across from Richie's desk.

"What about that train?" Phil asked. "Those people are still on it, aren't they?"

"As far as I know," Richie said. "I was just thinking about them, in fact."

"I'll take a walk down there and look in on them, if you want. Nice evening for a walk."

"No," Richie said. "No, I'll go down." He shook his head. "I want to have a look myself, see what's going on down there. I'm still curious about how they got through the storm last night."

"Okay," Phil said, and started to rise. "I'll check back with you—"

There was a firm knock on the door. Almost in the same instant, the door was pushed open and Stanton

Stokely, the ringmaster of the circus, stepped into the office.

"Good evening, gentlemen," he said. "May I come in?"

4:49 P.M.

Jimmy French gasped in fright. He whipped around and looked up into the broadly smiling face of a clown.

Unthinking, Jimmy jerked his hands up to cover his face, but the clown snatched at them and grabbed them first. Jimmy was shuddering uncontrollably, his knees wobbling beneath him, but the clown lifted his hands high and held them up, helpless, and smiled down into his face.

It was a terrible smile of red, distorted lips surrounded by white. Huge white rings encircled the eyes, lifting the black, bushy eyebrows high onto the forehead. A perfectly round red nose filled the middle of the face, and a shock of bright red woolly hair, like something cut from a mop, crowned it on top. The clown wore red and white satin in great diamond-shaped patches, immense floppy shoes, and had enormous white-gloved hands. It leaned forward and put its face close to Jimmy's, and the smile grew even wider.

Then it let go of him and took two floppy, exaggerated steps backward. As Jimmy fell back against the end of the train, the clown cocked its head far to the right, then to the left. When it suddenly clapped its hands together with glee, Jimmy wet his pants and was dimly conscious of the warmth turning to sudden ice on his leg. He stared up, barely seeing, and, impossibly, the clown's smile grew even bigger.

For an instant, one thing was crystal clear in Jimmy's mind, one fact that suddenly jarred his blurred vision into focus. The silent snow was passing right through the clown as it fell. But then it didn't matter because the clown's immense white hands were reaching for his head.

4:49 P.M.

"Please do," Richie said, and exchanged a quick glance with Phil Aymar that told the deputy to stay.

Stanton Stokely closed the door behind him and, with a look of satisfaction, seated himself in the one easy chair that stood beside the door, facing the desk. A few flakes of snow still remained on his shoulders, gleaming as they melted into the cloth. He placed his black gloves and the top hat on the floor beside the chair. Then he unwound a long black scarf—Richie could have sworn it was real silk—and carefully but quickly folded it and dropped it into the hat. His fingers were long and delicate and moved gracefully, like those of a man accustomed to doing card tricks. He unbuttoned his black overcoat but did not remove it.

"Ah," he said when he was settled. His pink cheeks were shining from the cold outside and now from the warmth of the office. "That's so much better. Such beastly weather, isn't it? This sort of weather almost won't permit a person to think of anything else." He rubbed his hands together briskly.

Richie kept his face composed. "We were just talking about you, Mr. Stokely."

Stokely beamed at him. "Were you? How very kind."

"Actually, we were wondering how you were getting along down there, you and . . . your people."

"Well, sheriff," Stokely said, and his face grew more serious as he leaned forward, "that's the very reason I've risked life and limb to come through the storm to speak with you. The very reason."

Richie felt his muscles tensing at the man's exasperating tone. He joined his hands together on the desk in front of him. "What reason is that, exactly?"

Stokely looked suddenly concerned and puzzled at Richie's tone of voice, and his face grew even more serious, almost solemn. "Why, I came to tell you how we're getting along. I was thinking how good it was of you to come looking for us, and—"

"It's my job, Mr. Stokely."

"Ah, of course it is," Stokely said, "but you'd be surprised at the reception strangers often receive in a small town. Oh, I could tell you such stories, I could indeed." He closed his eyes for a moment and seemed lost in thought, but he went on almost at once. "But you *did* come to see how we were, and I *was* thinking how very kind of you that was. And then I realized that you might be putting yourself to the trouble of coming down to the train again in all of this dreadful snow. And *then* I thought that I could save you the trouble by coming up to the hotel myself. And so here I am," he said, and spread his hands wide as if he were presiding over the grand spectacle of a circus.

Richie didn't smile. Out of the corner of his eye, he could see Phil Aymar staring at Stokely in disbelief.

There was a moment of dead silence in the room before Richie said, "So how are you?"

Stokely blinked. "Why, just fine, just fine. I'm happy to say that the illness that afflicted my company is . . . on the wane. In another day, or possibly two at the most, I am quite certain we shall all of us be up and about, and going about our business as usual. That is what I've come here to tell you, and to save you the bother of thinking further about us when you have so many other things on your mind.''

"That's very kind of you, I'm sure, Mr. Stokely,'' Richie said. He leaned back casually in his chair. "How many people did you say are on the train?''

Stokely seemed to hesitate for a fraction of a second before answering. "Eight,'' he said. "Plus myself, of course.''

"Eight?'' Richie asked, and couldn't keep the surprise out of his voice. "Your whole circus consists of eight people?''

Stokely dropped his gaze to the carpet. "Alas,'' he said quietly.

"I don't—''

"Oh, my good fellow, it's even worse than that,'' Stokely said solemnly. "We are, in fact, only six. Six clowns. The other two are the crew of the train. Plus myself, of course.''

"But how do you put on a circus with only six people?'' Phil asked.

"Six, plus myself, of course,'' Stokely said quickly, looking toward Phil. "Circumstances are not as they were, I'm afraid, and we are sadly reduced, very sadly reduced by . . . circumstances. But we carry on as best we can, and all of us do double and triple duty, both in the ring and behind the scenes. I assure you that, in performance, you would never know how few we actually are. To the average eye, we seem to be''—he paused an instant and cocked his head to one side, his face becoming more animated again—''many. Yes, many, indeed.''

Richie looked over at Phil, who lifted his shoulders in a shrug but said nothing.

"Do you have heat on the train?'' Richie asked.

"Oh, yes, we are well equipped with firewood, having learned from sad past experience. We are—"

"I thought you said that earlier today. Firewood?"

Stokely looked sad and a little embarrassed. "Our equipment is very old. Oh yes, quite old. Our train is actually a fine example of Victorian workmanship. That is to say"—he lowered his voice a little—"it lacks a heating system. But a stove and a wood fire do us very nicely. And safely, let me hasten to add. We are, I assure you, quite satisfied."

"Well . . ."

"Sheriff, if I can be of any help to you, please do not hesitate to ask. I am at your complete disposal. And as soon as my people are on their feet, which I expect to be very shortly, my entire company will stand ready to assist in any way that we can. And we shall place no burden upon you whatsoever. And now, if you'll excuse me, I shall take my leave."

As he said it, Stokely rose, gathering up hat, gloves, and scarf in one motion, and was at the door.

"Gentlemen," he said, and nodded to both of them, and then he was gone. The door was hardly open long enough for voices from the lobby to drift into the office.

Richie and Phil looked at each other.

"Jesus H. Christ," Phil said. "Will you look what the wind blew in!"

Richie just shook his head helplessly.

"You saw him earlier?" Phil asked.

"Yeah," Richie said, and told him about the meeting at the railroad station.

Phil sat back with his arms folded while he listened. "We have any laws against plain, old-fashioned *weirdness* in this town?" he said when Richie had finished.

"I don't think so," Richie said. "But if this snow goes on much longer, I'm going to start inventing some, because we'll *all* be going funny in the head." He shrugged, still looking doubtful. "Well, at least Stanton Stokely's Stupendous Circus won't be any trouble for us."

"Here's hoping. Well, I'll be on my way. I'll check back with you in a while."

When he was alone in the office, Richie recalled Susan pointing out something odd about Stokely, something he had said, that he should have asked the man about. But for the life of him, he couldn't remember what it was.

5:30 P.M.

The Centennial Hotel was warm and noisy, but all the rest of Deacons Kill lay cold and silent beneath the blowing snow. Drifts rose higher everywhere, and the few tracks that had been made through the snow during the day were obliterated, smoothed away as if they'd never been.

The wind had picked up in speed and ferocity since the afternoon's calm, adding snow that it whipped up from the ground to its arsenal of fresh ammunition. The frozen and glistening snow that now struck frosty windowpanes rattled grittily against the glass, a constant reminder to mortals of the strength and random savagery that moved outdoors.

Limbs tore loose from the older and stiffer trees of the Kill, felled by the combined weight of frozen snow and the rude push of the wind. Bushes, reduced now to bare, spidery sticks beneath the soft white mantle, rustled and creaked, as if begging the wind for mercy, yet trembling in fear of it.

At the corner of Anglican Way, on the west side of the square, the sign that jutted out from the brick wall above the Miller Bookstore swung violently in the wind, the steel hooks that held it rasping back and forth in pain. On the far side of the square, a paper sign announcing an after-Christmas sale that had been taped to the window of a drugstore flapped madly against the glass and then finally tore loose. It shot up against the glass of the next store, then whirled higher on the snowy crest of the wind, then shot level with the ground across the road toward the square itself, touched down and skated across the frozen surface until it crumpled tight against the dark trunk of a tree. It hung there, flapping and beating, as if it would gnaw its way through the wood until the wind itself released it.

On the hillsides around the town, farmers, bulking fat in their boots and scarves and hoods and sweaters, bent almost double to make headway against the force of the wind, stumbled blindly through the snow toward the barn and the chores that would not wait.

Elsewhere in the Kill, people who had stayed home and grown tired of looking out at the silently, endlessly falling snow returned cautiously to their windows to measure the storm once again. The windows were icy to the touch when they wiped them clear, and gritty snow clawed at the other side.

At the railroad station and the warehouse, the circus train stood as it had before, now even more thoroughly covered with snow and blending as one with the white landscape beneath the diffused gray light of an early moon.

In the market field beyond the depot and the train, in the whirling columns and sheets of snow that rode on the back of the whipping wind, dark figures held hands and danced in a circle, throwing back their heads to laugh with delight. One was tall and ungainly, with enormous floppy feet. One was very short and thick. They all danced in the snow but left no tracks, and another figure in a tall top hat stood nearby and watched them, smiling. They danced and danced, and

the blowing snow passed right through them, and the
wind caught their laughter and carried it away.

7:15 P.M.

Susan had gone home for a while after returning earlier in the day with Richie. To her surprise, Richie had only hesitated briefly before accepting her invitation to dinner. They had been standing in the snow in front of the hotel when she'd asked him. Richie had looked down the darkening square and up at the sky, and she'd seen him shiver at the gust of the quickening wind. Then he said he appreciated it and he'd be there. She'd told him to come at seven-thirty.

She was looking forward to it. She wasn't exactly setting her cap for him, but they were friends. He'd asked her out three times and been very nice to her, and he was going to overdose on coffee if somebody didn't sit him down and force him to eat something solid.

She'd taken a shower and washed her hair and brushed it and spent almost half an hour trying to decide what to wear. Finally she'd given it up and decided on jeans as the only thing that made any sense at all. How would it look if she greeted him at the door, with the wind howling and the snow flying in their faces, in lounging pajamas? Besides, she didn't own lounging pajamas or anything that even faintly resembled lounging pajamas. Susan, she told herself, you're just not the lounging-pajama type, and you never will be. Jeans it has to be.

The good ones, to be sure, but definitely jeans. She settled on a yellow sweater and decided not to think about it any more.

And then there was the question of food. She usually went shopping on Sunday, when it was less crowded, or after work during the week, but she'd gone to Cobleskill —could it really be only yesterday?—and, oh God, there was hardly a thing in the house to eat. After careful scrutiny of the freezer and the cabinets, she put together a dinner of chicken cutlets, mashed potatoes, and mixed vegetables. And God bless Stouffer's!

She looked at her watch. If Richie got away on time, he'd be here in a quarter of an hour. She laid out everything in readiness in the kitchen—with luck, she might even have all the parts of the meal ready at the same time—and set the table in the dining alcove.

It was 7:25, and Susan congratulated herself on being ready in time. She felt very much like a lady as she sat on the sofa and picked up the new issue of *Redbook* to flip through while she waited for her dinner guest.

8:05 P.M.

"He's not upstairs," Don French told his wife when he got back to the table.

"So if he's not upstairs, where the hell is he?"

"I told you, I don't know! I looked all over the place and I didn't see him. If I didn't see him, how should I know where he is?"

"Are you sure you looked everywhere?"

"Yeah."

"Did you look in the cellar?"

"I looked everywhere!"

"Do you suppose he had any dinner? I think they sent food upstairs for the kids."

"Jesus Christ. If I can't even *see* him, how am I supposed to know if he *ate?*"

Leanne thought about it.

"I guess he's okay," she said. "He probably ate, too. I never knew anybody who eats as much as that kid. He probably got something upstairs."

"Yeah," her husband said. "Never knew that kid to miss a meal. He's around someplace. Don't worry about him. He can look out for himself."

8:10 P.M.

Doc Warren's day had been quieter than he'd expected. One broken leg to look after, two badly sprained arms, a black eye that was young Freddie Ellenwood's souvenir of a fistfight, and three mild cases of frostbite, plus the usual run of winter complaints that he normally would have treated in his office. So far, not so bad. He finished writing out a card for the third frostbite case, then took off his half-glasses and pinched the bridge of his nose.

Well, he could certainly understand why Richie Mead was so on edge. Here he was himself, after what he had to admit had been a pretty light day's work, and he felt tired, strained. It was the tension, and the waiting. Yes, he'd gotten off easy today, it was true, but what would tomorrow bring? Doc had seen these mountain storms before in the Kill—and so had his father before him, and his father's father—and he knew what could happen. The injuries, the worry, the strain on aging hearts and sometimes on hearts that weren't even aging yet. And the old-timers, the ones who unaccountably seem to see a storm like this as a summons home to their maker. A large number of elderly people always die in bad weather.

Doc smiled thinly. And where, exactly, does that put me? he thought. Among the elderly, or the godly?

Looking suddenly grim, he placed his hands flat on the desk and stood up.

What's wrong with me? he thought, almost voicing the words in the empty room. What? I have never—I have *never*—thought like that, not for a minute in all my life.

Lips pressed tight together, he left the office quickly and walked out into the lobby. It was quieter now than before, less crowded, but the lounge and the Dining Room sounded busy. He acknowledged greetings from a few of the men who were standing talking, and strolled toward the front doors.

"Evening, Doc," Blanche Mackintosh said. She was mopping the floor at the entrance for the seventh time today.

"Hello, Blanche," Doc said. He moved close to the door and felt the chill that crept in from outside. The door rattled as a gust of wind raced onto the porch. He wiped his hand over the window and withdrew it instantly from the frozen glass. The door rattled again. He leaned forward and peered out at the snow swirling past in the road, the square, the town.

"Terrible," Blanche said beside him. "Just terrible. And going to get worse before it gets better."

Doc grunted. He put his hands behind his back and rubbed his cold fingers together, but he continued looking out at the storm.

"Frank Carpenter is resting nice and easy," she said. "I'll keep looking in on him."

"Thank you, Blanche."

"That's okay." She hesitated, studying his face, then asked, "See anything out there? I mean, besides the snow."

"Just snow," Doc said. "Is there something else to see?"

"Well . . ." Blanche said, and Doc noted that she had

lowered her voice. "A little while ago, I was looking out there, just like you're doing now, and I could have sworn there was somebody out there. Somebody out there in the square, just moving around but not going anywhere, and kind of looking over this way."

"Who did it look like?"

"Not like anybody. Just a dark sort of shape, moving in the snow. But funny-looking."

Doc turned his head to look at her at last.

"In what way?" he said.

"Doc, you're going to think I'm losing my mind or something."

"I won't, Blanche, I promise. How was the figure funny-looking?"

Blanche looked away for a second, then determinedly met his eyes. "It looked like a clown," she said. "And he was just standing over there in the square, like he was watching the hotel. It gave me the willies, I can tell you that. At first, I thought it was just the snow, you know, like sometimes it looks like something familiar when it's blowing around. But it didn't *really* look like the snow. It looked just like a clown, I swear it did. Does that sound crazy?"

"No," Doc said. "No, it doesn't." He turned back to look out the window again. "Because, just a minute ago, I saw him out there myself."

8:32 P.M.

Susan made Irish coffee and, after some urging, finally prevailed on Richie to have some. He protested that he was on duty, and would continue on duty, until the storm was over, but Susan insisted that nobody could be on duty for twenty-four hours a day. Richie smiled tiredly and finally agreed. He finished the first one, but settled for plain black coffee after that. They steadfastly avoided talking about the storm, and Richie declared that he hadn't been this relaxed in days.

John Chard's name had come up in conversation twice at dinner, and now, as they sat talking on the sofa, the sheriff's name came up again.

"He's probably out there in California, watching the news and hearing about the storm, and wishing he was back here," Richie said. "That's the way he is. In fact, he's probably burning up the phone lines trying to get through. I'll bet the first time we hear a phone ring in the Kill again, it'll be John Chard."

"The Kill," Susan said thoughtfully. "That's what I mentioned today, remember? That Stanton Stokely said 'the Kill,' as if he lived here, or at least knew the place. That's what struck me as so odd."

"Yes," Richie said, "I remember now." He leaned

forward on the couch, elbows on knees. "I should have asked him about it."

"How could you? I didn't realize or mention it until later."

Richie glanced sideways at her and away. "He came up to the hotel this evening."

Susan swung around toward him and tucked her legs beneath her on the couch. "He came up to the hotel? And you forgot?"

Richie gave her a look of mock annoyance. "I didn't forget. In the first place, my job doesn't require that I report everything that happens to you. In the second place, I . . . Well, it was a nice dinner and I didn't want to spoil it. Actually, it's been very easy to pretend for the past hour that everything is normal."

"So tell me about it," Susan said.

"About what?"

"Richie, you're just being difficult because you know I want to hear."

"About Stokely? He came up to the hotel and told me I didn't have to worry about his people, and I shouldn't bother checking up on them to make sure they're all right. What's to tell?"

"There has to be more than that."

"Oh, Susan, come on. Look, I'm sorry if this whole thing isn't quite as dramatic as you'd like it to be. I get the impression sometimes that you're treating this storm, and the fact that we're snowed in, as if the whole thing was a circus itself. It's not. We've gotten off easy so far, but that's not going to last. And the longer it goes on, the worse it's going to be. Even when the damn snow finally stops—if it *ever* stops, which I'm beginning to doubt—it's still going to be another day or two before we're in touch with civilization again. The whole damn situation is scary enough. Will you listen to that wind out there? It's getting worse instead of better. I've met this ringmaster guy twice and, to tell you the truth, he makes my skin crawl. But those people haven't broken any laws and they don't need any help, so I can't take the time to think about them any more. Susan, really, it's as simple as that. Okay, so the circus has come to town, but it's not as if . . . well, as if the circus had come to town, if you know what I mean.''

They were both silent a minute, until Susan said, "I'm sorry, Richie. Would you like more coffee?"

He didn't look at her. "Okay, yeah. Thanks."

When Susan returned with a fresh cup, Richie hadn't moved.

"You're right, you know," she said quietly.

Richie sipped the hot coffee. "About what?"

"About me, in a way. I was thinking about it while I was cooking before. All this—this storm and everything —it *is* kind of exciting. I know, I know, it doesn't seem that way to you, but it does, a little, to me. Or, rather, it did." She was speaking slowly, selecting the words carefully, as if they might crumble at her touch. "I'm on my own now, you know, and I . . . Well, I guess I'm sort of trying to prove myself."

Richie looked at her briefly. "You can only prove yourself when you stop trying," he said.

They sat in silence, hearing only the wind booming against the windows.

"Which, I suppose," Richie added after a moment, "is something I should remember myself." He glanced at her. "And let's not have any comments from you about that, okay?"

"I wasn't going to say a word."

They were silent again.

Then Susan said, "There's something else, though, Richie. I mean, there's a specific reason why I wanted to know what Stanton Stokely talked about, what he said. For one thing, I still think it's pretty weird how he referred to the town. And then you said he came up to the hotel. That's what you said: 'He came up to the hotel.' You made it sound as if he knew his way without even thinking about it.''

Richie had sat back on the couch while she was talking. He was watching her now. "I wasn't the one who made it sound that way. He did. It sounded so natural the way he said it that I never thought there was anything strange about it. Until now. Sort of. Go on.''

"Well, that's the kind of thing I'm talking about. Maybe it doesn't mean a thing, but I just think it's strange that he talks like that. Twice, anyway. And then there's the question of how the train got here in the first place. I guess it just plowed its way through the snow until it reached a town where it'd be safe to stop, but it . . . Oh, I don't know, it's just strange, that's all.''

"Okay, I agree. But it's here, which means it *got* here, which means it *could* get here. Yes, it's strange, but I don't know what else there is to think about it. I know it's bothering you a lot more than it is me, but . . .''

"I don't know what else to think, either," Susan said. She shifted her position on the couch.

"There's something else, too," she said.

"Tell me.''

Susan took a deep breath, held it, then slowly let it out. "Okay," she said. "But, remember, you asked me. I don't want to be sent off to the funny farm just yet.''

"Nobody's going anywhere till this storm is over, not even to the funny farm. What is it?''

As clearly and concisely as she could manage, Susan told him about her car going off the road the evening before, about walking across the market field toward the railroad depot, about the hands that had frigthened her in the snow, and about the clown at the window of the train.

Richie listened in silence. When she was done, he shook his head. "He didn't hurt you? Or threaten you?"

"No. He just scared the hell out of me."

"Nice time to be playing jokes on people." He straightened up. "C'mon, let's take a walk."

"To the train?"

"To the train." He stood up. "Now I understand why you've been so twitchy about it."

"I guess I have to go, huh?"

"That's a different attitude. Yes, you do. I want you to show me where it happened. Then maybe we'll pay another visit to our friends."

"Oh, no!" Susan said. "Go inside the train? Wrong. Uh-uh. No way. Get yourself another girl!"

Richie was at the closet, looking for his coat. "C'mon," he said. He looked back and pointed a finger at her. "Zap, you're a deputy. Now you have to do it. C'mon."

Susan walked reluctantly toward the closet. "Does that make it official? Aren't I supposed to get a badge or something?"

"You're supposed to get moving," Richie said. "I just wish you'd told me about this sooner."

Susan was pulling on her coat. "I half thought I just imagined it. And, anyway, I felt stupid about being frightened."

Richie paused with his hand on the front door, and turned back to look at her. "Believe me," he said, "it's not stupid to be frightened. Take it from one who knows."

Then he opened the door and the snow hit them in the face.

8:53 P.M.

Doc Warren had tried to read a couple of the journals he'd brought over from the office, but he quickly found that he couldn't concentrate and put them aside. He sat in the easy chair in his room, with his shoes off and his feet up on the side of the bed, but it did nothing to ease his thoughts.

He hated being helpless like this. He felt trapped, just as he knew Richie Mead did, and a lot of the other people in town too. It was a good thing the Centennial Hotel was here, or they'd all be trapped in that cold and bloodless school building. But they were still trapped, he thought, condemned to do little more than hang around and wait it out. He missed his comfortable home, his library, his chair. He missed driving the red Mustang that John Chard always kidded him about. He missed John, too, and hoped he was well out there in California. It had taken a lot of pressure to get the man to leave, even for his own good, but Doc knew that John would be champing at the bit as soon as he heard about the weather in this part of the country.

Thoughts of John Chard made him think again of Richie Mead. When John had confided to him that he was going to leave Richie in charge during his absence, Doc had briefly wondered about the wisdom of it.

Richie was a fine young man, but Doc had thought he lacked the degree of self-confidence that would give him automatic and unquestioned leadership ability in a crisis. John had replied that you only learn those things *in* a crisis, and Richie would do fine. Doc had seen Richie at work and, so far, he seemed to be doing all right. He was edgy and impatient, but he was doing all right. Of course, it hadn't gotten really bad yet. Not near as bad as—Doc was sure of it—it was going to get.

He grunted with disgust at his own gloomy thoughts, then stood up and crossed to the window. Cold air, coming in through crevices around the wooden frame, fluttered the curtains.

He looked out at the snow. Heavier than before, he thought. And the wind was worse, too. He pulled his suit jacket closed across his chest.

The view out the window reminded him of the last time he'd looked at it. He could have sworn he'd seen the unmistakable figure of a clown out there in the snow, just standing out there, looking at the hotel. And Blanche Mackintosh thought she'd seen it too.

And that ringmaster. Strange fellow. Doc had had a good look at him as he passed through the lobby earlier, after talking with Richie. Odd cut to his clothes, as if they were very old but well preserved. And that top hat. And that hearty smile. Phony and hateful, Doc thought sourly. And wasn't it strange that he and his fellow circus folk, the whole troupe of them, were staying down in that train?

Circus troupe, Doc thought.

Stanton Stokely's Stupendous Circus.

He could almost have sworn he'd heard the name before. He searched his memory, but absolutely nothing came to mind.

Doc stood there another minute, tapping the toes of

one foot against the cold floor. A circus and clowns.
Well, then. He turned abruptly from the window, went
back to the bed, sat on the edge, and began putting on
his shoes.

9:17 P.M.

"Do you get the funny feeling you've done this before?" Susan whispered.

"Yes," Richie answered, "and it's not so funny."

They were halfway down the familiar space between the warehouse and the station. The wind was whistling through it and hurling gritty snow in their eyes.

Susan took hold of Richie's arm. "I'm right behind you, chief," she said. "Lead on. Just like General Custer."

"Thanks. That makes me feel really good."

They moved slowly toward the corner of the building, blinking in the flying snow. Then Richie turned the corner and collided with a tall dark shape.

9:22 P.M.

The van just wouldn't move another inch, no matter how hard Leon tried.

They had been sitting in the van for hours, with the storm growing in ferocity all around them, snow drifting against the sides and climbing up against the doors toward the windows, blurring the dark outlines of trees and road and hills that surrounded them. The windshield was completely covered with snow. Leon had been running the engine for heat, just enough to warm up the interior of the van, then shutting it off to conserve fuel, but he had stopped doing that when he began to fear that the engine would refuse to turn over the next time he tried it. After that, the engine had run and run until, finally, its fuel exhausted, it had coughed and sputtered and died. The heat inside the van died minutes later.

Sally had kept herself warm by railing at him the whole while.

"It's all your fault! You had to take this road, didn't you! You knew best. Sure you did. Sure you did! And now look. We got this far, and now we're stuck here and you can't get this thing to move another inch. If you knew how to drive it, this never would have happened. We never would have gotten stuck like this, and not even a house in sight. Look at this mess we're in now. Just look!''

Leon looked, but there was nothing to see. The window on his side was open just a crack at the top to let in a little air. Through the narrow slit he could see more snow falling.

Earlier, when the van had first bogged down forever in the snow, Leon had fetched blankets out of the back. They all pulled them closer now to preserve a little body warmth, what little they still had. Between her parents, Alice, leaning against her father's side, shivered and huddled beneath two blankets. Leon could feel her shivering through the thickness of his coat and he could hear her teeth chattering. Except for Sally, he would have cried.

"Get out and see where we are! This has to be someplace familiar. There must be a house around here somewhere.''

Leon looked up at the crack of space above the window. Snow blew in at him and touched his cheeks.

"I said, get out and see where we are! Walk along the road till you come to a house. You got us into this, Leon, so you can damn well get us out of it!''

Leon didn't know what to do. He tried to think but he couldn't. They were in danger, he knew that, but he couldn't think clearly enough to get them out of it. To get *Alice* out of it. Oh, my baby! Leon was afraid Alice was going to freeze to death, all huddled over, right there on the seat beside him.

"Go on!''

He had gotten out twice before to look around and walk some distance along the road, scanning the darkness for a lighted window, some sign of life, some promise of help. But the snow had worked dark magic on the hills, changing their shapes and lines, and he

couldn't figure out where he was. The first time, the
swirling snow had blinded him so badly that he could
see nothing. The second time, it had been a little calmer
out there, and he had trudged some distance along the
road, back the way they'd come, but there was nothing
there to see, no houses, no lights, nothing. What could
he see now? Should he go? Should he stay? He looked at
the top of the window again, and tears filled his eyes.

He had to go out. He had to see if there was a way to
save his little girl. He hunched himself deeper inside his
coat, grasped the door handle with his gloved hand, and
opened the door.

He jumped down quickly and slammed the door shut.
Even so, he caught a glimpse of Alice drawing back in
fright from the rush of cold air.

He looked around. All he could see was flying snow
and the darkness beyond it. The snow bit with icy teeth
at his face. He shuddered, thought for a second, then
began plowing his way toward the side of the road and
the dark line of trees. Maybe he'd see a sign or something this time. Please God, let there be a sign.

He walked right into it, hard, and yelped with fright.
A signpost. A tall metal post with signs on it. Blinking
the snow from his eyes, Leon reached up with both
hands and frantically wiped the signs clean of snow. He
was hoping and hoping as the letters came clear, but he
already thought he knew where he was. He squinted up
and tried to read the words in the reflected light of the
moon.

The sign on the bottom told him that Oneonta was
twenty-two miles away. The sign on top told him he was
leaving Deacons Kill and he should come back soon.

Leon stood there, panting, face wet with snow, looking at the signs and trying to choke back the sobs. Now
he knew where he was for sure, and there were no

houses along here for miles. They were all going to freeze to death. Alice was going to freeze to death.

He turned away from the signpost and wearily slogged back through the snow to the van. When he reached the door, he took hold of the handle, yanked it open, and put his foot up to jump in.

Instantly, Sally began yelling. "Now, look—"

Her yell was choked off by an enormous pair of white-gloved hands that reached around her throat from the darkness at the back of the van.

Leon had one foot up on the floor. He stared, bewildered, at his wife's face as her eyes grew large and her tongue was forced out of her mouth. Then he saw the grinning face of the clown just behind her head. The clown's grin broadened at once into a merry smile. It tightened its grip on Sally's neck, and then it began to twist her head to the side.

Leon snatched across the seat at Alice and pulled her away from Sally's thrashing body. He heard a snap and a strange tearing sound, and then Alice was in his arms and he was running, running, running, and stumbling and running again through the snow with his baby in his arms.

9:24 P.M.

"Doc, you scared the shit out of me!" Richie said.

Doc Warren muttered an apology and the three of them sorted themselves out.

"What are you doing here?"

"The same thing you are, I suspect," Doc said. "Snooping around to look at the circus train. And in weather like this, I think we should go ahead and do it before we freeze." He had to raise his voice to make himself heard above the wind.

Without another word, the three of them started toward the train.

They had just reached the platform of the last car when the door above them flew open and Stanton Stokely called out, "Hurry, hurry, or you'll all catch your deaths."

With difficulty in the snow, they pulled themselves up the steps to the platform. Stokely held the door open. Doc and Richie hurried inside. Susan, who had held back as they climbed onto the platform, hesitated an instant longer, then followed them.

It was a different world inside, warm and bright and cozy. A fire crackled quietly in a potbellied stove in one corner. Gas lamps threw a pleasant yellow light everywhere among the overstuffed chairs, they heavy Victorian draperies, the colorful circus posters on the paneled walls, the worn rugs. There were even several potted palms. Ceiling fans hung silent overhead. On a table beside the sofa along the wall, a decanter of red wine gleamed in welcome. Four glasses, already filled, stood beside it.

"Please," Stanton Stokely said, and picked up two of the glasses. He held them out to Susan and Doc Warren. They took them, looked at each other, but didn't drink. Stokely picked up the remaining two glasses and handed one to Richie. "Please," he said. "I saw you out there in the cold and thought I'd have this ready for you. Before anything else, you must take some wine to warm yourselves." He lifted his own glass to them and took a drink.

Richie replaced his glass on the table and pulled off his gloves. "We didn't come here to drink, Mr. Stokely."

Stokely put his own glass down and gestured them all into seats. "I would think not," he said, "on a night like this. Please, won't you make yourselves comfortable?"

"Mr. Stokely," Doc Warren said, "I'd like to introduce myself, since we didn't have a chance to speak earlier. My name is Elbert Warren. I'm a doctor, and I understand you've had some illness here."

"Dr. Warren, I'm so pleased to meet you. And thank you so much for your concern. Yes, it's true, we have had illness. Indeed, my whole poor company has been affected. As you see, however, I myself am fully recovered, and I am pleased to tell you that all my friends are well on the road to recovery themselves."

"What exactly was the problem? Have they had medical attention?"

Stokely waved a hand in the air. "Some winter ailment,'' he said. ''Nothing serious, nothing to be concerned about. And nothing, I might add, that is contagious, so there is no cause for alarm. Winter colds, nothing more. Some slight fever, but all of that is gone now. May I ask . . . is that what brings you here this evening, in this terrible weather?''

''Yes,'' Richie said.

''How very good of you,'' Stokely replied. ''How very, very good. Even after I told you it wasn't necessary. Would that we received such a warm welcome everywhere.'' His glance moved back and forth between Richie and the doctor. ''I thank you both very much.''

Doc, looking troubled, said, ''I'd be glad to—''

''Not at all,'' Stokely said. ''They're all sleeping comfortably—I looked in on them just a little while ago —and I think that tomorrow they'll be as good as new.''

Doc, helpless to insist, pressed his lips together and looked at the rug.

''Mr. Stokely,'' Susan said suddenly, startling the others.

Stokely turned toward her. The light from the lamps was reflected faintly in the pink of his cheeks.

''When we met you this morning, in the station, you referred to Deacons Kill as 'the Kill.' Only people who live here, or come here a lot, call it that. Why did you call it that?'' Susan looked embarrassed and added quickly, ''I'm . . . I'm just curious.''

''Did I?'' Stokely said. ''Well, I hope you haven't taken offense at my familiarity. It's nothing more than a habit one picks up, traveling around as much as we do. There are so many small towns in this land, and so many whose names are constructed like this one, especially in the northeastern part of the country. There's oh, Oxrun Station in Connecticut, for example. People just call it 'the Station.' It's really a very ordinary sort of thing to do. So naturally, without even thinking about it, I called Deacons Kill 'the Kill.' Nothing more than that, I assure you." His easy glance took in all three of them.

Richie Mead cleared his throat. "Where is everybody else?" he asked.

"They are sleeping, as I told you," Stokely said, "in the other coach." For the first time, there was the slightest hint of annoyance in his voice. "I hope there's no objection to that, sheriff. They have all retired early in the hopes that another good night's sleep will see an end to their indisposition."

With that, the ringmaster rose to his feet. The others rose with him.

Stokely extended his hand first to the doctor, and now the moment of irritation was gone. "Let me thank you again for your concern." He shook hands with Susan, then with Richie, and Richie found the man's handshake surprisingly firm and forthright.

"It is my hope that we shall find a way to repay your kind welcome before it is time for us to leave," Stokely said. "I hope that very sincerely."

And he showed them to the door.

9:53 P.M.

Blanche Mackintosh thought they were out there again.

They were. She could see them from the window of her room—just fleeting glimpses in the whirling curtains of snow in the square—but they were out there and she could see them. Oh Lord, how she hated the snow.

They were dancing and tumbling in the drifted snow, all around the dark trees of the square, and every now and again, she thought she saw a flash of color, though that was clearly impossible in the dark. Even so, she could have sworn she saw a bit of color and, for the life of her, didn't they look—just for those fleeting instants —Lord, didn't they look like clowns!

10:16 P.M.

"I can make more Irish coffee, if you'd like."

"No," Richie said, "but thanks."

They were standing just inside Susan's front door. The two of them and Doc had pushed their way through the snow back to the square in silence, forced on them by the cold and the wind and their own thoughts. They had left Doc at the hotel, and Richie had walked Susan back to her house.

"If you want to talk about anything . . ." Susan said.

"I better get back."

"Okay."

Neither of them moved, and for an instant they both thought Susan was going to ask him to come back later when he was done. And in the next instant, they both thought he was going to take her in his arms.

"I better get back," Richie said again, and this time he reached for the door.

Susan nodded.

He turned back to look at her. "Will you be over early tomorrow? At the hotel?"

"I promise," Susan said.

"Good," Richie said. He hesitated for a second, then opened the door and went out.

10:27 P.M.

Doc Warren couldn't sleep, but then he hadn't expected to. He couldn't get the face and voice of Stanton Stokely out of his mind. There was something so wrong about the man.

Stanton Stokely's Stupendous Circus.

He could swear he knew the name from somewhere. Something about a circus. He was sure of it.

12:00 MIDNIGHT

Midnight held the Kill. Pale shadows, as pale as moonlight, crept slowly through the town, lurked behind trees, watched at front doors, peered into windows.

The shadows flickered in the wind as trees swayed heavily beneath their burdens of snow. They crawled across the flat, white surfaces, blending with the dark, chilling everything they touched.

The wind made the only noise.

There was no movement anywhere in Deacons Kill, except in the market field.

In the market field, figures moved. Brightly colored figures with distorted human bodies, great hands, big feet, huge heads, long noses, red and blue and yellow and green, and the tall black figure in the top hat stood in their midst. They danced, capered, frolicked in the falling whiteness, jumped and tumbled and played leap-frog, and left no mark in the snow.

TUESDAY
January 18

7:45 A.M.

The arrival of Tuesday's dawn had been slow and painful in the Kill. The town itself was white and frozen, scarred only by steel-blue shadows beneath a slate-gray sky. The snow had tapered off a little around first light, but the air was still not free of it. Glittering sheets still whirled up from the ground, swirling upward as others glided down. Roads and sidewalks and yards were gone. Windows were coated with frost. Doors were stuck with frozen snow. Trees stood as if with heads bowed, yielding to greater force.

The air was filled with bitter, stinging ice, ice that jarred the teeth, froze delicate membranes in the nose, bit at the cheeks of those few souls brave enough, or foolhardy enough, to venture out, or who, not believing there was still snow left to fall, or curious to learn if it could still be that cold, opened their doors a crack to test the air, then closed them instantly with a violent shudder and a worried shake of the head.

Deacons Kill, like a lifeless body in the winter woods, was cold, and gray, and still.

8:10 A.M.

"Ask around again," Richie said. "He has to be here someplace."

"Richie, I've asked," Phil Aymar said. "Nobody's seen him since Sunday night."

"Well, I passed the house myself yesterday and he was there. Susan Lester and I stopped for a second to . . . uh, look at a snowman the little girl had made. Her mother was at the window, so Leon has to be around here someplace. It's not like him to just disappear. And he was at the meeting Sunday night, so he knows the score."

Phil shrugged. "That wife of his rides him pretty hard. Maybe she won't let him go out to play in the snow."

"From what I hear," Richie said, *"she* should be *made* to go play in the snow. Look, just ask around, okay? There might be somebody you missed who lives over that way. And if he doesn't turn up soon, then take a stroll on over there."

"Hey, no problem," Phil answered airily. "That sounds good. Maybe I can get a nice suntan on the way."

"Maybe," Richie said. "Get one for me while you're at it."

"Listen, there are a couple of other items, too."

Richie leaned forward on the desk. "Go ahead," he said. "I can take it."

"Well, there have been several people unaccounted for since Sunday. Most of them have been accounted for by now, one way or another. Either they're just holed up, or somebody else knew they were out of town and probably couldn't get back, or something like that. But there are still a couple of others. I'd say the only real problem case is Evan Highland."

"Guy who drives a bus for Trailways?"

"Right. As far as anybody knows, he's always home on Sundays. He has enough seniority now so he doesn't have to work the weekends. Nobody's seen him."

"Phil, has anybody—"

"I was there myself. The garage door was open and the car was gone. You should have seen the inside of the garage. It was up to your eyeballs in snow."

Richie thought about it. After a moment he said, "They have two cars, right?"

"I think so, yeah."

"Well, if the cars are both gone, I think we have to assume they were both out of town. I don't know what we can do, under the circumstances. And it's really not possible to send out search parties for everybody we haven't seen, if there's some reasonable explanation for their absence. I think we better just wait on that. Let me know if he turns up."

"Okay," Phil said. He checked his list and frowned. "There's one other thing. You're not going to like this one at all. Jimmy French."

"Little brat," Richie said. "What's he done now that we don't have time to be bothered with?"

"Disappeared, it looks like."

"Oh, swell. Well, we know he wasn't kidnapped because nobody'd want him. What are the other possibilities?''

"Seems to me like the kid is always underfoot, but his folks say they haven't seen him since yesterday afternoon.''

Richie made a sour face. "They've been parked in the bar since the first snowflake fell on Sunday. I doubt if they're *able* to see anything. When did they miss him?''

"They only told me about it half an hour ago. Nice, huh?''

"Nice. Have you checked around? That kid's a holy terror. He could be anywhere.''

"I've checked. No sign of him. The only thing we know is that his coat is missing. And they only told me *that* on my way in here.''

"Oh, no.''

"I checked around the building, but didn't see any sign of him. He could be stashed away someplace, playing a trick on us. I wouldn't put it past the little monster.''

"Neither would I. Well, listen, get his father and another few guys—make sure they can all see straight—and you'll just have to slog it all over town. And I'll just bet he's nice and snug somewhere in the hotel. Can you get back to me by, say, ten o'clock?''

Phil glanced at his watch. "Richie, if you haven't heard from us by ten o'clock, send the Saint Bernards out looking, okay?''

"Okay. Anything else?''

"That about covers it for now. We're running low on milk and perishables, but nothing critical yet. I expect we'll be seeing a lot of new people coming in today, looking for food. Frank is up in his room, keeping tabs on what we've got on hand and working out a plan for distribution.''

"Good. Okay, then."

Phil rose and started for the door.

"Phil, have you seen Doc Warren?"

"Just saw him finishing breakfast a little while ago."

"Ask him to come in, will you?"

"Sure."

When Phil had gone out, Richie leaned forward on the desk and rubbed his eyes. So far, he thought, Jimmy French was the biggest problem they had, and very likely that would mean nothing more than inconvenience and aggravation. Everything else seemed at least to be under control. His glance fell on the manager's white telephone. He picked it up and held it to his ear. Nothing. The hollow silence, where usually there was a familiar buzz, unnerved him a little and reminded him that things were still far from normal and far closer to critical.

8:29 A.M.

Phil Aymar had taken two men and quickly searched through the Centennial Hotel again for Jimmy French before taking a group outside. The search turned up nothing.

He divided up the twelve men who were going to search the town, sending parties in four directions around the square. He went himself with one of the groups, fanning out up Hill Street and into the streets that ran off it to the northwest of the square. Each man was taking a block, and then they'd rendezvous at a designated corner.

Phil took the farthest street from the square for himself. As he plodded his way through the snow, wishing he were back in the warm hotel, he began to really worry for the first time, now that he felt the bite of the wind, about what could have become of the boy. If he actually had left the hotel for some reason, there was no telling where he might be or what might have happened to him. Christ, he could be right here at my feet, Phil thought, buried under the snow, stiff as a log. He could be—

A sudden sharp gust of wind made him turn around, putting his back into it to protect his face. As he turned, he caught a glimpse of a blurred figure coming toward him through the curtain of blowing snow.

"Oh God," he said after he blinked and saw clearly what it was. "Oh my Jesus God!"

8:31 A.M.

Richie thought Doc Warren looked more tired than he'd ever seen him. Usually the doctor was strong, healthy, energetic, known to all the residents of the Kill as tireless in his work and unsparing of himself. He kept his regular office hours on Hill Street, but there was never a time, day or night, when he couldn't be located and counted on. Now, for the first time in Richie's memory—and Doc Warren had treated him since he was an infant, as he had treated most people Richie's age and younger—the doctor's face was lined, weary, showing his years.

"You okay, Doc?" Richie said.

Doc looked at him, eyes flaring briefly. "Of course!" he said. "Why would you ask a thing like that?"

"You look tired."

Doc sat back in the easy chair, suddenly looking very relaxed, and easily crossed his legs. "Well," he said, and his voice was gentler than during his momentary outburst, "you and I must sit some evening and discuss medicine. I wasn't aware that you'd completed a degree. Did it by mail, did you?"

"Not exactly. You just look tired, that's all."

Doc replied placidly, "I am perfectly free, so far as I am aware, to look any way I choose to look. Now I'm

236

quite certain, Sheriff Mead"—he looked Richie straight in the eye as he addressed him—"that your professional time is fully as valuable as mine, so I'd suggest we get on with business."

Richie asked the doctor to fill him in on illnesses, injuries, medical supplies available, what the doctor anticipated if Deacons Kill remained cut off from the outside world for much longer. Doc's report was straightforward, precise, undramatic, given in a tone that was businesslike and factual. Nevertheless, Richie saw at once that the doctor thought the outlook was bleak, even though illnesses and injuries so far had been less than expected.

"The rate of injuries will increase," the doctor concluded. "The number of frostbite cases will increase, since people can't remain indoors forever. And there's always the usual run of normal illnesses—heart attacks and so on—with no communications available and no transportation. It could turn out, when this is over, that we learn of deaths out on the farms, especially old folks. I know you're trying to look in on everybody who might be in trouble, but these things will happen anyway. Just be glad we don't have some exotic little flu virus taking up residence here—at least we don't yet—because if we do, you can rename this place the Centennial Hospital. I'm sorry it's not a prettier picture."

"So am I."

The doctor's voice was low, the way Richie remembered it from his childhood, when he said, "Richie, you can only do what it's possible to do, and not one bit more. As long as you do all that, you can rest easy."

"Maybe *I* should remind *you* of that."

"Maybe," the doctor said.

They sat in silence a moment.

"Has somebody looked in on all those people who are

cut off? The ones out in the hills?"

"Yes," Richie said. "I have a list here somewhere."
He rummaged through papers on the desk. "We did a
list from the map, the big one, and somebody checked
up personally on everyone on the list. I saw a lot of them
myself. Here it is."

He pulled a smudged, handwritten list of names,
three yellow pages stapled together, from a pile at the
corner of his desk. The list was a mess now. Richie had
crossed off some of the names himself on Monday, and
three of the deputies had also made markings on it from
their own lists of people in different areas. Near the
bottom of the second page, there was one name that
hadn't been crossed through.

"Torvey," Richie said as he looked up. "The
Torveys, on West Hill Road."

Doc sat up straight. "They're not checked off?
Nobody's seen them?"

"Very likely somebody has." Richie stood up.
"Somebody must have been there and just forgot to
cross them off. I'll check on it."

"They're in their eighties," Doc said. "The old
fellow's in a wheelchair."

"I know, I know!" Richie said.

Doc followed him quickly out into the lobby.

Behind them, in the office, the telephone rang.

8:36 A.M.

"Nobody's seen them. Shit!" Richie said quietly to Doc. They were standing in the lobby, near the front doors. "Unless Phil saw them. He and Tom Planck covered adjoining areas out that way." He thought for a second. "Unless each one thought the other had seen them." He was breathing hard from worry. "Damn! And Phil is out looking for the French kid!"

"Maybe Phil checked on them," Doc said.

"Or maybe he didn't, and we all thought—*I* thought —they were okay, when actually they're out there freezing to death."

"Even if nobody saw them, Richie, that doesn't mean they're in danger."

"No, but they could be in danger without our knowing it. When we could have been there. Goddamnit, I should have checked that list more carefully! Jesus!"

"Richie," Doc said, and shook his head.

"I should have been more careful. Sure, everybody's responsible, but I'm the one who's responsible for everybody else." He pressed his lips together and stared blindly at the thickly frosted glass in the front door.

When the door flew open, he was so lost in dark thoughts that, for an instant, he didn't react. Then he saw Phil Aymar's face.

239

"Phil," he said, "did—"

"Give me a hand," Phil said. He'd lost his hat, and his hair was covered with snow. "They're nearly frozen to death!"

With swirling snow stinging their hands and faces, Richie and Doc Warren leaped forward to help Phil and Don French. Half standing, half slumping between them, was Leon Bissell and, in his arms, his daughter Alice.

8:40 A.M.

"In here!" Doc said. "In my office!" The tiredness was gone completely from his face as he hurried ahead of the small group that was helping Leon Bissell across the lobby. Someone tried to take Alice from his arms, but Leon opened his mouth and croaked something wordless, unintelligible, and refused to give her up. He held her tight against his chest, wrapped in a blanket, with her face barely showing beneath the edge. The men held his arms as they helped him into Doc's temporary office.

"Christ, look at his face!" someone said.

Leon's face was the ashen-gray color of frostbite. His lips were cracked and blue, his eyes glazed, nearly sightless, his eyebrows white and thick with rime. He moved stiffly, turning his whole upper body together, as if his neck were frozen immovably to his shoulders and Alice forever frozen in his arms.

Doc eased him down onto a couch.

"All right, Leon," he said gently. "It's all right now, you're both safe and you'll both be fine. I'm going to take Alice now."

Leon slowly looked up at him, glazed eyes dully searching his face. His mouth opened slightly but he said nothing, only stared. There was ice frozen around

his eyes and down the sides of his face where tears had
run.

"I'm taking Alice now," Doc said, more firmly this
time.

He had to pry the little girl from Leon's arms. Her
clothing and the blanket Leon had been clutching
around her were stiff from the cold. Reluctantly, Leon
allowed the doctor to pull his fingers loose.

The room was filling rapidly as people crowded in
from the lobby. Blanche Mackintosh stood outside,
stretching up on tiptoe for a second, then resolutely
pushed her way through. Loudly and firmly, she told
everybody to move back, get out of the room, leave the
doctor to do his job in peace. "Go on, now," she said.
"Go on! There's nothing to see, so don't stand there
looking. The doctor has work to do."

Gradually the crowd fell back, at Blanche's repeated
urging. When she pushed the door closed, only Doc
Warren, Phil, and Richie remained with the patients.
Don French, who had helped to bring Leon in, had disappeared somewhere with the crowd.

"What do you want me to do?" Blanche said to the
doctor.

Doc Warren didn't reply. He had Alice in his arms
now and gently laid her down on the desk he was using
as an examination table. His movements were effortless
and practiced as he pulled her clothing open. Quick
fingers felt at her wrist and throat, then held back first
one eyelid, then the other.

He straightened up. "Blanche, there's a private stair-
way through this door. Take Alice upstairs and put her
to bed in one of the rooms." More quietly, he added,
"Just lift her the way she is. And come right back."

As Blanche, grim-faced, gathered the child into her
arms, ignoring the wet snow that melted onto her own

clothes, Doc turned his attention back to Leon. The man was lying stiffly on the couch, his eyes following Blanche as she carried Alice out of the room.

"She'll be all right, Leon," Doc said. "She'll be all right. Now we're going to take your clothes off and take care of you."

Leon croaked something, and Doc replied, "She'll be all right, Leon. We have to take care of you now." Without looking up, he said, "I need electric blankets, as many as you can find. Richie, I need a bottle from that shelf. It's marked 'tetanus toxoid.' And boil one of those needles, over there by the hotplate. It's all set up."

"Tetanus?" Richie said as he located the tiny bottle.

"For frostbite. Just get it."

Doc had already inserted a thermometer in Leon's mouth and was now taking his pulse. When he finished with that, he pulled at the man's clothing to free one arm and, frowning, began taking his blood pressure. A minute later, when he removed the thermometer from Leon's mouth, he read it and murmured, "God."

Phil Aymar had left at once to find blankets. He returned now with an armload and dumped them on the desk. "I'll find some electrics," he said, and went out again. As he opened the door, they could all hear the excited questions thrown at him by people in the lobby. Before the door closed, Susan Lester slipped in.

Doc and Richie were stripping off Leon's frozen clothing, moving his stiff limbs as gently as they could. Richie snapped a glance toward the door, then relaxed slightly when he saw it was Susan.

"Can I do something?" she asked.

"Get those blankets ready," Doc said without looking up.

By the time Doc had given Leon the injection of antiserum, Phil had returned with three electric blankets. Doc was carefully examining Leon's toes and fingers, his ears, his cheeks, the tip of his nose.

"There's a stretcher over there," Doc said, nodding toward the corner. Richie brought it and opened it out on the floor beside the couch. They tightened the blankets around Leon, then eased him onto it. Lying there on the floor, wrapped in a brown blanket that nearly hid his face, his eyes closed and his skin chalk-white, he looked like a corpse.

Doc and Richie bent, and lifted the stretcher from the floor, then set it down, at Doc's direction, on the desk.

The rear door of the office opened, and Blanche Mackintosh came in. She closed the door behind her.

Richie and Susan both looked at the doctor at the same time. "Doc," Richie said, "what about Alice? Shouldn't—"

"She'll be all right. I'll look in on her as soon as we have Leon settled comfortably. Get a couple of men to take him upstairs. Blanche, I'd like you to go with him. Take the electric blankets and set them up around him. The single most important thing is to raise his body temperature back to normal as quickly as possible."

Richie went to the door and pulled it open. The crowd in the lobby fell silent when they saw him. Richie pointed at the two men standing closest. "You and you," he said.

The people in the lobby, silent and embarrassed now, moved back from the door as the two men, led by Blanche Mackintosh, carried the stretcher with Leon Bissell toward the stairs. Doc watched from the doorway for a second, then closed the door, and turned to face Richie, Susan, and Phil.

"Doc," Richie said, "what about Alice? Shouldn't—"

"Alice is dead," the doctor said. "I'd guess she's been dead about eight hours."

9:21 A.M.

The little girl ran across the ballroom.

"Mommy, Mommy, I saw a clown. I was out in the hall and I looked out the window and I saw him!"

"Margaret Louise—" her mother began. She looked tiredly at Nora Ellenwood and Mikey Yoshioshi, with whom she was sharing ballroom duty. The ballroom was lively with the sounds of children playing.

"But I did! He was in the square. I saw him. He was standing on his head."

"Margaret Louise, we have a long day ahead of us. A *very* long day. And I won't—"

"But they said there's a circus."

"I will not have you telling tales this early in the day." She pointed across the ballroom. "Look at all the nice games we got for you children. There's a set of Chinese checkers over there by the wall that nobody's using. Go ahead and get it and find somebody to play with. Go on."

"But, Mommy, he was real! I saw him!"

"Margaret Louise!"

The girl arranged her face into a very exasperated look, then went slowly off toward the Chinese checkers. After a few steps, she stopped and turned back to look at her mother.

"He was real," she said. "I saw him." Then she went off slowly to find someone to play with.

The women looked at each other, cast their eyes heavenward, then shook their heads helplessly.

9:29 A.M.

Leon's eyes were still glassy, but he could talk a little now. His face was as white as the pillowcase that cushioned his head and the sheet tucked under his chin.

"Tell me," Doc said.

Leon painfully tried to clear his throat. When he got out the first words, his voice was gravelly, guttural. Doc unobstrusively pulled his chair a little closer to the bed. Beside him, Richie Mead crouched down.

"Cold," Leon said.

Doc nodded. "Yes, I understand. Go on."

"Cold. Dark."

"Yes."

Leon moved his head from side to side a little. Then, for an instant, a look of terrible fear filled his eyes. "Alice," he managed to say. "Alice."

Doc nodded again. "I told you, Leon. She's all right. I'm more concerned about you right now. I want you to tell me what happened."

"Snow," Leon said. "Cold." He closed his eyes.

Doc glanced at Richie and shook his head. Richie sighed and stood up. Together they looked at Leon a moment, then quietly moved toward the door.

In the corridor, Richie asked, "Will he be able to talk soon? I'd really like to know what they were doing outside. I'll send somebody over to the house to look for Sally."

"I hope so," Doc said. "Maybe in a couple of hours. Richie, I don't want anybody in that room. I don't want him to know about Alice until he has more strength."

"Okay. Jesus!"

"He must have carried her all night," Doc said.

Richie turned away until the lump in his throat went down enough for him to speak.

"Call me when you think he can talk."

"I will," Doc said.

Richie nodded, shoved his hands in his pockets, and walked toward the stairs by himself. Behind him, Doc Warren followed slowly.

9:38 A.M.

Susan was in the hotel kitchen when Richie found her.

The women who had been working there the last couple of days had at first tried to talk to Susan, then left her alone. She was out of sight, sitting on a straight chair back in the corner, near the big ovens used for baking. Her head was down and she was hugging herself tightly, but she wasn't crying anymore.

Richie stood beside her. Neither of them said anything, but Susan moved a little closer to him. After a minute, he put a hand on the back of her neck. She lowered her head further but raised one hand and touched his fingers. After a while, he stroked her cheek gently with his left hand.

Susan shuddered and Richie held her tighter. Without looking up, she said, "Promise you'll let me help."

"I will," Richie said. "I promise."

"Not a sign of him," Phil said. "The last guys just came back. They were all over the place, at least as much as they could through the snow, and they couldn't find a trace of him."

Richie stared at the door past Phil's shoulder and tried to think.

"Where could he be? Where the hell could a kid get to in weather like this? He can't be far. He *can't* be!"

"I know he can't. But I don't know where he is."

"I'll go out with you myself. God, I wish we had Frank. What's it like outside?"

"Don't ask."

"Christ."

12:05 P.M.

Leon Bissell's eyes were open and looked less glazed than they had before. Doc Warren and Blanche Mackintosh sat beside the bed. Blanche made a show of fluffing up the pillows.

"How do you feel, Leon?" Doc said. "Tell me how you feel."

Leon shook his head impatiently and tried to clear his throat.

"Alice," he whispered after a minute.

"She's sleeping," Doc told him. "Leon, I want you to tell me what happened. Where's Sally? What were you doing out in the snow?"

"Snow," Leon said, and dozed off again.

12:41 P.M.

Richie's group was the last to arrive back at the hotel. They had divided up the town systematically and carefully into seven different areas, and each area was covered by a team of three or four men. There was no sign of Jimmy French anywhere. Richie had taken for himself the area that included the railroad station. When he knocked at the train, Stanton Stokely had answered at once, but he had no knowledge of the boy.

They were all nearly frozen when they came back into the lobby, stamping snow off their boots, blowing their noses, and rubbing their hands together to restore the circulation in numb fingers.

Richie took the Frenches into his office and tried to talk to them, to calm them down, but he hardly knew what to be saying. He had been out there himself for two and a half hours, and had seen nothing that might give them even a clue to the boy's whereabouts. The only thing he knew for certain was that, if the boy had been outside the hotel all night, he was surely dead by now.

After ten minutes of anguished conversation, he persuaded Don French to eat something, get some food into him to build up body warmth, before going out again with another search party.

When they were finally gone from the office, Richie put his head in his hands and made a conscious effort to breathe deeply and try to relax. It only helped a little.

Then he jerked upright. The telephone. The phone had rung earlier, he was sure of it. Hours ago, just about the time they brought Leon in. . . . He reached for the white phone at the corner of the desk and put it to his ear. There was no dial tone. He slammed it down and stalked out of the office.

He found Phil Aymar eating a sandwich in the Dining Room. The place was crowded. It had been noisier early in the day, but news about Leon Bissell and little Alice, as well as the news that Jimmy French was nowhere to be found, had quieted the room to a low hum of nervous conversation.

There were five other men at the table with Phil. Richie ignored them.

"What's with the phones?" he said.

"They're still dead. They—"

"It rang before. I know it rang before."

Phil swallowed the food in his mouth. "I know, I know. They rang all over the place. It happened a couple of times. Some people were even able to make calls the first time, before they went dead again. There were five or six calls to the station. It lasted maybe five minutes, maybe ten, I don't know, then they went out again. It happened again twice after that. The company's probably working on them."

Richie stood a second, staring down at the table, tapping the fingers of his right hand against his leg. Then he said, "Okay," to no one in particular, turned, and went back to the lobby.

He was just reaching the door of Doc Warren's temporary office when Susan hurried up beside him.

"Want company?" she asked without smiling.

Richie didn't answer, and she followed him as he knocked on the door with one hand and pushed it open with the other.

The doctor was putting a lightweight brace on the arm of John Winter, who had been bested painfully in a wrestling match in the ballroom. John's mother, Lynne, watched with a look of both anger and worry on her face. John's younger brother, Stevie, watched the procedure with more fascination than concern.

Doc chatted lightly with the youngster and his mother while he worked. Richie stood against the wall, looking impatient. Susan tried to engage the boy in conversation to distract him from what the doctor was doing.

When the patient and his family were finally gone from the office, Richie said, "The Bissell house is empty. No sign of Sally. Were you able to talk with Leon?"

"No."

"Well, when—"

"When he's able to talk," Doc said. He held up a hand to silence Richie. "When he's able. Which could be in another hour, or another couple of hours, or possibly never. Does that answer your question?"

"Sorry, Doc."

Doc waved his hand. "Any sign of the French boy?"

"Nothing."

Doc sighed. Now that the tension of necessary work was gone, he looked tired again.

"I thought I heard phones ringing," Doc said. "Am I imagining things?"

"No, they . . . Oh, God, the Torveys! I completely forgot about them!"

Doc closed his eyes for a second. "I did too," he said.

"I'll have to go out there myself. I can't leave it for somebody else to do after forgetting it so many times."

Susan said nothing, but she moved closer to Richie and touched his arm.

"Richie," Doc said quickly, "we all forgot. I forgot too. There have been plenty of other things to think about."

"I'll have to go out there now."

"Fine," Doc said. "That's a good idea. You can go right after you eat something."

"Doc, I can't stop to eat now." He was already turning toward the door.

"You've been outside in that weather for a couple of hours, on foot. If you go out again now without plenty of hot food in you, you'll never come back. What do you think of that?" Doc looked at him over the tops of his half-glasses.

"He's right, Richie," Susan said. "You have to eat to keep warm. I'll come with you and get you something fast, starting with plenty of hot coffee. Come on, let's go."

"All right," Richie said, "on one condition. We go up and see Leon. At least we can see if he can talk. If he can't, then he can't. But we give it a try. Now."

Doc lifted his eyebrows slightly as he looked at Richie, then sighed and said, "All right. Just remember that I'll be the judge of whether he can talk or not."

"Fair enough."

"Follow me," Doc said, and they filed out of the office.

1:28 P.M.

Doc sat in the chair beside the bed with Richie and Susan standing behind him. Blanche Mackintosh, who had stayed with Leon, sat on the far side of the bed.

"Leon, do you feel up to talking?" the doctor asked.

Leon nodded. When he spoke, his voice was a hoarse whisper.

"I carried her," he said. "I carried her all wrapped up in a blanket."

The others leaned closer to hear him better.

"She was so cold. . . ." His voice trailed off as he remembered.

Gradually, in broken phrases and with many repetitions, Leon told how he had carried Alice and kept her wrapped in the blanket all through the night. He talked about how cold it was and how sometimes he couldn't see in the dark and how he had fallen in the snow. He told them that he remembered hearing that the snow could keep you warm and that, when his legs wouldn't carry him any farther, he had sat down and rested in a snowbank. He'd come to a house along the way and it was empty, but the cellar door was open and he'd gone down there for a while. It was pretty cold, but at least they were out of the wind and the blowing snow. Then he'd pushed on again. He'd found an abandoned farmhouse and, later, an empty barn, and had taken shelter in both of them for a while. But he'd always pressed on toward the town, later even passing by lighted windows, to get back to the hotel and the doctor he knew Alice needed. And always he had kept the child close to him, always held her in his arms to keep her warm, always kept the blanket around her, and never put her down once. Not once. Finally, he was crying and had to stop.

The others, embarrassed at the man's tears, moved away from the bed while Blanche dabbed at his wet eyes with a tissue.

Doc gestured to Richie and Susan, and the three of them went out into the hall. Doc closed the door.

"I'll stay with him a while longer," he said, "and see if I can find out what happened to his wife. He may be blanking it out. But he'll have to be allowed to tell it, if he even knows it anymore, in his own way and at his own pace. I can't put too much pressure on him. He's going to have a very rough ordeal ahead of him. If he hadn't found even the shelter he did, he'd be dead now himself. He could be up and around by tomorrow, but he'll have a lot more than weakness to deal with."

"Okay," Richie said. "Then we'll get going. I'm really worried about the Torveys. If you find out anything about Sally, tell Phil."

"I'm getting worried about you," Doc said. "Richie, you be careful with the snowmobile. And see to it that you eat before you go out. You'll be no good to anybody if something happens to you." He looked at Susan. "Are you going with him?"

"Yes."

"Good," Doc said. "See to it he doesn't do anything foolish."

"Doc, we have to go."

"You have to *eat* before you go anywhere," Doc said firmly. "Doctor's orders."

Richie and Susan had started toward the stairs when Doc said, "Richie, one more thing."

They turned to look at him.

"If you find . . . bad news . . . when you get out there, remember that nobody can do everything or be every-place at the same time."

"Sure, Doc," Richie said. "I'll remember. I just hope I don't have to."

They searched each other's faces for a moment. Then Richie and Susan hurried down the hall, and Doc went back to see Leon.

1:49 P.M.

With gentle coaxing and much patience, Doc gradually drew the rest of the story out of Leon.

The man told how Sally had insisted on leaving town, how he had struggled with the truck, forcing it through the snow, how they had finally bogged down and he hadn't known at first where they were and it was so cold and he was worried about Alice because she was shivering and then . . .

Doc Warren had to press his teeth hard together to keep all expression from his face when Leon told about the clown. At the other side of the bed, Blanche joined her hands together.

"Go on," Doc said softly. "Tell me, Leon."

Shivering and sobbing, Leon told him what the clown had done. Then he lapsed into silence and closed his eyes.

Doc murmured, "Oh, my God." He rose from the chair and moved around the bed to the window. The snow, as if knowing he was there, rattled loudly against the glass.

A moment later, he turned back to the room. "Blanche . . ." he said, but Blanche was already going out the door.

Doc looked out the window again. He could feel the

cold from outside. It chilled his fingers and made him shudder.

"Oh, my God," he said again.

2:05 P.M.

"You missed him by about fifteen minutes," Bob Booth told Blanche in the Dining Room. "He ate two sandwiches as if they were the last sandwiches in the world. Susan Lester was with him. They wouldn't even sit down, just ate the sandwiches standing up, and dashed out of here. They're far away by now. I just saw Phil Aymar go into the office, though, if you want him."

Blanche walked slowly out to the lobby, but instead of looking for Phil, she went toward the front doors. The floor was wet and muddy because she'd been busy most of the day with the doctor and hadn't had a chance to think of it. She paid no attention to it now.

She stood at the doors for a moment. Then, ignoring the icy touch of the glass, she wiped the steam from the inside of the window and looked out. Across the street in the square, a brightly costumed clown waved gaily to her.

2:09 P.M.

Susan and Richie had each been lost in their own thoughts as they grabbed something quick to eat and headed for the snowmobiles. She had tried to think of something to say that would let him know she was with him, that she understood how he felt, but the only words that came to mind sounded inane and adolescent. Finally, she decided that the best thing she could do would be just to stick close and lend support by her presence. When he wanted to talk, she'd be there to listen.

She had more time to think while the two snowmobiles glided through the white and silent countryside. They followed the roads out of the Kill, moving along what were normally green and pleasant residential streets—green even in winter with a profusion of fir trees. Now they were white, white everywhere, the trees only shadows of darkness, and the windows of houses seeming blind and blank, reflecting only the glare of snow and the gray of a slate-colored sky.

Richie, in the lead, kept the speed down, moving more slowly than they had yesterday. Susan hoped that meant he was heeding Doc Warren's advice.

Then the houses grew more sparse. Now there were wide stretches between homes, and the homes them-

selves were bigger, great Victorian mansions left over
from the height of the Kill's prosperity. The big white
houses, most of them kept in lovingly good repair,
looked gray against the snow, and snow had blurred the
outlines of their gabled roofs and their intricate gingerbread woodwork.

The road took a wide, long curve around the base of a
steep hill and slowly began to climb. It circled the hill,
then dipped a little, swung the other way, and climbed
again.

Richie looked back over his shoulder, and it made
Susan feel good to know that he was checking on her.
She waved to him and he turned back to face the road
ahead.

The hill sloped up steeply now on their left, a solid
expanse of unbroken white. On the other side, it dropped
off, sloped downward for a short distance, then
curved out flat into a wide, long valley. Susan could just
make out, through the blur of blowing snow, two farms
in the valley. Smoke rose from the chimneys, and she
wished suddenly that she were in one of those houses,
curled up by a big fire, and the only thought she'd have
to give to the storm and the snowfall would be how
pretty it all was.

Too late for that now, she thought. I wanted to get
involved, didn't I? I wanted to be helpful. I wanted to
be a full-fledged adult member of the community and
come through with flying colors when the chips were
down, and assorted other cliché-type things like that. So
here I am, out in the cold and the snow, racing off to *do
the right and brave thing* with the sheriff, like some
frontier gal in a cowboys-and-Indians movie, and we'll
be getting off easy if we don't find this sweet old couple
frozen as stiff as logs on the doorstep.

She pulled her knit hat down lower on her forehead

and tried to snuggle deeper inside her coat. Her fingers were beginning to feel stiff from the cold. And she was trying very hard not even to think about her feet.

Some heroine, she thought.

On the other hand, she was actually doing something to help, right? Right. Good girl, Susan, she told herself. Boy, I really do love it out here. To think I could be curled up on the couch at home, eating bonbons, with a nice fire crackling away merrily, and reading the new Judith Krantz or looking at the latest make-overs in *Cosmo*. Nope, not me, nosirreebob, not when there's danger in the air and hard work to be done.

Oh, please God, let the Torveys be all right.

Richie looked back at her again and she waved to let him know she was doing fine.

2:15 P.M.

"Leon," Doc said gently, "I just want you to tell it to me again, and then, I promise, I'll leave you alone so you can sleep."

Leon nodded weakly. He closed his eyes for a few seconds while he thought and sorted it all out again.

After a moment, he said clearly, "I carried her back. She . . . She was so cold."

"No, Leon, not that part. I understand about that part. I want you to tell me again about what happened before that. About what happened at the van. Tell me what happened to Sally."

"Oh," Leon said. And, more thoughtfully, "Oh, I understand now. That part. All right."

He thought it through again and then began.

As much as Doc Warren wished it otherwise, Leon Bissell, in his tired and raspy voice, told the story exactly as he had before.

2:23 P.M.

They passed the truck without stopping, and it was a full minute later before Richie realized what he'd seen. He slowed the snowmobile to a halt and waited for Susan to pull up beside him.

"Did you see that back there?"

"All I can see is snow, as far as the eye can see." Her hair had come loose from under her hat, and she took the opportunity now to push it back.

"I think it was a truck or a van," Richie said. He was squinting at her through the snow. Then he looked past her, back down the road the way they'd come. The scene was white and desolate, empty of all life. "I think it was a van," Richie said.

Susan looked but couldn't see a thing.

"What color is the Bissells' van?"

"Blue."

Richie shook his head. "That's what I thought. I don't know, though. Could be. I'm going back for a look."

He started the snowmobile, circled around and started back. He didn't look at Susan. After a moment, she followed him.

The hills seemed even more silent than before. Any sound or sign of life, any movement or breath of living creature, was muffled and stilled by the blanket of snow on the ground and the moving snow in the icy, brittle air. The snowmobiles, as they moved slowly on the road, seemed to growl like nervous animals at the mute landscape.

They stopped near the van. It was parked, if that was the word for it, on the wrong side of the road. Where blowing snow hadn't adhered to its surface, it was blue.

They climbed slowly out of the snowmobiles and their feet sank into the drifts, making walking slow and difficult. They moved closer to the van.

Susan was first to spot the crude lettering on the door, partially obscured by snow.

"It's Leon's," she said, and the cold made her voice catch in her throat.

Richie made his way around the front of the snow-encrusted van, and now he could see that the door on the driver's side was open. Without looking back, he stretched a hand out behind him and gestured to Susan to stay where she was.

Susan stood for a few seconds as Richie moved toward the door. Then she pressed her lips together and followed him.

Richie reached the door, hesitated for a second, then moved around it. Snow completely covered the windows and windshield of the van, and the interior was dark. He leaned forward.

Snow had blown and drifted in, covering the dashboard ledge, the steering wheel, the floor, the bench seat, and a lumpy bundle that rested against the far door. Richie leaned into the van through the doorway and looked in the back. It was empty. He withdrew a bit, then leaned in again and brushed some of the snow from the lumpy bundle on the seat. The snow fell away easily. The bundle was covered with cloth . . . like a

coat. Richie clamped his mouth shut and brushed
quickly at the snow, not allowing himself to think about
this for one second more . . . until he was looking at the
body of Sally Bissell.

"Richie, what—" Susan said behind him.

He jumped violently at the sound of her voice and
cracked the top of his head hard against the roof of the
van. He lost his balance and fell backward against
Susan. She reached out instinctively to catch him and, in
the same instant that his full weight struck her, she saw
the uncovered body of Sally Bissell on the seat. It lay in
a heap, crumpled unnaturally, with the shoulders turned
toward the open door and resting against the back of the
seat. Where the head had been was only a torn and
ragged stump of neck, covered with dark, frozen blood.

"Don't . . ." Richie said as he sprawled in the snow.
Then everything went black and he passed out.

2:29 P.M.

At Blanche Mackintosh's urging, Doc Warren finally consented to take his own advice and get something to eat.

The Dining Room had emptied out a little and, when Blanche found him there, he was sitting alone at a booth in the corner, with a half-finished bowl of pea soup in front of him. A plate beside it had two untouched slices of buttered whole-wheat bread.

"You're not eating it," Blanche said.

Doc had been lost in thought. He looked up when he heard her.

"You're not eating it," she said again. "You're not supposed to be just looking at it. It's not all that good to look at, anyway. You're supposed to *eat* it. Doctor's orders."

"Do you want something, Blanche?" There was the slightest hint of controlled irritation in his voice.

Blanche sat heavily on the edge of the seat across from him and slid herself into the booth.

"I want two things," she said. "The first thing I want is for you to eat that soup. And both pieces of that bread. When you'e done that, I have something to tell you that you obviously haven't heard yet."

Doc looked down at the soup, picked up his spoon,

stirred it, and began to eat. Neither of them spoke until he'd finished. Then he wiped his mouth and looked at her.

"Well?"

Blanche's stern look melted away.

"I'm glad you had that much, at least, Doc, because when I tell you this, you won't have much appetite. I just heard it a few minutes ago when I passed by the ballroom where the children are." She joined her hands tightly before her, as if in prayer.

"Tell me," Doc said.

"About ten minutes ago—while you were in here, I guess—that ringmaster from the circus, from down in that train, came on up here and slipped by without anybody in the lobby seeing him at all, and of course Richie Mead is on his way to the Torveys, and all the deputies are outside somewhere looking for that Jimmy French again. He just marched right upstairs to the ballroom, so it seems, and introduced himself to the mothers who were up there—and let me tell you, they're going out of their minds with those kids all cooped up like that—and he says he has a surprise for everybody in Deacons Kill. Then he calls over all the children and announces that his circus is putting on a free performance for the whole town, everybody who can get there, tonight. Tonight at six o'clock, and they're going to do it in that old warehouse down there by the train station."

The doctor stared at her for a second, then began to push back from the table. "Is he still there? While I've been sitting—"

"He's gone, Doc. He was gone before I got there. It was the children making so much noise after he left, they were so excited, that made me go by that way to see what was going on."

"At six o'clock," Doc said, his voice a monotone.

"That's right. And, Doc, I can tell you, after getting a look at that creepy ringmaster earlier today, and after seeing what I've been seeing out there in the snow, I just know there's something wrong about the whole thing. The thought of it just chills me through and through."

"Yes," Doc said. He pushed the soup bowl away from in front of him and leaned forward tiredly on the table. "Yes," he said again.

2:29 P.M.

Susan was kneeling in the deep snow beside the van, with Richie's head in her lap.

"Richie, *please!*" she said again.

He had been unconscious for several minutes, and she'd been calling his name and rubbing his face and his wrists, but he was only now beginning to stir. Susan had carefully avoided looking inside the van again, although her gaze was constantly drawn there and she had to stop herself deliberately.

"Susan?" Richie said suddenly. He jerked upright before she could stop him. The pain made him groan.

It was another few minutes before he could talk or felt he could move without having the world spin away from beneath him. Susan cushioned the back of his head as best she could. Even the long johns beneath her jeans felt wet and icy now, and her feet felt as if they were frozen solid.

When Richie could talk, she told him he had a lump on his head that was bigger than he wanted to know about, and that, no, he shouldn't try to touch it. It looked terrible but the skin wasn't broken.

"I feel like my head is broken," Richie moaned. "Christ, what a stupid thing to do."

"Richie, I didn't mean to—"

"Not you. Me! Oh God, my head hurts. I should have had my wits about me better." Without moving his head, he lifted his eyes and looked inside the van. "Jesus," he whispered. "Susan, don't look in there."

"I already did. Once. That'll do me."

Wincing with the pain and leaning on Susan for support, Richie struggled into an upright position. The two of them sat there in the snow.

"This may sound grotesque," Susan said, "but under other circumstances, this would be something to laugh about."

And suddenly they were both laughing. There was nothing of humor in it, only a reaction to the sight of the headless corpse on the seat of the van, plus the fright of Richie's injury, and they both knew it, but they sat there in the snow, both of them covered in white, and they laughed and laughed anyway.

2:43 P.M.

When Doc Warren fell in the snow on Hill Street, he had to rest there for a minute, on his hands and knees, until he caught his breath. Then he carefully got to his feet and resolved to go slower the rest of the way. He could see where his office was from here, so it wasn't that far to go. No need to hurry so much that he'd lose his balance and fall again. Then he stopped and looked all around and up to the sky. It was dark—darker, he thought, than it should be for this time of day, even in a winter snowstorm—but he thought the snow was letting up a little and the wind easing off. He looked all around again. Yes, the weather was definitely easing off a bit. He thought the air might even be a little less cold than it had been.

At least, he thought, nobody will freeze on the way to the warehouse, especially the children.

Especially the children.

He stopped suddenly and drew in his breath.

Ahead of him, across the street, he could see the door of his office clearly. The air was clear and the wind had died. It had stopped snowing.

When he started moving again, he was hurrying as quickly as he could go.

2:50 P.M.

Richie was too dizzy to walk by himself, and Susan had to help him back to the snowmobiles. When they got there, he sat back against the side of his own, ignoring the snow beneath him. He kept muttering alternately, "I'll be all right in a minute," and, "Oh, Christ, I'm so dizzy!"

"Richie, you won't be able to drive this thing."

"I will, I will! Just give me a minute till my head clears. I told you, I'll be all right."

"You've already had about *fifteen* minutes, and you're not all right. You could have a concussion or something."

"I don't have any concussion. Just stop shouting, will you? I'll be okay in a minute."

Susan was breathing hard with tension, her breath forming a white cloud in front of her. She looked up and down the empty white road, and realized with a start that the air was clear. The wind had died down, and it had stopped snowing.

"Be grateful for small blessings," she murmured.

"What?"

"It stopped snowing."

"Terrific. And maybe my head'll fall off. Oh Jesus, what a thing to say!" He pushed away from the snowmobile and tried to stand by himself, but he swayed at once and fell back against it.

"That's it," Susan said tightly. "That little balancing act just made up my mind." She took hold of his shoulders. "Tell me I'm a deputy."

"You're a pain in the ass."

"I'm serious. Tell me."

"Okay, okay. You're a deputy."

"You can give me the badge later. C'mon, you're getting into this thing."

"What?"

"Get in! I just suspended your driver's license, so you're a passenger and I'm driving. Get in! I'll help you."

Richie lifted his head slowly and looked her in the face. Their eyes met.

Very serious, Susan said, "I'm not kidding."

After a second, Richie nodded, then instantly closed his eyes. When he opened them again, he silently reached out and put his arm around her shoulders for support.

3:03 P.M.

The children playing in the ballroom could not contain their excitement at the thought of seeing a circus performance this evening after three days of being confined. It seemed to the harried women in charge as if the boys were multiplying by the minute, especially if you judged by the noise they were making. Freddie Ellenwood, with his arm in a cast, was playing tag with five other boys. But the girls weren't much better. Margaret Louise Kennedy, Carol Trenchard, and some other girls were jumping rope, chanting rhymes to the beat of the rope slapping the floor. None of the children could concentrate long enough to get involved in a game unless it required constant frantic activity.

The mothers on duty for that hour—an hour at a time was definitely all that a mere mortal could stand—tried not to look too closely at the children and to block out the noise. Any attempt to quiet the children at this point would be hopeless.

Kathleen Kennedy was one of the women on duty now, taking her turn "in the barrel," as the women had been quietly and grimly joking among themselves all day. Her daughter, Margaret Louise, whom she had earlier in the day sent off to play Chinese checkers, was walking toward her.

"Yes, Margaret?" her mother said, hoping there was no real problem that had to be dealt with. The hour from now until four o'clock, when she'd be relieved, and the two additional hours until the time for the circus, stretched out endlessly before her.

Margaret looked up at her mother. With no expression whatsoever in her face or voice, she said, "I told you there was a clown," and turned and walked away.

3:10 P.M.

Doc Warren knew only that something had drawn him away from the hotel and back to his office on Hill Street. He was old enough to have long ago learned to trust such unconscious impulses. There was a reason for them, some reason perhaps deeply buried in the mind, but a compelling reason, even so. Yielded to, given a chance to grow and flower, fed with the right stimuli, the meaning of such an impulse might rise to the surface of conscious thought.

So far, sitting at the rolltop desk in his office and staring unseeingly before him, he didn't have a clue.

For the first couple of minutes, it felt good to sit in the office, in the familiar leather chair that was molded to his body with years of constant use, at the familiar desk, surrounded by the comfortable shapes and shadows of his life. He straightened some drug order forms and a small pile of journals, took off his glasses, rubbed his eyes, put his glasses back on. But he still didn't know what had brought him here.

Something about a circus. Or about the name, Stanton Stokely? But what had brought him *here,* to the office? He didn't know. He trusted the impulse, but he didn't know where it was leading.

He leaned back in the chair and, placing his heel on

the floor, swiveled around toward the rest of the room. His eye immediately fell on the door to his inner office, the examining room. He turned away and tried not to think about it. Earlier, after Leon Bissell was safely put to bed in a room by himself, with Blanche Mackintosh watching over him, Doc had spoken to Will Burke, one of the two morticians in Deacons Kill. The Burke & Lewis funeral home and facilities were too far away to take Alice's body there through the snow, so Doc had asked Burke to move the child's body over to his office. It lay now, he knew, on his examining table, wrapped in a sheet and frozen by the air from the window Burke had opened in the other room.

The doctor had dealt closely with death all his life, doing his best to hold it at bay as long as possible, but knowing that, in the end, it would win every contest. But he had never gotten used to it. Not when he quietly explained to a man that he had six months left to live. Not when he had to come out of a room and announce to a waiting family that the father, mother, child, was dead. Not when he did it on the telephone. Not when he visited the flower-scented rooms of Burke & Lewis. Not when he went to the supposedly comforting religious services. Not ever. And least of all with children. Only the sternest self-discipline could hold the pain at bay.

He sighed with resignation, gave in, rose, crossed the office, and opened the door of the examination room.

The air was bitter cold. In the gray light from the window, he saw the small shape beneath the sheet on the table. He stood in the doorway, looking at it—forcing himself to look at it—hoping it would trigger some thought. The thought that struck him was as icy as the air: some vague memory of a circus, coupled with the . . . visions?—could he call them that?—of circus figures that he and Blanche Mackintosh had been having, had brought him into this room, where he now stood looking at the covered body of a child, dead of exposure.

No, he thought, enough is enough, and he backed out of the room and closed the door. The chill air seemed to cling to his clothing. He went back to his desk and sat down.

He tried to think no further of Alice Bissell, but the thoughts wouldn't leave him alone. And among them was the thought: how she would have enjoyed the circus tonight.

No, wrong, he told himself. It was the promised circus performance that had brought him here, that had triggered something long buried in his thoughts. But what? And why was he so afraid of this Stanton Stokely? And why was he seeing clowns in the snow?

Seeing clowns in the snow. But he *had* seen them. He had.

And Blanche had seen them too.

And Leon.

Leon said a clown had torn off Sally's head.

It was all madness, nonsense.

Doc raised one hand and massaged the side of his face.

This was no good. He couldn't put any of it together. All this was doing was making him feel foolish and even more confused. He had to do something more concrete, something more reasonable.

He rose from the chair again, went to his filing cabinets, and began searching through old files of past patients to see if there was a Stanton Stokely among them.

He had no hope of finding the name, no conscious hope at all, but he looked anyway, quickly but thoroughly, impulse guiding his fingers.

3:13 P.M.

The snowmobile was harder to handle with the extra weight, and Susan had been taking it very easy the rest of the way to the Torveys'. Thank God, it had stopped snowing and she could see the road ahead of her, or at least she could see where the road was *supposed* to be. It wasn't always easy to tell where the road ended and a field began, and Susan was afraid of hitting a low fence or boulder or even a bush that was buried in the snow. If she did, it would be the end of them.

She steadfastly blocked from her thoughts what she'd seen in the van back there. She didn't know how long she'd be able to avoid thinking about it, but she meant to for as long as possible.

And she was still praying that the Torveys would be all right when they got there.

At first, Richie had tried to talk, but he'd given that up now. He sat silently in the snowmobile, carefully holding his head as steady as possible.

Susan saw a house ahead.

"I think that's it, Richie. Is that it?" She raised one hand long enough to point.

Richie focused his eyes on the scene ahead. "That's it."

There were no other houses in sight, only this one, its

283

gray paint badly weathered and peeling, set far back from the road against the treeline. A snow-covered lean-to at the side of the house sagged with age. Susan slowed, tried her best to locate the lane that led to the house, and turned in toward it.

She was concentrating so much on handling the snowmobile that she had brought it to a halt in the yard before she realized what she was looking at.

The front foor of the house was open about three inches.

"Oh, no," she groaned. "Oh, please God, no."

Richie was already climbing out. She put a hand on his arm to steady him.

Richie was looking at the door. "Maybe you better stay here," he said.

"No, thanks," Susan said quickly. "Apart from the fact that I'm scared silly, I'd only have to pull you out of the snow again. If we're going, let's go."

She held on to his arm, and they supported each other across the white yard and toward the door. A few feet from the steps, Susan stumbled over something in the snow. She looked down and gasped.

Mrs. Torvey's body lay face down, most of it covered with snow. She'd been wearing a long brown coat that reached to her ankles, but her gnarled hands were bare. Susan had tripped on the woman's frozen wrist.

"Don't look," Richie said. "Just let me hold on to you." Moving slowly, he crouched by the body and looked at the woman's face. He pulled off a glove and touched her, then quickly put the glove back on and stood up. He looked at Susan, who was holding her free hand over her mouth. "I think you better stay out here," he said.

"No," Susan said.

Placing their feet carefully on the steps, they moved

up to the door. Richie reached out and pushed it back. It creaked a little in the silence of the snow-smothered world.

He was able to see into the house before Susan. "He's dead," he said quietly. He stepped through the doorway and Susan followed him.

The room was just as cold as the world outside. Old Mr. Torvey still sat upright in his wheelchair, facing the door, with arthritically swollen hands folded neatly in his lap. Richie crossed the room and examined the man quickly, but of course he was dead.

3:20 P.M.

Everything was jolly in the hotel kitchen.

Mary Booth and some of the other women had thought of baking cookies to take to the circus tonight, and others had eagerly joined in, warmed by the idea itself, but drawn also by the warmth of a communal effort, by the need to be doing something positive and constructive, and by the camaraderie of the kitchen. There had been sad expressions of shock and sorrow at the death of poor little Alice Bissell, and further worry about her missing mother, but not too much. There was also secret relief that Sally Bissell wasn't around, dead or alive, to spoil everybody's fun at the baking. Besides, the snow had now definitely let up, no question about it, sparking talk that maybe the worst of the storm was over and pretty soon now things would be getting back to normal.

Trays of oatmeal cookies and sugar cookies covered most of the counter space in the gleaming kitchen. It would be cold in that old warehouse, Mary Booth kept saying, at least until body heat did a little to take the edge off, and everyone would be glad of something to eat.

Then Lynne Winter thought of making popcorn. It was cheap, the children would love it, and they could make barrels and barrels of it in no time at all. They checked the supplies and, sure enough, there was plenty of popping corn on hand. Everyone agreed it was a terrific idea.

Now the hotel kitchen was filled with talk and laughter, and the air was warm and sweet and homey with the smell of baking, and the popcorn popped and rattled away.

3:26 P.M.

There was nothing in the files. Doc hadn't expected to find anything, but he was disappointed anyway.

His back was paining him from bending, and he returned to the desk and sat in his chair.

Although he'd found nothing in his files, he now had the unmistakable feeling, although he couldn't explain it to himself, that he was getting warm, getting close to finding what he was after. The half-formed thought persisted that the name Stanton Stokely was somehow associated with . . . what? His files? Doc snorted. Too bad he didn't know what he was after. That makes it a little hard to know when you've found it. His father had always said that, he recalled, when he had a patient with a complaint that was hard to diagnose.

His father.

Maybe there was something in his father's files.

Doc leaned forward and reached into the top-left pigeonhole on the desk. He pulled out a heavy, old-fashioned key, contemplated the cold weight of it in his palm for a second, then rose and walked quickly out to the hall.

3:30 P.M.

While Susan sat on the edge of the sofa and looked at Mr. Torvey, frozen solid in his wheelchair, Richie went outside alone to move Mrs. Torvey's body. Susan wanted to help him but, although Richie was still unsteady—she saw him holding onto the doorjamb as he started down the steps—he insisted on doing it alone. Through the angle of the door, she could just see him bending over, trying to lift the woman's frozen body. Richie grunted loudly with the effort, and Susan called out, "Richie, are you okay?"

"I'll do it," he shouted back, and Susan could hear the bitter anger and self-reproach in his voice.

She rose from the couch and went to look for the kitchen. Maybe she could make tea or coffee, anything hot, before they started back. She was half-numb with cold and fright. It was going to take a long time getting back to the Kill, with the two of them in the snowmobile, and something hot would stand them in good stead. Little as she liked the thought of using the poor couple's food and utensils, she went into the kitchen. She found the pipes frozen and the refrigerator almost empty, and felt suddenly embarrassed at this intrusion into the Torveys' privacy.

She heard Richie at the door, and retreated farther

into the house, looking for the bathroom, hoping for something stronger than the first-aid kit's aspirin that would help to ease his headache and dizziness. God, she should have realized he'd jump when—

"Stay in there," Richie grunted from the hallway. She heard something thump against the wall. She didn't want to think about what it was. She stood silently at the bathroom sink, her head lowered, hand clutching the bottle of Excedrin she'd found, her back toward the door.

A minute later, she heard Richie pushing the heavy wheelchair down the hall and into the bedroom. Then the bedroom door closed and Richie said. "It's okay now."

She followed him to the living room and saw that he was unconsciously touching a hand against the wall to steady himself. Without saying a word, they sat beside each other on the couch. Susan handed him the bottle of Excedrin. He opened it, dumped out four of the white tablets, put them one by one into his mouth, and chewed them.

After a while, Susan looked at him and placed a hand on his.

Richie turned his face toward her. His eyes looked dark and tired. "She must have been getting wood for the fireplace," he said.

Susan nodded.

"Jesus," Richie said.

3:35 P.M.

Leon Bissell stirred in his sleep. Blanche Mackintosh leaned forward in her chair by the bed.

Suddenly Leon sat up. "Alice!" he called out, staring sightlessly before him, then slowly sank back to the pillow. He stirred uneasily for a moment, then mumbled, "Sally, where are you?" Then he was quiet again.

Blanche rose from the chair, one hand covering her mouth, her eyes bright and sad. She looked at the man in the bed for a minute, then quietly went out, hurried down the corridor, and let herself into her own room.

She stood there, hugging herself, until the threat of sobbing had passed. Then she crossed the room, pushed the drapes back, and slid the window open. Cold air rushed in at her, surrounded her, filled the room. She ignored it.

She leaned on the cold windowsill and looked out. The sky was gray, and the town and the square were gray beneath it. She looked at the place across the street where she'd seen the clown. There was no one there.

"I don't know what's happening," she said, her words puffing out in a thin white cloud. "And I don't know how and I don't know why. But with the help of God, we're going to beat you."

Then she closed the window with a bang and went back to watch over Leon.

3:40 P.M.

Doc Warren's father had used this same office before him. In those days, around the turn of the century, it was common for a doctor, especially a country doctor, to keep consulting rooms in his home. But Doc very clearly remembered his mother speaking out on that very subject: she'd have no sick people traipsing through her house and that was the end of it. His father had been a placid man and, for the sake of household harmony, had agreed.

His father had also been a very generous man and dedicated to the spirit as well as the letter of his profession, and therefore totally incapable of referring an indigent patient to a doctor in some other town. Doc's mother, although in many regards the kindest of women, was also fiercely protective of the family's meager fortunes and would hear none of this. Her husband had treated such patients anyway and simply neglected to mention the fact at home. He kept his medical records for them as diligently as any others, of course, but he took the precaution, since Mrs. Warren came into the office once every month to straighten out and supervise his financial records, of filing them in a place known only to himself. He had passed that confidential bit of information on to his son only after the son had earned his medical degree and begun aiding him in his practice, preparatory to taking it over himself.

Doc would have smiled at the memory if he hadn't been so intent on his search. He was down on his hands and knees, searching through faded and musty records in the storage room. After ten minutes, he found what he hadn't known he was seeking.

He carried the folder with his father's faded hand-written notation, "Circus Fire," back to his desk, adjusted the light, and began reading. It suddenly seemed much colder in the office. He shivered and tucked his hands between his knees for warmth, but his fingers remained as cold as ice.

3:48 P.M.

They had been sitting on the couch, talking quietly while Richie waited for his dizziness to fade a bit, but now he wanted to leave and start back for the Kill. Sally Bissell had been murdered, her body horribly mutilated, and he had to get to work on it in spite of the storm. Susan wanted to get away from the house herself, with its two dead bodies in the bedroom—she had never seen a dead person outside a funeral home before today, and today she had seen four—and she wasn't looking forward to the ride back. Besides, it was beginning to get dark out and would be full dark long before they reached town.

Nevertheless, she squeezed Richie's hand and said, "Sit a few minutes longer. You'll be glad of the rest once we go out in the cold again."

For a second, she thought he was going to stand up and insist on going, but then he sat back against the cushions.

"Richie," she said slowly, "you're not blaming yourself for . . . for what happened here, are you?"

He was silent a long time before he answered. "No," he said at last. "I did when we arrived, right at first, but . . . No, I guess I don't. Partly because I don't want to, I suppose, and partly because I don't have the time to. If that makes any sense."

"It does."

"Good," Richie said. "Then you can explain it to me someday."

"I will," she said.

Richie put his head back, sighed, and closed his eyes. "Another couple of minutes," he said, "and then we'll start back."

3:48 P.M.

The whole story was there, in his father's faded but precise handwriting on the medical records, and in two very yellowed newspaper clippings, one from the Albany *Union* and one from a long-defunct Cobleskill paper. Doc had to assemble the story from bits and pieces of information. He was shivering by the time he'd put together half of the tale.

On a snowy evening in January of 1909, Stanton Stokely's Stupendous Circus had arrived in Deacons Kill. It was a small circus, apparently, with no more than twenty people, including both performers and roustabouts. They had a private train—the article from the Cobleskill paper suggested that it was quite luxurious; its coaches, at least, were thought to have been obtained from the estate of a wealthy but failed entrepreneur of the nineteenth century—and they used the train to travel around the country, making a living in all the small towns they visited but a great reputation in none. The company, it seemed, offered little in the way of visual spectacle, having no wild animals and only two "aerial acrobats." But its posters and handbills did promise the sight of "a cacophony of clowns" who would "caper and cavort capriciously" and "capture the hearts of young and old alike."

The circus arrived in Deacons Kill, that evening of 1909, at the very beginning of a terrible blizzard. After a couple of days—all of the information was not here, but Doc was piecing the story together as best he could from what he found—the circus put on a performance in a huge shed that had stood alongside the railroad tracks in the market field.

In those bittersweet turn-of-the-century days of candles and gaslight, fire was a common hazard, and it was during that otherwise welcome circus performance that a fire broke out in the shed. The results were terrible, although dramatically less so for the residents of Deacons Kill who were in the shed at the time than for the circus performers themselves.

With the exceptions of only a few minor injuries and one broken arm, the residents of the Kill escaped unharmed. Not so the members of Stanton Stokely's Stupendous Circus. Trapped among sawdust, ropes, and makeshift wooden platforms, hampered further by clumsy costumes—the fire flared up suddenly during the "cacophony of clowns" number, both papers reported —and even further by desperate efforts to release and save the company's prized team of six performing horses, almost every member of the circus, including the frenzied horses, perished hideously in the searing, rushing flames.

Not all of them, however, died at once. The ringmaster—Stanton Stokely himself (the doctor's neat handwriting described him as "a man of approx. 60-65 years, of robust appearance")—six of the clowns, and two of the roustabouts, although horribly burned, lived in agony for some days after the event. Stokely himself, despite his terrible pain and anguish, was yet conscious enough several times to lament loudly the deaths of his fellows and, even more loudly, the awful suffering of

those others who still survived. He outlived the last of
the others by a day, and was clear enough in his mind
near the end to insist on knowing the condition of the
rest. When told that those remaining had finally been
spared further suffering through the kind ministry of
Death, he had lapsed into a silence from which he never
returned.

Neither the newspaper clippings nor the doctor's
handwritten notations gave any indication of the final
disposal of the bodies.

Doc's fingers were white and trembling as he closed
the folder and pushed it away from him. He sat back in
the chair and wrapped his arms tightly around his chest
for warmth.

He sat there for many minutes, head sunk on his
chest, staring unseeingly at the desk.

What he was thinking was impossible, of course, and
he was losing his mind.

And of course it could not be otherwise than the
truth, because he had seen Stanton Stokely himself, and
the circus train with the name painted on the side, and
he had seen the clowns, seen them all with his own eyes.
Phantoms, apparitions, men of flesh and blood—whatever they were and from wherever they came—he had
seen them.

This is the sheerest sort of nonsense, he told himself.

And in the same instant, he thought of the circus performance scheduled for tonight in the warehouse, with a
couple of hundred of the Kill's residents shut up inside.

Tonight, he thought numbly. He unclasped his arms
and looked at his watch.

No, it was madness, all madness.

Six of the clowns and two of the roustabouts, as well
as Stokely himself, had survived the fire, only to linger
in agony for several days afterward. In many ways, the

ringmaster's agony had been most terrible of all, knowing how his entire company had suffered and knowing of the additional suffering of his last eight colleagues. Knowledge like that, working in concert with excruciating pain, could unhinge the mind of any man. And in fact, according to the record, Stokely, although conscious, had lapsed into silence until his own suffering reached its end.

Earlier that day, Stanton Stokely had said that his circus was now much reduced and there remained, besides himself, only two men who operated the train, and six clowns.

Doc choked back a cry of fright, then reached for the telephone on his desk, whispering a prayer that it would work.

3:55 P.M.

"So I'll be dizzy," Richie said. "And, yes, it still hurts. But I can't help it. We have to go. I have to get back. Will you be able to handle the snowmobile?"

"I have to," Susan said.

"Yes, but do you think—"

"I will. I have to, so I will."

They looked at each other a moment, then Richie said, "Okay."

They pulled their hats and gloves on and fixed scarves tightly around their throats. Richie, making a deliberate effort to walk steadily, crossed to the door and waited for Susan.

When she came up to him, she glanced back toward the bedroom. "I guess we just leave them," she said flatly.

"We have to," Richie said.

Susan looked away from him.

Richie suddenly pulled off one glove and touched his hand to her cheek. "Susan," he said gently, "you're keeping a lot inside, I know, and you're doing it to help me." He lifted her face to his. "It's helping a lot, I want you to know that."

Susan nodded but couldn't say anything. She pressed her face against his hand.

Then they moved apart and Richie opened the door. The telephone rang.

They both started violently at the sound. Richie sprang back into the room, almost losing his balance, and looked around for the phone. He spotted it on an end table by the sofa and grabbed at it.

"Doc!" he said. "What—"

He listened, his mouth open. Susan came and stood close to him. When he shuddered inside his coat, he tried to turn away and conceal it from Susan, but she saw it anyway. After a moment, he looked quickly at his watch.

"That's two hours from now. . . . Yes. . . . Doc, don't do anything yourself. . . . No, I'll be there. . . . Doc? . . . Doc?"

But the line had gone dead, Doc's voice cut off by a hollow silence.

Richie turned to Susan to try to tell her what Doc had just told him. As he turned, the living-room lights flickered, dimmed, brightened momentarily, flickered again, and faded down into darkness.

3:59 P.M.

Doc Warren grunted in disgust at the dead telephone and put it down. For a second, he sat with his hands on his knees, then stood, moved into the center of the office, stopped uncertainly, and found himself facing the door of the examining room. He took a step toward it, reached out, opened the door, and looked through the dimness at the white-sheeted body of Alice Bissell. The freezing cold in the room hit him hard. He shivered and clutched the lapels of his jacket across his chest. Then the lights in the office flickered twice and left him in the dark.

3:59 P.M.

"Go on," Blanche said. "You have to finish it, every bit of it."

Leon Bissell was sitting up in the bed, his back propped against pillows. In his hand was a cup of steaming-hot beef broth. A larger bowl of it stood on the night table beside him.

"Go on," Blanche said again. "Every bit."

Leon dutifully sipped at it.

"It's good," he said.

"Of course it's good. Although that's not much of a recommendation. Almost anything would taste good after what you've been through. Take some more. There's a whole bowlful left."

Leon sipped again but he didn't smile. He swallowed and drained the cup.

Blanche stood at once and refilled the cup from the bowl. She handed it to Leon. As he raised it to his lips, the lights in the room flickered, dimmed, and went out.

"It's all right, Leon," Blanche said. "You go on drinking that soup. I'll see what's happening."

Moving carefully in the darkness, she made her way around the bed to the door, groped for the doorknob, and pulled it open. The corridor was pitch black. In the direction of the stairs, off to her right, someone shouted. She heard voices raised down in the lobby.

She went back into the room and crossed slowly, feeling her way along, to the window. She had closed the drapes earlier to shut out the sight of the snow. Now she pulled them back on one side and looked out.

The last gray light of day was dimming now, edging toward darkness. All the lights were gone, as if the town itself had been swallowed up by night.

She found her way back to the bedside and sat again in her chair. "The power lines are down," she told him.

"Will Alice be all right?" he asked at once.

Blanche was thankful for the darkness. "I don't imagine it will make much difference," she said, her voice level and controlled. "Now go on and finish that soup."

3:59 P.M.

In the kitchen of the Centennial Hotel, Mary Booth
and the others were just beginning to gather the cooling
cookies into plastic bags. Popcorn was still popping
away merrily, and more plastic bags had been found to
hold it. The bags were being piled in cardboard cartons
on the floor near the door, ready to be taken over to the
warehouse. When the lights dimmed and went out, there
were four big pots of popcorn all going at once, making
a pleasant, warm, homey sound and adding to the sweet
scent of the cookies.

"Oh, no!" somebody groaned when the darkness
caught them.

But the cookies were finished, and most of the popcorn, and they chose to be glad they'd gotten that much
done, and not to think at the moment about what the
darkness and loss of electricity would mean in the night
and the days ahead.

3:59 P.M.

The sudden loss of electric power dropped a gray pall over the Kill, and the town cringed beneath it. The air was clear now, for the first time in days, and the wind had ceased its blowing, but the still, cold air felt black with an edge of ice. With the wind gone back to the hills, the snow-smothered silence was even deeper, emptier. No lights showed, nothing moved, and shadows filled even the open spaces.

After a while, a solitary figure appeared here and there in the silent streets. The thin beam of a flashlight flared pale yellow against the blanket of unmarked snow, darkening even further the shadows at the sides of houses and beneath the burdened trees. A shout from one house to another broke the brittle silence for an instant, another shout came in reply, and all was still again.

Flashlights moved in houses too and swept briefly, brightly, across the black, cold glass of windows. Still later, fires began to flicker indoors, burning the wood saved carefully for just such need—no pleasure in the fires, only cold necessity, and worry about the long night to come—and the flames danced yellow at the windows, though none of their light or heat could hold back the swelling darkness outside.

The Centennial Hotel loomed gray and chill above the square. Inside, in the Dining Room and lounge and ballroom, fireplaces crackled with sudden flames and candles gleamed against the wood paneling of the large rooms, but none of the light reached outdoors.

Outdoors, early darkness held the Kill, silent, cold, and deep.

The only sign of life was at the warehouse. All around it were cold snow and creeping black, but the warehouse itself assaulted the dusk with slivers of yellow light. They knifed out between narrow cracks, between the ragged, weathered edges of decayed boards that covered windows. Sometimes the beams of light held steady, and sometimes a wispy shadow floated across them, darkening them for an instant, then moved away. There were sounds too, very faint sounds, very like voices, talking, humming, sounds of men eagerly at work, and sounds of saws and hammers, and tinkly, tuneful circus music, faint in the brittle dark outside.

4:06 P.M.

Richie had told her Doc's story quickly, breathlessly, as they stood close together in the darkness of the house.

"It's crazy," Richie said, "but Doc sounds . . . I don't know. He sounds like he believes it."

Susan was huddled deep inside her clothing, her shoulder touching Richie. "I believe it," she said. Her teeth were suddenly chattering.

"But it's not possible. It's—"

"No, it's not. But it makes sense. It's crazy, but it makes sense." She looked into his eyes. "Richie, I saw that clown. I swear to God I did."

Richie looked away.

"And that ringmaster's name."

"I know."

"We have to get back right away," Susan said.

"Doc said it was a fire. They all died in a fire, except the ones who lingered. And the numbers fit." Richie shook his head no. Then another thought struck him, what Doc Warren had been starting to say when the line went dead. "If they're real, they're reenacting it. And with all the power out, they'll have to use . . . candlelight in the warehouse."

"Same as before."

308

"Susan, I don't believe a bit of this, and at the same time, it scares the hell out of me. Let's go."

"Richie, hug me for a second. Just for a second."

He put his arms around her shoulder and touched the back of her head with his gloved hand.

"I'll be all right," she said after a moment.

"You better be," Richie said. "I need you."

They moved apart and looked at each other, both of them startled.

"Come on," Richie said. "I don't know what speed we can make, and it's already pitch black out there."

At the door Susan said, "This is really happening, isn't it? And we're really going to do this."

"Yeah," Richie answered quickly. "We are."

He opened the door and they went out into the cold.

4:17 P.M.

"Good afternoon, ladies. Although, I must say it seems more like evening outside."

"Oh, Mr. Stokely. Please come in."

He moved gracefully from the doorway and into the ballroom. Kathleen Kennedy, who had stayed in the ballroom after her tour of duty ended, Rosemary Stell, Nora Ellenwood, and a few other women gathered around him. Some of the children spotted him too and came hurrying to gather around. Candlelight danced warmly on the walls, gleamed on the hardwood floor, and stretched the children's distorted shadows across the width of the room.

Stanton Stokely, holding his top hat respectfully in his gleaming pink hands, smiled all around the room and said, "I've come to reassure you."

"What does that mean?" Stevie Winter asked in the now silent crowd of children.

The ringmaster looked benignly in his direction. "An excellent question," he said. "Well, I shall tell you what it means. It means . . ." His sparkling gaze swept slowly from face to eager face. "It means that we shall have a circus tonight, *that's* what it means."

The children cheered and the adults smiled with relief.

"We were worried when the lights went out," Rosemary Stell said. "We weren't sure you could still go ahead and perform."

"My dear lady," Stokely said, "Stanton Stokely's Stupendous Circus is absolutely reliable. When we have an audience that cries out for us, how could we fail them? Never! We need no electricity for our circus. In fact"—he lowered his voice and bent slightly toward the excited children—"we have all the power we need. We have at our beck and call the most wonderful power of all, the power of magic, the power to make you laugh . . . and the power to make you cry. But," he added at once, and forcefully, so that the children all stared wide-eyed at his face, "I promise you, there shall be laughter at the end. There shall be the jolliest laughter heard in Deacons Kill for years and years and years. The cacophony of clowns! I can tell you with absolute certainty, my dear children, it will thrill you, it will chill you, it will bring tears of laughter to your eyes. Because"— and here his voice mysteriously, enticingly, dropped even lower—"after the magic of the circus, there is always and forever laughter at the end."

He straightened up suddenly and beamed at them all. "Will that suit you?"

"Yes!" the children shouted.

Stokely turned toward the small group of adults. "I like to begin on time, and we're set for six o'clock. My people are building platforms and benches for everyone, and I'd like the audience to be seated by six o'clock, on the dot."

They assured him everyone would be there by six. Graciously, he took his leave, and a moment later he was gone.

The children, stilled with awe at the thought of a real circus ringmaster actually come among them, held their places in silence for a moment. Then the spell broke and

the boldest of them rushed to the door. They looked up
and down the corridor, but the ringmaster had already
vanished.

4:31 P.M.

They weren't going fast because the darkness was deep and thick enough to keep moonlight from touching the ground. All Susan could see was gradations of black. Whether the shapes that floated up before her eyes were trees or houses or merely darker shadows, she couldn't tell. They crawled along through the cold and chafed at the slowness that kept them from the town.

When the snowmobile hit the drift, it lurched clumsily to a halt and growled like a frightened animal.

Wordlessly, they climbed out, Richie holding on to the side, and began pulling it away from the drift. Susan's feet went from under her and she landed on her side in the snow. Her sleeve was pushed up and chilling wet snow crept under the wristband of her coat and into her glove.

When they had the snowmobile free, they stood, panting, for a minute, to catch their breath. Richie fumbled at his sleeve and finally had to take off his right glove before he could work the little button that lighted the face of his watch.

"We have less than an hour and a half," he said.

Then they climbed back in the snowmobile, Susan again taking the driver's seat in front, and started off.

4:43 P.M.

Doc Warren had spent three-quarters of an hour, sitting in his office, in the cold darkness, trying to think it all through. It made no sense. And it made perfect sense.

Finally, after struggling with it as long as he could, he gave it all up. True or not, mad or not, impossible or not, one thing, he knew, was certain. Stanton Stokely's Stupendous Circus was going to give a performance in the old warehouse at six o'clock. Most of the residents of Deacons Kill would be there, and most of them, Doc was certain, would be trapped in a fire by the . . . No, he wouldn't even permit himself to *think* the word.

And there were the others, too. Alice Bissell lay dead in the next room. The knowledge of her death, though it was the result of her weak condition and prolonged exposure to the cold, still darkened all his thoughts and seemed a part of the larger danger that threatened Deacons Kill. Alice's mother, according to Leon's report—every word of which Doc believed to be true—had died a terrible death at the . . . hands . . . of a clown. Jimmy French was still missing. It should not have been possible for a child simply to disappear like that, but Jimmy French was gone, and no amount of searching for him had revealed any hint of his whereabouts. Other people, other residents of the Kill, were missing too, although less mysteriously and ominously than Jimmy French. But where were they? Could something have happened to them that had no easy explanation? Something related to the ringmaster, the circus, the clowns . . . and the circus fire that had brought death so many years before?

Yet, if it were true, why hadn't a story like that survived in the Kill? Stories of darkness and death live lengthy lives in country towns. But so many years had intervened, and then a war that had taken away so many of the town's young men, and then a depression, and another war, and a full generation after that. Too many years, he thought, and too many changes. And the tale itself was one best put out of mind.

As he had so many times before, he rose and went to the window. The snow in Hill Street looked black now, shadowed, uneven, a landscape made for the purpose of nurturing fear.

He should tell Phil Aymar. He'd meant to say that to Richie but they hadn't had a chance.

But what would he say to Phil? The circus isn't real? The clowns aren't real? The ringmaster you saw has been dead for three-quarters of a century?

Could he stop people from going to the warehouse tonight? Could he keep them away from the circus?

He struck the window frame, hard, with the heel of his hand, and it rattled angrily back at him.

4:50 P.M.

Richie shouted in her ear, "Do you want me to drive? My head's a little better."

Susan shouted back over her shoulder, "I'm okay. We'd only lose time stopping."

But the noise of the snowmobile and the wind sliding past them was too loud. Richie patted her firmly on the shoulder, hard enough so she'd feel it through the heavy clothing, and Susan nodded her head to tell him she understood.

Moving at only a quarter of the speed they wished for, as much as Susan dared, they glided on through the landscape of night, threading their way past a gauntlet of frozen black and shifting shadows blacker still.

4:59 P.M.

Blanche knew that Leon could hear the children shouting and laughing and running in the corridor, and she wished to God they'd stop.

Leon had dozed a little more, but now he was wide awake. Even by the flickering candlelight in the room—luckily the Centennial kept an adequate supply of candles on hand—she could see that some of the color had returned to his face. He still stared into the room, lost in thought about his daughter and his wife and his long night in the bitter snow, but his condition was much improved since morning. Several times he had turned to Blanche and looked as if he were going to ask her something. Blanche had dreaded that look in his face, and the question she knew was eating away at him and the answer that she feared he also knew, but the look had subsided each time, and Leon had sunk back into his own silent thoughts.

Now, however, with the children shouting loudly just outside and the sound of their running feet pounding by, he turned his head and looked toward the door. Blanche pushed herself out of the chair and began fussing with the pillows and bedcovers to distract him.

"You should be sleeping," she said. "You need all the sleep you can get."

"Where did the doctor put Alice?" Leon asked. He spoke slowly, but his voice was clear and it startled Blanche.

She stood up straight beside the bed, glad that her body blocked some of the candlelight so that Leon couldn't see her face. She took a deep breath.

"She's—"

"She's dead," Leon said. "I know she's dead." He turned his head without moving it from the pillow and looked up at Blanche.

"Leon," she said softly.

"I know it." He was silent for a minute, staring at her, past her, through her. "I know it."

Blanche sat on the edge of the bed. Leon bent forward, rolled on his side, and curled up with his head on her lap. She cradled him there, stroking his forehead, brushing the hair back gently from his face, hoping her hands felt warmer to him than they did to her. With her other hand, she pulled the loose covers close around his back to keep him snug.

They were still sitting like that, with the cries of children reaching them faintly, as if from another world, when there was a quiet knock on the door and Doc Warren came in.

Blanche looked up at him and, even in the dim yellow light of the room, Doc saw from her face that Leon knew. He came and sat on the other side of the bed.

"Leon," he said.

Leon cringed a little closer into Blanche's lap, burying his face against her.

"Leon," Doc said again, and placed his hand on the man's shoulder.

Leon stirred then, moved away slowly from Blanche, and sat up straight on the bed. He turned his face toward Doc.

Doc touched Leon's arm. "I'm so very sorry," he said.

The room was cold and dark with a terrible silence while they all looked at each other and tried to realize the import of the fact.

Leon was the first to speak. "The clown killed her," he said, his voice flat and steady. "The clown killed her. I know it. The clown scared her to death. It frightened her to death."

Instinctively Doc opened his mouth to speak, to explain, to comfort, but stopped himself at once.

"Yes, Leon," he breathed after a moment. "Yes, I believe you're right."

"Hold my hands," Leon said, his voice constricted now, tight and painful, beginning to choke. "Please hold my hands."

Each of them took his hand, Blanche on one side and Doc on the other, and held it tight. Then Blanche reached across him with her free hand and Doc immediately grasped it. They sat there, the three of them, in the flickering light of the candles, making a fragile circle to protect them from the night.

5:12 P.M.

Susan brought the snowmobile to a gliding stop and leaned back wearily in the seat.

"Are you all right?" Richie asked anxiously, leaning over her from the back.

"I'm okay," she said. "I just can't drive any more. I'm frozen and my arms are stiff from holding this thing so tight. And my eyes are giving out on me. I'm afraid I'm going to get us killed."

"I'll take it," Richie said. He was already climbing out. "Come on, get in the back."

They switched places, and Richie looked over his shoulder to make sure Susan was settled.

"Are you sure you're okay?" he asked.

"I'm okay," she said. "I'll be better when we get there."

Richie turned back to the wheel, grasped it, and pressed down on the pedal. The snowmobile roared but didn't move. Instinctively Richie glanced down toward the floor. When he looked up, the white face of a clown was looming out of the darkness in front of him, its red mouth looking as dark as the hills that surrounded them. The clown was leaning forward on the front of the snowmobile, holding it in place, and grinning at him.

"No!" Richie shouted. "No, no no!" He tromped down as hard as he could on the pedal, and the snowmobile wailed loudly and leaped forward. The clown sailed up into the air, tumbling, tumbling, right above their heads, and came down behind them as the snowmobile shot away.

Susan swung around to look behind them, where it had landed. Even in the darkness and the rapidly growing distance, she could see the clown, as if it generated its own luminescent spotlight on the snow. It was lying on its back, feet kicking in the air, and holding its sides with rollicking silent laughter.

5:23 P.M.

The hotel was a little quieter than it had been. Parents had taken children off to their rooms to wash their faces and get them dressed to go out. Many people were leaving for the warehouse already, eager to get the first choice of seats and, anyway, it was easier to humor the children by going now, as soon as they were ready. Besides, it would be a long walk there for the youngsters, making their way through deep snow. Thank God, everyone said, that the wind had died and the snow had stopped falling; they didn't know if they'd have risked taking the children outside if the storm hadn't let up like this.

Doc stood against the wall at the side of the lobby, his hat and coat still in his hand, and watched the families —the Trenchards, the Booths, the Plancks, the Mercers —come down the stairs, cross the lobby, and go out into the night.

And no way to stop them.

Yes, yes, of course, he'd be there, he told them when they asked if he was coming.

Phil Aymar came by after a bit and walked over to talk to him.

"You coming down, Doc?"

Doc had to draw his thoughts back from the dark

places they'd been. "Yes," he said. "I'll be along in a few minutes." He avoided the deputy's gaze.

"That damn ringmaster had us going there for a bit," Phil said, "but he turned out okay in the end. Too bad Frank Carpenter has to miss this. Should be a good show."

"Yes."

"I just hope Richie makes it back in time. This whole thing has been rough on him. It'd be too bad if he missed it."

Doc looked toward the door.

"Doc, is something wrong?" He lowered his voice as people passed them. "I mean, other than what we know about?"

Doc managed a smile. "No," he said, "I'm just very tired, that's all. Why don't you go ahead, Phil. I'll see you down there."

After Phil left, Doc continued to stand there, watching the stragglers hurrying out. He had still said nothing to Phil about Leon's story of Sally Bissell's death. It might all have been Leon's imagination, he kept telling himself. And kept trying to believe it. But if it was Leon's imagination, then it had become Doc's imagination too.

During a moment when the lobby was empty of other people, Blanche Mackintosh came and stood beside him. She had her boots on and a bulky sweater that made her look immense and a scarf around her throat. She was carrying her coat and gloves and hat.

"I'm ready, Doc," she said. "We'd best be going."

"Yes," Doc said. "I wish Richie were here. And Susan. I'm worried about them." But he began pulling on his coat. Blanche helped him with it.

"Doc, Leon is coming," she said quietly.

Doc turned around. "He can't. He has to—"

"He begged me, Doc. He begged me to find him some clothes and let him come. I think he has to come."

Slowly, Doc settled his hat on his head. "Yes, I see," he said. "I guess he does, for better or worse." He sighed. "All right."

There was a footstep on the stairs, and they looked up to see Leon coming toward them. The clothes he wore were all too big for him. Under other circumstances, someone might have smiled, but not now. He came carefully down the stairs and joined them.

"Don't send me back, Doc, please," he said.

"No," Doc said. "No."

Together, the three of them moved toward the door.

When they reached the porch, they saw it was wet and sloppy from so many people tramping over it. Carefully, they helped each other down the slippery steps to the pavement, then started out across the darkness of the square toward the circus that awaited them.

5:31 P.M.

They were approaching the outskirts of the town when the ringmaster appeared suddenly in the road ahead, his arms extended in a grand gesture, one hand holding a baton, and his black cape flowing around him like liquid night. The lining of the cape flashed blood-red silk as he swept it aside and doffed his top hat in a low, sweeping bow.

Richie groaned something wordless and swung the wheel hard to avoid the figure in the road. The snowmobile swerved too sharply and slid sideways, out of control, toward the side of the road. Richie tried steering out of the slide but he was too late. The snowmobile slammed into a snow-covered wall of bushes and ground to a vibrating halt.

"You okay?" they said breathlessly to each other.

Together, they looked back toward the road. There was nothing there but the unbroken, silent dark.

It took almost five minutes to free the heavy snowmobile from the bushes and make certain it wasn't damaged. They were both sweating inside their heavy clothes and shivering in the cold and wet. Their hands were numb by now, their shoulders stiff from tension, their cheeks stinging from the cold.

Before they started again, Richie took a second to look at the dimly lighted face of his watch.

He only breathed the curse, and then they were moving again.

5:40 P.M.

The clown glided silently as a cold breath of air through the deserted corridors of the hotel. It looked at the rows of empty, silent rooms, and it smiled and smiled.

But a woman's voice was raised in one room. "Margaret Louise, you've already gotten your father angry. I just hope he can save good seats for us, that's all I have to . . . *Here* it is! Margaret, for heaven's sake, you must have kicked it under the bed. Now put it on. Margaret, will you *move!* Put it *on!*"

The door of the room was ajar and the clown floated toward it, its big floppy feet barely touching the floor. Inside, mother and daughter were struggling to get the boot on Margaret's foot.

The clown placed one white-gloved hand in the middle of the door and slowly pushed it all the way back. Kathleen Kennedy and her daughter, Margaret Louise, looked up.

It stood in the doorway where only the child could see it. With its painted grin stretching from ear to ear, it gestured at her, arms flying in exaggerated mock panic, to hurry up, hurry up, hurry up! Then, before she could say a word, it popped out of sight and was gone.

5:44 P.M.

"We must be the only ones who've seen them,"
Blanche said.

She and Doc and Leon Bissell huddled together in the
darkness by the side of the railroad station. Although
the cold was noticeably less intense than it had been,
they stood close together, shoulders touching, hands
thrust deep into pockets, arms pressed against their
sides. The black night felt immense around them.

The last stragglers from the hotel, a few of them
armed with flashlights, came stumbling through the
snow that was now trampled and uneven from the
passage of many feet before them. The pale beams of
the lights moved back and forth unsteadily, winking out
of existence for an instant, then flashing back and forth
the other way, lighting a dim moving patch that blurred
away on the shadowy snow, and casting only enough
light backward to reveal a huddled shape and an out-
stretched arm. The cold took away the breath and no
one spoke, and the only sound was boots crunching
frozen snow. Above the Kill, no stars shone and no
moon, and the sky was the black of night.

But from the great looming bulk of the warehouse came
the dull roaring sound of hundreds of people, people
who were excited and warm, who had been promised

amusement and laughter, who were relieved at the waning of the storm, and who were joyful for an unexpected pleasure. The sound they made contained shouts and laughter and the faint crying of a baby and the heavy thud of booted feet on boards. The wide double doors, three sets of them across the broad expanse of the building, were kept closed against the cold, but the sound drifted out to the night and floated lightly across the snow.

"We have to do something, Doc," Leon said, his voice barely a whisper.

Doc shook his head slowly. "This is more than I'm ready for."

Blanche pulled a hand from her pocket and clutched at his arm. "Don't be talking like that."

"We can't get those people out," Doc said. "We can't go in there and shout 'Fire!' If we did, I don't think they'd believe me in the first place, especially now when they're ready for the show to start. They wouldn't believe us. And if they did, there'd only be panic."

"But, Doc—"

"I don't know," Doc said. "Maybe Phil Aymar could do it, but there's no way to convince him that we've been seeing . . . what we've been seeing. Or Richie, but he's not here."

They turned as one and looked out at the darkness. One flickering flashlight moved toward them, coming down from the square: a taller figure and a short one, a child. They were hurrying, stumbling a little on the rough surface, then crossing the final open space toward the door of the warehouse and the warmth and welcome inside. They reached the door and the taller figure pulled heavily at it. A sliver of light knifed out, and the garbled sound of many voices. The two slipped in and were swallowed by the building.

"Yes," Doc said. "All right. We have to."

Doubled over against the cold and the fear, they moved away from the station toward the closest doors of the warehouse. Out here in the open, with nothing at their backs, they felt the size of the night around them. They heard more clearly the voices from inside and saw the slivers of light coming through the crack between the double doors.

"They're gonna kill everybody," Leon said, "just the way they killed Alice and Sally."

"No," Doc said. "They won't." He was staring at the door.

5:51 P.M.

Inside the warehouse, now magically converted—with red, white, and blue bunting and a red-and-white striped curtain—to resemble somewhat the inside of a circus tent, the people of Deacons Kill were eating popcorn from big plastic bags and passing packages of fresh-baked cookies along the rows in the wooden bleachers.

A few of the younger children, too excited after their long confinement in the house or the ballroom to sit quietly beside their parents, climbed up and down the steps, up and down and again, shrieking and giggling and struggling in their pink and red and blue snowsuits. Children a few years older, equally excited at the imminent prospect of seeing a circus, ran back and forth in the makeshift aisle between the first row of bleachers and the bright curtain, racing, laughing, calling to their friends. Whenever any of them got down on hands and knees to peek under the curtain's weighted bottom, or patted its shivering surface to find the opening and steal a look through it, an adult voice immediately yelled a name from the bleachers and the children at once ran off, shrieking and laughing even louder. The teenagers in the crowd, too old to act silly but young enough to be thrilled at all the excitement, squirmed in their seats, grinned, and dug each other in the ribs.

A few of the adults had thoughtfully provided themselves with bottles to help keep off the cold and to increase the evening's conviviality, and the bottles, with much winking and grinning, were being passed from hand to hand by the men, around the backs of the ladies, who pretended they saw none of it.

George Yoshioshi was there with his family, and the Winters and the Ellenwoods and Bob and Mary Booth and Norman Kite and Rosemary Stell and Jeff and Joan Prisco and grouchy old Ed Shalvey, all of them waiting eagerly for the circus to begin.

5:52 P.M.

"What should we do, Doc?" Blanche whispered. "I'm praying as hard as I can, but we have to do it by ourselves."

Doc was between the two of them, Blanche and Leon moving half a step behind him, each of them holding on to one of his sleeves. He took another couple of steps closer to the door, then suddenly stopped, jerked his face up toward the sky. Hard, icy snowflakes, almost pellets, had struck his cheeks. The others felt it too and looked up.

It was snowing again, suddenly, fiercely, furiously, a white swirl of snow lashing down at them from the blackened heavens, and with the same cold suddenness came the wind, whipping the icy snow, flinging it at their blinded eyes, biting at their faces, creeping into their clothing, cutting at their skin. It eddied around them, cutting them off even from the night, as if it had picked them out as its particular victims. They clutched at their clothing. Scarves flapped madly at their faces, and Doc's hat was whipped from his head. They tried to duck from its force, from the screaming wind, from the snow that cut at their eyes, but there was no place to go. They swung around, tried to put their backs to the wind,

333

but the wind was everywhere at once and pushed them cruelly where it willed.

Blanche fell heavily in the snow and screamed her fright. The two men struggled against the pushing wind and fell to their knees beside her, hands reaching blindly to help. Blanche struggled up and got to her knees, holding the men for support. "Oh, Lord!" she breathed, but the wind snatched at the words and hurled them away.

They they heard it, the sound carried to them by the wind, muting its roaring as if it meant them to hear. From inside the warehouse came the lively, bouncing music of a calliope, dancing on the frozen air, amid the whirling snowflakes, and with it, the sound of the crowd. The shapeless roar grew louder, peppered with applause and yells, but the music swelled louder still and seemed to fill the night and the snow-smothered town.

5:54 P.M.

The music of the calliope roared from all around them, from every direction at once, filling the entire warehouse with its sound, filling the very air.

At the first note, everyone jumped, then laughed, then burst into a roar of applause and cheers and yells. The cold was forgotten, and the snow, and the worry about the storm. Now the only thing was the roaring, bouncing music, the smell of popcorn, the happy warmth of the crowd jammed tightly together on the bleachers, and the red-and-white curtain that would open any minute now, *any second,* to reveal the clowns and the start of the circus.

Parents yelled at their children, over the din of the cheering and the music, to come and take their seats *right now, right this instant!* The children scrambled up, breathless with anticipation, squeezed into the narrow spaces saved for them on the wooden boards, and clapped their hands with everyone else.

Phil Aymar was over in the entrance aisle near one of the doors at the side. He was grinning along with everyone else but sedately kept his hands joined behind his back. In spite of his smile, however, he was worried about Richie Mead. He'd been gone an awfully long time. Phil was also a little worried about the size of the crowd packed so tightly into the warehouse. You had to be careful with crowds. It had crossed his mind earlier to wonder if the town had any ordinances about this sort of thing, but it was too late now to do anything about it anyway.

Phil had been careful to take a look at the bleachers, to see if they seemed secure. He'd even climbed under them before they were filled and pulled at a few struts to make certain they'd hold the weight of the crowd. They were solid, plenty solid. Plain old-fashioned workmanship. The circus guys had done a good job.

He walked forward to where he could look along the aisle in front of the seats. Still smiling, he scanned the people in the bleachers. The crowd was noisy but, considering the excitement, pretty well behaved.

Big Al Vredenburgh was sitting at the end of the second row with his tiny wife beside him. Phil's eyes met Al's. As the music of the calliope swelled even louder, building to a huge crescendo, Al gave him the thumbs-up sign, and Phil, grinning, gave it back.

5:55 P.M.

"The door!" Doc gasped, almost choking on the wind that filled his mouth like an icy gag. On hands and knees, they inched toward it.

The wind raged at their backs and then, behind them, swelling and dying on the caprice of the air, something else roared louder still and a light swept across them, freezing them to the snow.

Doc shakily struggled to his knees and then to his feet, stretching a hand to the dark shape of Blanche beside him. Nearby, Leon was getting up slowly and turning around.

"Richie!" Doc said, hardly moving his lips.

The snowmobile lurched and skidded on the rough snow in front of the warehouse. It slewed around and came at them sideways, its light cutting at the moving wall of snow. For an instant it roared louder; then it stopped moving and the sound of its engine whined away into silence. As it died, the lively music from inside swelled again to fill the night, and the wall of snow danced madly to the bouncing tune.

"Thank the Lord!" Blanche said when Richie and Susan stumbled out of the night. She stretched her arms out and Susan fell into them.

Richie covered his mouth against the wind and tried

to take a deep breath before talking. "Did they start?" he gasped out to Doc.

"No, I don't think so! We should have a couple of minutes!"

They had to yell above the wind, the music from inside, the pounding of blood in their ears.

Richie pulled Doc close to him. "Doc, you believe this, right?"

"I do," Doc said.

"Okay," Richie yelled.

A gust of wind rocked them, and they tried to turn away from it.

"What do we do?" Doc said.

"We yell 'Fire!' " Richie said. "Is Phil in there?"

"Yes, I think so."

"Come on!"

5:58 P.M.

As the music neared its thumping, pounding peak, the red-and-white curtain began to shudder as if responding to the deafening roar.

Suddenly, a narrow slit opened at the center of the curtain.

A white-gloved hand appeared, grasped the edge of the material, and slowly pulled it back. In the opening was only darkness.

Then the white-painted face of a clown popped into view, grinning broadly with its bright red mouth, and turned its head slowly from side to side, looking at everyone in the crowd with its big wide eyes.

The crowd went wild, pounding their hands together in even louder applause, the yelling and cheering and pounding of booted feet on boards threatening to drown out even the music.

The clown stepped out from the opening in the curtain, its big floppy feet slapping on the floor. An immense burlap sack hung from one shoulder and dragged behind it.

From somewhere in its satiny white pants it produced a cigar that must have been two feet long. It stuck the end of the cigar in its mouth and pretended to be almost toppled over by the weight. Then it started patting its costume, obviously searching for a light. An idea struck it. It bent over, the cigar still in its mouth, and dipped one arm deep into the burlap sack. After a moment of rummaging around, it discovered what it wanted. It straightened up and, its painted grin seeming even wider, produced a four-foot-long wooden match.

5:59 P.M.

Still bent to make a smaller target for the wind and the slashing snow, the five of them stumbled toward the closest door.

They reached it, clustered tightly together, and touched its snow-chilled rough wood almost gratefully. From inside, the music of the calliope wheezed and pounded out at them, recalling circus tents, amusement parks, merry-go-rounds, popcorn, laughter, clowns.

Richie reached for the latch and, in the same instant the sliver of light from between the doors was darkened and then broken.

He pulled on the latch as hard as he could, panting with the effort.

"It's bolted! They've bolted it!"

"The others!" Doc yelled.

"No, they'll be the same," Richie shouted over the thumping music from inside. He stepped back, braced his feet as best he could in the slippery snow, and lunged at the door. His shoulder struck it hard. The door rattled and must have complained loudly at the blow, but the sound of it was drowned out by the music.

"Richie!" Susan yelled.

He lunged again and hit it harder. The door vibrated but held.

Then Leon Bissell was tugging at Richie's arm, frantically pulling him away with fingers like claws.

"I'll do it!" Leon shouted. "I'll do it!"

He hurled himself at the door, shoulder first, mindless of the pain. The door shook, and angry snow sprayed off it into his face. He lunged again. The door seemed to wobble, but still it held. Calliope music filled their hearing, killing all other sounds. Leon gathered himself once more, lunged furiously at the door, and this time they all heard something snap. The double doors flew open and slammed back against the wall with a terrible crash, hard enough to fly back again into the doorway.

Richie and Leon leaped forward, grabbing at them, pushing the shivering doors out of the way, and rushed inside, with Susan, Doc, and Blanche right behind them.

The place was blazing with light, yellow light that filled it with the brightness of day.

Blinded after the darkness outside, eyes tearing in the sudden heat of lights and hundreds of bodies, the five of them stopped where they were.

Wooden bleachers rose up on either side of the aisle from the door, six levels high and filled with people yelling and cheering and laughing as the music crashed out around them.

The air was warm with the odor of melting wax and redolent with the friendly circus scents of sawdust and popcorn.

At the end of the aisle, in front of them, in front of the eager crowd, they just caught sight of a clown ducking out of view behind a red-and-white striped curtain as the audience roared with laughter. Even as Richie's gaze focused on it, Stanton Stokely, in his full costume of black tailcoat, flowing cape, and high top hat, parted the curtain and stepped in front of it to the cheers and applause of the crowd.

The music wound down to a lower level as Stokely raised one white-gloved hand and put a finger across his lips for silence. The crowd instantly grew quiet. A few children giggled nervously.

"Welcome!" Stokely shouted, one arm upraised.

"*No!*" Richie screamed. He sprang forward.

But in the very instant he shouted and jumped toward the ringmaster, the music swelled loud again, the red-and-white curtain flew back, and the crowd roared at the sudden spectacle.

Six clowns formed a pyramid: three on the bottom, then two, and one, his arms stretched wide, at the top. Their costumes were a glittering, satiny patchwork of every color in the rainbow, their hands and faces white, lips red and grinning ear to ear, woolly hair standing on end. The audience applauded, and the top clown leaped to the ground, flipping over in a somersault and landing in a comic pratfall. While the others scampered away in every direction, he magically produced a pink parasol from his baggy pants. He held it over his head and it seemed suddenly to fill with air and yank him away. While he struggled with it, running this way and that, the five other clowns ran into view again. Two of them leaped onto the shoulders of two others, and the pairs squared off, facing each other. The music of the calliope seemed to bounce with every movement they made. The fifth clown took his position between the two pairs, gestured wildly to the audience, and dipped dramatically into a huge burlap bag he wore slung over one shoulder. He pretended to grope around in it for a second, leering at the audience and winking with giant eyes. Then he seemed to find something, and his face lit up with joy.

"No!" Doc yelled. "Don't!"

"No!" Richie screamed.

He leaped forward and sprang onto the second level of bleacher seats at his left, where the audience could see him.

"No!" he screamed again at the top of his lungs. "Get out! Everybody get out!" With relief he didn't have time or awareness to consider, he saw Blanche and Doc running across in front of the seats to open the set of doors on his right, while Leon and Susan ran to the doors on his left. He caught a blurred glimpse of Phil Aymar's startled face. The audience quieted a little, distracted and puzzled, and eyes came into focus on him. "Fire!" he shouted. "Go carefully, but *get out!*"

He leaped down from the bleachers as a few stunned people rose to their feet. Behind him the music crashed, drums and tympani pounding in a rattling crescendo. He ran forward, toward the clowns, where the audience could see him. He saw only a blur of color. All he could hear was the music.

He screamed again, feeling the aching tightness in his throat, "Fire! Get out!" He pointed at the doors in front of him and yelled again, but his voice was almost gone.

The crowd was moving now, surprised, bewildered, staring at him, but moving. Too stunned to rush, but moving. Richie could hear Leon's voice bellowing something above the noise, something he couldn't make out, but they were coming down from the stands now, men and women and children, and moving toward the three open doors.

Richie was gasping for air, fighting the rawness in his
ᵃt so he could yell again, fighting the ingrained
ɗge that you don't shout *"Fire!"* in a crowd,
he shortness of breath and the hammering in

his chest and the fear that the crowd would panic, and it was then that he smelled the smoke.

He whirled around, looked past the clowns and saw the yellow flames dancing behind them, looked above and saw the flames overhead, racing across the dry wood of the ceiling, looked down and saw the flames leaping across the sawdust on the floor, racing toward him, racing toward the clowns.

He spun again toward the doors and saw the last few people clambering down the bleacher steps, hurrying now and yelling, leaping to the floor and scrambling out into the blackness of the doorway. He saw Susan wave an arm frantically at him, cup her hands around her mouth, and shout something he couldn't hear.

Music roared in his ears and flames roared toward him, licking at everything, consuming the warehouse as if with ages-old hunger, now free and unrestrained. Flames devoured the curtains and licked their way up the walls. The clowns, grinning broadly, juggled madly among the flames and the deafening tumult of music.

Richie sprung away, leaped toward the door, and crashed hard into Leon Bissell. The others had been running toward him, to pull him away, to pull him out. Together, the five of them stumbled toward the gaping black doorway, feeling the roaring heat of the fire pressing at their backs.

"Wait!" Doc shouted. His voice was weak, trembling. "We have to be sure!"

They stopped and, panting, helping each other stand, looked back. Sheets of flame, yellow, red, white, flickering blue, danced and leaped everywhere they looked, moving from the back of the warehouse toward the front where the doors were, consuming ropes, curtain, cables, sawdust, floor, walls, ceiling, and starting on the bleachers. At one side, on a high platform, Stanton

Stokely stood with his arms out and his head thrown back, embracing the flames. As they watched, the fire reached him and licked hungrily at his cape. He arched his back and threw his head even higher, welcoming the fire with a look of relief and joy, a man released at last to eternal peace. The fire swallowed the platform and raced on toward the clowns. Above them, a portion of the ceiling roared, split, gave way, in a crashing, falling din of whirling flames and tumbling wood and crackling sparks. Still the clowns juggled, still they grinned—grinned more broadly and juggled more quickly—outlined against the dazzling light of sheeting flames, two still standing on the shoulders of two others, and the two remaining tossing the round objects up and up and up and up to the two others on top. Back and forth and around, top to bottom and bottom to top, across and across and back and again, they tossed and tossed and tossed, and in the final few seconds before the clowns were engulfed in the rushing flames, Richie and the others could clearly see what the clowns were juggling so madly, could clearly see the head of Sally Bissell and the head of Evan Highland and the head of Jimmy French and of others and others and others, and then the flames reached the clowns and climbed up their bodies, turning them to torches. More of the ceiling collapsed, and the clowns, madly juggling still, were taken at last by the flames.

"Oh, my God!" one of them said, and none of them knew who it was.

They turned together, the five of them, and ran, fell, stumbled, toward the blackness of the doorway, gasping for breath, and then they were outside, feeling cool air on their faces, on their tears, and falling headlong into the cold, wet, welcoming snow.

7:35 P.M.

By the time the first few weary people had made it back to the Centennial Hotel, the power was on and lights were shining everywhere. Telephones were ringing in the lobby. The snow had stopped, the wind had died away to nothing, and a few people swore that the temperature had warmed up a few notches.

It was an evening of fright and confusion, although, mercifully, none of the townspeople had actually seen the ringmaster and the clowns go up in flames, and they had been distracted from seeing the objects the clowns were juggling. That, at least, cut down on some of the evening's horrors for Deacons Kill. But everyone knew that all the members of the circus had died in the flames, beyond hope of rescue. There had been no chance of saving the warehouse, and they had been forced to stand there and simply watch it burn rapidly to the ground. There was little talk as people returned to the hotel.

Richie had found Phil Aymar in the confusion outside the burning warehouse, and had gotten him to hurry people away from the fire as quickly and as firmly as possible. Phil, hearing the tone in Richie's voice and seeing the look on his face—and on the faces of the four

others who stood with him, never once looking away
from the fire—had obeyed without question.

Of the five of them, only Doc Warren had stirred,
moving away from the little circle long enough to deter-
mine if there were any injuries that required medical
attention. There were not, and he returned silently to
the others and watched the flames.

The old building burned quickly, loudly, and
collapsed in on itself, still burning until the flames were
smothered in melted snow. The innocent railroad
station beside it was spared.

After a while, when only a few timbers smoldered in
the ruins, the five turned away. They left silently,
knowing they'd be back shortly and knowing too that
only smoking ruins would await them.

When they reached the front of the hotel, they stood
for a long moment in silence.

"I hear telephones," Richie said. "I have to go to my
office."

"I'll go with you," Susan said.

"We'd best not say anything," Doc said to him,
"until we . . . well, until we know what we want to say.
There were a lot of people dead. It'll be bad enough as it
is."

"Yes," Richie said.

Blanche took Leon's arm and said, "Leon here is still
a patient. I'll see that he gets into some dry clothes. And
that's what you should do, too." She looked at all the
others.

"Well," Richie said quietly.

They moved apart slowly, reluctantly, unwilling to be
separated now.

Doc leaned heavily on Blanche's arm as he climbed
the steps, and Leon carefully supported Blanche on the
other side.

Richie and Susan walked slowly toward the corner of Hill Street and, without even realizing they did it, put their arms around each other.

10:43 P.M.

They met again by the ruins of the warehouse. Doc was first to arrive. Leon and Blanche found him there, standing alone, head bowed into his collar, hands shoved deep in the pockets of his coat. A few minutes later, Susan and Richie joined them. No one said a word. The moon had appeared and, as if newly returned to the world and eager to please, shone bright on the snow at their feet. Where snow had melted in the heat of the fire, they could hear it trickling and faintly dripping. The night was quiet around them and the air felt almost soft.

Only a few wisps of smoke came from the ruined warehouse now, and the open space here, beside the railroad station, looking out toward the market field, seemed immense.

"The train is gone," Doc said quietly.

"Yes," Richie said. "We knew it would be."

"Yes," Susan said.

"When I was at the office," Richie said, "I talked to the troopers in Albany, and the Weather Service." His voice was flat, simply telling them, without comment, what he knew. "The storm never really materialized in Albany. They had flurries, a little snow, that's all. It

350

was the same all around here. We were the only ones who got it. Only this area. Only Deacons Kill.''

''Is it over now?'' Leon asked, his voice as pale as the moonlight.

''Oh, yes,'' Blanche said softly. ''Yes, Leon, it is.''

The five of them moved closer together, huddled together in a tight circle against the possibilities they had come to know. Blanche Mackintosh, the black woman who had known from years before what the snow could do, who trusted even so in the Lord, and who had raised her hand against the night. Doc Warren, an elderly man learning wearily to admit his years, who had seen much in his time and more than he'd wanted. Leon Bissell, who had lost his love even while she lay in his arms, a man to whom much of the world had always been, and now would always be, a thing of chance. Susan Lester, no stranger to death, older than she'd been on Sunday, and much of the pain still fresh. Richie Mead, who had known the possibilities all along, and now had seen their faces. They stood together, touching, arms embracing, for a long, long time before, reluctantly, they parted and moved slowly back to the town.